BLOODY MARY

Ricki Thomas

A Wild Wolf Publication

*This second edition Published by Wild Wolf
Publishing in 2016*
Copyright © 2011 Ricki Thomas

Second print

ISBN: 978-1-907954-17-7
Also available as an E-Book

www.wildwolfpublishing.com

Also from this author

Unlikely Killer

Deadly Angels

Bonfire Night

Black Park

Rings of Death

Hope's Vengeance

I dedicate this book to Dave, to honour a lovely man. And also to my mum, my brother Alan and his wife, Bek. And, as always, to my children.

A Lost Family

I watched them all, my nearest and dearest, forever loved and never forgotten. I watched as their bodies, one by one, were fed through the curtains to the heat of the incinerator. Except for the one lonesome soul who had escaped the bloodthirsty day and, not unreasonably, wished she hadn't. Because now she was alone in the world, too scarred to hope or believe; too scared to love or trust again.

I wanted so badly to hold her, hug her close and tell her it would be alright, but I knew that would just be feeding her false hope, and that wasn't my way. So I continued to watch her drown in her sorrow, vilify her body as punishment for things which weren't her fault and ultimately lose the final chance of joy she had left.

When I began my plot of vengeance a year and a half earlier it was never meant to end this way…

Chapter 1
The History of Revenge

Manipulation; that's what I'm good at. Manipulating people's minds. Don't get me wrong, I'm not a bad person, it's just when you've had the two people most precious to you cruelly taken away through no choice of your own, it leaves a lifelong and overwhelming hatred towards the world. To those surrounding you, the bustling public, people you thought to be friends who turn out to be purely acquaintances with a need to gossip about you viciously when your back is turned. And the most vitriolic revulsion to those you once loved, but had made the choice to take your precious gifts: your first born.

My twins.

After that, nothing is forgivable. Nothing. So I decided to achieve what I wanted throughout life, and if that meant messing with people's minds, carefully controlling them until they did what I wanted them to do - be it money gain, marriage, or murder - then so be it.

When I had first set eyes on Harry, I was instantly in love. He was a gentle man, yet suave, sophisticated, and he exuded intelligence in such an unassuming manner. I was visiting Birmingham Polytechnic on a rare open day with a view to studying there once I left school when his striking looks and easy manner struck me. Mesmerised, I walked over to him for a chat. A lecturer of biology, which wasn't the course I was interested in, he was a lot older than me, which made him more of a temptation, yet less of a challenge. Or so I thought.

I wanted him so much, but when I flirtatiously locked eyes with him and made the suggestion, he told me he was married with a family. That didn't deter me. Instead, I took a subtler approach, following him to his social haunts, appearing in places 'coincidentally', and using my young - childish - feminine charms to tempt him to stray. And when I finally found him at a restaurant with his wife, I knew I'd win the game if I persisted long enough.

She was plain, Beryl. Nervous, fidgeting with her fingernails, stuttering in her lack of confidence, her whole demeanour pitiful, and I instantly despised her because she had what I wanted. But in contrast I was young, my figure athletic and pert, with a mane of glossy and flowing black hair. And I knew that my striking blue eyes twinkled with cheekiness like the blinking stars at night. She was no competition.

Intent on winning the battle, I turned up at his office the next day, knowing from a previous conversation he would be working late. I'm far too individual to follow fashion, but - and think about this from my point of view - why would you *not* wear tiny hot pants if you were determined to win a man. For the first half an hour I sat beside Harry with my long coat on, discreetly inching towards him, twirling my hair through my fingers, batting my eyes innocently as he unassumingly answered my questions.

He stood and turned his back, preparing a glass of juice for each of us from the tray on the filing cabinet, and I went in for the kill, dropping my coat to reveal my lean legs beneath the tiny denim shorts, and as he turned, I stretched my arms up seductively, feigning a yawn. His deep brown eyes nearly popped out and he

10

faltered, words tripping over themselves as he tried to look away, anywhere but at the body I knew he would soon be taking. I sidled up to him provocatively, softly stroking his fingers, and his stuttering silenced. I knew he wanted me. And he had me.

However, my wiles only worked that one time and his rejection after that single perfect evening was devastating. If I 'accidentally' saw him in the places he socialised, he would disappear; if I came to his office his secretary would make his excuses. After a few weeks I had no choice but to accept that our first night of lovemaking would also be the last.

Two months later - Christmas had been and gone, taking the New Year with it - my mother became concerned. 'You're not eating enough,' she would say, 'you're not working hard enough for your exams', or 'you need more sleep'. And when my eyes, frequently tearful from the pain of losing my first love, became sunken and hollow, her worry increased. 'What's made you like this, Mary, why are you so unhappy?' And finally, 'If this carries on I'll have to take you to the doctor'.

But one day the nausea and expanding waistline, the inexplicable 'knowing' feeling emanating from within me, added up and I realised with glee that I would never lose my Harry after all. I had him inside me, a part of him that would never spurn me the way he had: I was carrying his child.

In nineteen eighty, unmarried mothers were frowned upon and my parents were devout Catholics, so I hid my pregnancy for as long as possible. But Mother realised when I was seven months gone and the vitriol she and my father spat was frightening. Before I knew it I was sent away to a distant aunt I had never even met and hidden indoors while the bump I was so proud of, so full of love for, grew to bursting.

The pains started and my aunt calmly drove me to what I believed was a hospital. I was wrong, it was a home run by the church. After Anna and Andrew, as I proudly named them, were born I cherished their sweet faces, tiny hands and feet, marvelling with wonder when I cradled them. The staff were uncaring and abrupt, but that didn't hinder the unbelievable love and protectiveness I felt towards my babies. I knew motherhood would be hard work, but I would have done anything for them.

Then the fateful and totally unexpected day came. It seemed so normal to begin with, the nurses taking my babies to the nursery for a sleep, but I never saw them again. My parents had signed the adoption papers without giving me a chance to prove myself as a mother. And by law they had every right to: I was fifteen years of age.

I was discharged to my aunt's care and soon my father pulled up in his car and we travelled to our home in Birmingham in silence. I had already decided to visit Harry at the college and see if he could help me to get my babies back. Little was I to know that my parents had already found him a couple of months before, having demanded to know who the father was, and strongly warned him never to come near me again. I cried all the way home when I discovered he had relocated to another college, the details of which personnel couldn't, or wouldn't, give me.

I had no choice but to continue with life and leave behind the brutally painful yearning for my children. But the venomous seed of hatred had been planted deep inside my heart and I intended to get my revenge no matter who suffered in the process.

Over the next two years, I flunked my exams and let myself go physically. My hair, now cut short, dulled to a matt black through lack of care, I no longer used cosmetics, and my clothes, due to unhappy weight gain, were a necessity rather than a tool for attraction. I no longer cared about anything except loathing anyone and everyone around me, and carefully plotting my future. First, I landed a job in a small garage as a receptionist. The work was tedious - answering the phone, filing, making tea - but that wasn't the point, it was part of a cleverly designed plan. As was flirting with Reg on the first day.

I made the process of courting me easy for him. He wasn't a clever man and had no idea of my ulterior motive to putting up with his acne-covered face, yellowing teeth and greasy, shaggy locks. We became an item and he met my parents soon after. My father, a habitual penny-pincher, was impressed by his work as a car mechanic and I could hear the cogs whirring as he interrogated Reg about his job. It wasn't long before the question was out and a date made for Reg to service Father's car.

It was equally easy for me to persuade Reg to adjust the brakes, tearfully fabricating a story about my father sexually abusing me from a young age. So at the age of eighteen my initial plan came to fruition: I became an orphan when the car skidded from a bend into a tree, both parents dying at the scene of the accident. If Reg ever found out, it wasn't from me; I'd already dumped him. And the monotonous boredom of the garage.

With no qualifications, I would never find a job that would inspire my mind, but the meagre inheritance from my parents was too paltry to see me through more than a couple of years, so I needed a husband to support me, and quickly. Harry had been my first love and I intended him to be my last - I would never let somebody under my skin again to reject and humiliate me - so I settled for the first decent offer and, just shy of my twentieth birthday, I married Kev.

At first he appeared to be hardworking, soon relocating us to Derby when he found a better paying position. The early days passed in a swirl of nappies and baby sick as I produced three sons for him in quick succession, but just after the last was born, Kev was made redundant and money became tight, our savings dissipating rapidly. It was only a matter of time before we faltered on the mortgage and lost our house. The council list was long and we lived in a dingy bed and breakfast for over a year, during which time Kev spent more and more time at the pub, abandoning me and the kids for a quieter life in that smoky, soggy hovel.

By the time we were given a two-bedroom flat, the damage to our marriage was irreparable. We stayed together, but living separate lives, his mostly in the local, mine dragging up the boys with little money and less hope. The only thing to keep me going was finding my only love - the man who had cruelly spurned me - and the revoltingly timid wife he had chosen over me all those years ago. With nothing else in my life, I wanted revenge.

Over the years, my sons became men, if you could call them that. Copying their father's laziness, they were thugs who preferred crime to work and I had no respect for the men I lived with. Eventually I'd had enough: Kev needed to go.

Without hindrance from my drunken bum of a husband, I kicked the boys out one by one, preferring not to keep in contact, and when I was finally alone, I trundled through each day, managing on the pittance from the dole office, scraping the pennies together for food and bills. And to while away the boring hours I read, and this led me to Beryl in a roundabout way. The wish for retribution that had simmered for nearly thirty-one years was at last a possibility.

Chapter 2
Mystical Madam Mary

Amid the retailers under the block of flats I lived in was a grungy charity shop, the type that smells cloyingly of stale body odour as you step through the door. With such a low income it was all I could afford to replace my tatty clothes, but soon I began to frequent the second-hand book section. I started with novels, but soon tired of the cheesy tales of the type of life I'd never have: career girls falling in love; single mums falling in love; happy families enjoying love. One day, while hunting for something more gripping, an instruction book on reading tarot cards stood out from the others.

With both scepticism and curiosity, I handed some small change to the lady behind the counter and took it home to study. After skimming through the pages over a period of a few days, I realised I could potentially earn money if I learned the meanings in depth, advertise under a different name to give people daft enough to believe such rubbish a chance to give me money in return for me telling them what they wanted to hear. So I bought a cheap deck of cards.

It took no time at all to memorise the pages, and an advert in the Derby Evening Telegraph, under the guise of 'Mystical Madam Mary', led to my first reading. I didn't charge much, and the woman was pleased enough to recommend my services so, along with a weekly advert, punters for my 'talents' slowly increased.

The extra income - undeclared, of course - gave me two main benefits: I could pay the bills and even have the heating on in winter; and I could purchase more materials to do with the occult. Over the next few years my living room was littered with spiritual goodies, which gave the place a believable atmosphere, and whacky books. I researched and practised until I could offer fortune-telling services with runes, dice, tealeaves, palms, auras and crystal balls. In short, although never wealthy, life was manageable.

I remember with clarity the shock of seeing Beryl's unmistakable face on my doorstep. She had phoned that afternoon, distressed, and was clearly relieved when I told her to come at six. She gave her name as Mrs Waller. It had been a glorious July and was a sunny and warm afternoon, but despite the cheery weather there was nothing bright about Beryl. She had aged over the past thirty years, but better than I had, and I felt a pang of jealousy. Then it occurred to me that I wouldn't have fared so badly if Harry hadn't destroyed my life. There wasn't a flicker of recognition in her eyes, but why would there be? She had only met me once and I was now the opposite of the striking fourteen-year-old I had been then, the day before I screwed her husband.

I moved aside and she entered, eyes flitting about the murky hall as I guided her to the living room. We sat at the purple-cloaked table and I regarded her, ready for some welcome fun. Now she was here, her anguish was evident. "I've never done anything like this before," she admitted with embarrassment.

I removed the cover from the crystal ball, lifting it before me. Beryl seemed confused. "I thought you read the tarot cards, that's what I came here for."

I pulled a few expressions - crowd pleasers - and waved my hands slowly. "I will read your tarot, but my spirit guides are telling me to use the crystal ball." I had mastered a mysterious tone of voice over the years. "I sense your name begins with a B... Be... Bella... no, wait... Beryl. Are you Beryl?"

She was visibly taken aback, gasping 'yes', and I wanted to laugh, but restrained myself. "I see a man. Fair hair," I kicked myself mentally as I realised he was probably grey by now, "dark eyes. I think he's your husband, and the letter H is coming to me... Harr... Harry. Is it Harry?"

"Harold, he likes to be called Harold." Amazement.

The consultation with the crystal ball continued and from the depths of my memory I recalled Harry mentioning once that he had a young son. I couldn't remember his name, but I could fish for that; most clients gave clues without realising it. "I can see another man, younger, maybe mid-thirties, his name... his name... oh dear..."

"That'll be my son, Steve." A light smile, brief, and the anxiety returned. "Can you see my daughter, Sophie? It's her I'm here for."

So that bastard Harry had continued to fuck his wife after ruining my life. Fury rose through me and I wanted to lean across and squeeze the life out of the bitch before me, but first I had to get to Harry; he needed his comeuppance too. "Your daughter lives in Derby too?" I was probing subtly, but Beryl missed it.

"Yes, well, a village nearby."

Now I knew Harry was alive and lived in Derby. Still a needle in a haystack, but a smaller one than ten

18

minutes before. Appearing to come out of my trance, I covered the crystal ball and took the tarot cards from the table, shuffling, and without speaking, dealt the Celtic cross format. There was no way I could tell what cards were where, but I intended to twist the meanings to hurt Beryl, leaving her desperate to see me again.

She kept her decorum during her visit and it was difficult not to respect her, considering my advice to give her daughter an ultimatum. I told her to come back in a week, asking if she would consider using my psychic skills, which would give more depth than the tarot. I didn't have such powers, but this meant our consultations would involve interaction, and hopefully lead to more about Harry. She was understandably upset at my advice regarding Sophie - my stab in the dark had clearly hit a raw spot - and paid cash after making a further appointment.

Slowly bumping along the driveway towards Iris Cottage, Sophie noted Darren had already arrived and slapped the steering wheel in frustration, glancing at the clock on the dashboard. 'Damn him,' she whispered, and switched off the engine, waiting in the car a while to buy some time before the inevitable argument.

Her thoughts drifted to the previous night, of preparing his meal as he drank at his local, debating what mood the alcohol would leave him in this time. It hadn't been a good one, and once more she had received his angry blows and spiteful words. She had driven to her parents' house during her lunch break, the quiet and peaceful atmosphere of the home she had grown up in always calmed her, taking her mind from the horrors she frequently experienced in her marital cottage. Her mum had seemed uncomfortable, upset, which was uncharacteristic, but being in the homely surroundings still pacified her.

After ten minutes with no sign of life from the cottage, Sophie wondered if Darren had gone out and decided to test the water, brave going inside. Closing the car door quietly, she crept to the oak door of the home she had purchased three years before meeting Darren and turned the key, tentatively stepping inside. She relaxed; although she often complained about the time he spent at the White Horse, today she was glad of his absence.

Dropping her handbag and briefcase on the kitchen side, she was about to make coffee when the phone trilled. Sophie answered, clamping the handset between shoulder and ear, but once her mum had spoken, the drink was forgotten. "Mum, what are you talking about? You can't do this, it's crazy."

Beryl's tone was firmer than usual. "It's gone too far, Sophie, we've been in this place too many times, and somewhere a line has to be drawn. We will always love you, but if you insist on staying with that violent bully we will have no choice but to cease contact with you. At least until you come to your senses."

She was stunned. "But Mum…"

"No, Sophie, I'm sorry. Truly sorry. But we can't constantly pick you up every time he gives you a hiding. If this is what it takes to make you see sense, then this is what we have to do. Leave him, or deal with him on your own." The stern voice was replaced by the dial tone.

Sophie's chocolate eyes dropped as she comprehended the choice - husband or parents - and she drew a hopeless breath, deep, holding it for too long. She replaced the receiver and poured a large brandy from Darren's stash. Her wedding vows had been heartfelt, and she reluctantly accepted her marriage had to come before everyone, even her parents.

Tears of anger and confusion sprung and, not usually a drinker, Sophie knocked back the warming liquid and took the bottle upstairs, hoping sleep would come quickly, that she would wake to discover this was a bad dream.

She heard the snoring before opening the door; fully clothed, Darren was slumped haphazardly on the bed, an empty glass clutched in his hand. A litre of vodka that he must have picked up after work was two thirds empty and a spent carton of orange juice lay on its side, leaving an orange stain on the covers. Sophie sighed and left the room, considering calling her mother back as she tiptoed down the stairs.

Another brandy beckoned; if Darren could get himself wrecked, then so could she. But she was too angry to share the bed and threw a sleeping bag on the sofa, downing the second glass as she snuggled into the folds. Should she call her mother? Maybe her father; he was more easy going. But anger surfaced: how dare they force her to choose between them and her husband. Stubborn, Sophie reached for the bottle and poured again. If a reconciliation was ever going to happen, it wouldn't be instigated by her.

Unaccustomed to the alcohol, she was asleep in seconds.

Feeling herself jolted, her husband's Mancunian lilt filling her ears, she opened her eyes to near blackness, the moon casting an eerie hue through the window, and Sophie cleared her throat, her head thumping. "What?"

Darren flicked the light switch and she threw her hands over her eyes, recoiling. "I said why are you sleeping down here?"

Thinking quickly, unable to gauge his mood just yet, "I, um, I saw you were asleep and didn't want to disturb you. No other reason." Sophie inched back instinctively.

Grinning, he slumped on the sofa and she relaxed. "Ah, sweet, you should have climbed in with me, we could've had a cuddle." He winked.

Today - or was it yesterday, she had no idea how long she had been sleeping - seemed to be a bad day for making choices. "I'm sorry." She wasn't.

Darren took the brandy bottle and glass from the carpet and glared accusingly, before pouring a large measure and gulping it back. "Got yourself tanked up, did you?" His hypocrisy was overwhelming but she refrained from answering. "So what did the old dragon-in-law have to say for herself today, then? More whingeing and whining? A bit of emotional blackmail, maybe?"

The dreadful conversation flooded her memory and she wriggled from the sleeping bag to get a fresh glass from the kitchen. "No, she was fine. Yeah, fine. Er, did you contact your mum?"

"Yeah, we had a really long talk. I told her we were trying for a baby and she nearly cried, she was so happy. Said it was about time I gave her a grandson. She was dead proud of me."

Sophie was pleased to have turned the conversation around, unable to tell her husband about the ultimatum just yet. She poured another drink, emptying the bottle. "That's nice, I'm glad she was happy."

"Oh, and great news too. They've got a buyer for their house, a youngish couple. They offered full asking price and said they'd buy Dad's car too, with the house, you know, so Mam and Dad won't be car-less until the day they move to Mallorca. Fantastic news, isn't it?"

Sophie was genuinely shocked - some people were so lucky - but smiled widely. "Yes, great news. That's brilliant. So when's the villa going to be finished? How are they going to tie it in?"

Darren waved as he downed the dregs from the glass, refilling it immediately from a whisky bottle he found in the sideboard. "The buyers have agreed to wait for completion until the villa's built, but that's not so far ahead anyway, three months or so. It's all worked out perfectly." He took cigarettes and a lighter from his pocket and offered her one, and she reached across the table for an ashtray and emptied it into the bin before setting it on the sofa between them. They both inhaled deeply, lost in their own thoughts: Sophie irritated that her in-laws had sold their house within days, yet her cottage had been on the market for months; Darren smug at the rosy news from his mother.

It was as if he had read her mind. "I don't suppose you've heard from the estate agents at all?"

She shook her head, expelling blue smoke swiftly. "No, nothing."

Darren glanced around the cosy room, taking in the darkened oak beams and cream painted lime plaster for a millionth time, and she knew the familiar spiel verbatim: "You made a bad decision when you bought this place, Soph. The thing is, people want modern places nowadays. I mean, three hundred years old, uneven floors, woodworm-filled beams all over the place and inefficient heating."

The cottage had been her pride and joy before she had met her husband and Sophie was defensive. "Hey, you know I had the heating installed by a good plumber. And that the woodworm and damp were treated professionally. It's a cottage full of character."

Darren scoffed, his arrogance biting her. "Whatever, I still think you should have got a modern place like I did, my apartment sold on the first day it was advertised. Modern is what people like."

Sophie took a sip to stop herself responding; she wasn't in the mood for an argument. It was true, his studio flat had been in a desirable area and was neat and minimalist, economical to run. He had made a good profit in the three years he had owned it before selling up to move in with her. Not that she had seen a penny from the proceeds, which he kept hidden in some lucrative savings account somewhere while she paid for the bills and food with her growing loans and credit cards. It grated that she had no choice but to sell her cottage to pay off those debts, the house she adored and worked hard for as she climbed the career ladder. The temptation to slap the self-righteous words from his pompous face grew fierce.

Time for bed. Sophie drained her glass, standing. "Come on, we need to get some sleep, we've both got work tomorrow."

He sniggered as he finished his drink, stubbing dead the cigarette with yellowed fingers. "You should have bought a modern place, Soph, that's what people want."

Sleepless due to the interminable rasping, Sophie lay in turmoil. The minimal glow from the new moon through a gap in the curtains lightly illuminated her husband's features, his clothed body. Was he handsome? She had thought so at first, well, in a quirky way, but nowadays his cocky sneer irritated her. Yellow-brown eyes, a crooked nose and slightly greying dark hair. His job as a joiner kept him muscly, but his belly was bloated from alcohol excess and takeaway food.

But it was the growing violence that depressed her most. Caring and protective in the wonderful early days, he had treated her like a precious princess, with compliments, gifts, cuddles, kisses. But as his drinking increased, so did his beatings, and every punch reduced the respect she had for him. And for herself.

She rolled over and wondered for the second time since the ultimatum if she should have chosen her parents. Unfortunately, she considered gloomily, divorce did not appear in her personal dictionary.

In Darren's hometown of Bolton, his parents, Maureen and Bob, sat with best friends, Peggy and Bry, by the expensive, polished walnut table, each with a large glass of wine raised. Bry was the most vocal, but Bob took credit for being the most inebriated. He was a happy drunk, or so he would have people believe, and the occasion for celebration made him happier: the imminent move to Mallorca. It had held the entire conversation from the meal at the local Harvester at the beginning of the evening, to this early-hours-of-the-morning toast.

Bry stood, steadying his drunken wobble against the table, and raised his glass. Slurring, he said, "I'd like to take a moment to congratulate our good friends on their wonderful news today. As we all know, we've known each other since our schooldays, we've had our families together."

Bry stopped briefly for an ill-disguised belch, giving Peggy a chance to get a word in: "Get on with it."

His glass shook a little, the aubergine liquid splashing onto the varnished wood, prompting Maureen to snatch a tissue and mop it before it stained. "I'll thank you, my good wife, not to interrupt me while I speak." They all chortled drunkenly. "We've seen our children grow up as friends, move on into adulthood, get married. We've lived our lives alongside each other." He glanced at the grinning group, reddened faces glowing in the soft light. "So I'll cut the speech short, all I can add is you'd better damned well make sure we get plenty of holidays with you in sunny old Mallorca."

Bob took a swig and chuckled as Bry sat. "You bet, mate, but on one condition: you make sure you look at villas for yourself when you come and stay; we want to see you follow us out there."

Peggy giggled. "I'll definitely drink to that." She tapped her glass with a manicured ruby fingernail. "I'd also like to make a little toast myself. Our Davy's Claudia's just found out she's having our first grandchild. We're over the moon, aren't we, Bry."

Maureen glared at Peggy before settling a practised smile on her pink-stained lips. "Well done, Davy and Claudia, we're very pleased for you, Pegs, Bry," she smiled, Mona Lisa, "but if we're talking babies, of course I wasn't going to say anything yet, you know, I like to keep a little decorum, but our Darren and his wife are also having a baby, a son."

"But…" Bob started, incredulous, hastily silenced by a withering stare from his wife. Crestfallen and irked by the instant upstaging, Peggy smiled politely and returned the congratulations.

Harold and Beryl's household in Littleover was quieter, the pleasant semi-detached house in darkness as they lay in bed. Harold purred softly, but Beryl was sleepless after the altercation with Sophie. She had been tossing, turning, heaving and contemplating for hours, often wishing she hadn't consulted Mystical Mary, or whatever she called herself. If she had just stayed at home…

Harold and Beryl liked a refined start to the day, and every evening she would set the table with a choice of cereals, the toaster, the crockery and cutlery. As always, the alarm was set for six, which gave Harold time to read his morning newspaper without rushing before leaving for work at seven thirty. He was close to retirement, and Beryl knew he would miss lecturing at Derby University, but the languid days ahead appealed to her. At least they had before the reading.

Beryl's worries eventually became too much and she realised that if she were to sleep at all before daybreak, she would have to be selfish and wake him.

"Harold." She shook his shoulders and he stirred dreamily.

"What is it, darling?" He rolled over to face her.

"I can't sleep after what happened today. I shouldn't have woken you, but please can we talk it through?"

Harold gently took her hand. "Of course. Look, I know it's upset you, and whether it was the right or wrong decision, I don't know, but you have to remember how upset you are every time you see her covered in bruises. Sometimes you have to protect yourself, and at the end of the day Sophie's a grown woman."

"Yes, I know that, but maybe we should support her. I mean, was it fair to essentially suggest she leave her husband?"

Harold hurt too at Sophie's reluctance to end the destructive relationship, but there was little they could do but wait in the background until their daughter was ready. He contemplated Beryl's indecision for a moment before breathing a reluctant sigh. "I don't know. It's such an awful situation. For all of us."

Beryl sat, hugging her knees to her chest. "You should have seen her this time, Harold. Her make-up was plastered on so thickly but the bruises still showed through. Why does she tolerate it? Why doesn't she admit it to us? I've even passed her leaflets about domestic violence and watched her discreetly throw them in the bin. It's just too hard to stand on the side-lines and see that happening to my child."

Harold wriggled up wearily, hugging her to his chest. "I know, darling, I know, and if that's the case then you've done the right thing. In a way we only have ourselves to blame…"

Beryl sat straight, aghast. "Us? How dare you, Harold Waller. We brought our children up to respect people and be respected in return, we…"

"Shh, you've misunderstood me. Darling, we have a wonderful marriage, we rarely argue, and even when we do it's a sensible discussion rather than a shouting match. Sophie has grown up to believe that once married, forever married, you know, until death do us part. We're her role models and that will have made her determined to make her marriage work."

Beryl sighed, relaxing into Harold's shoulder. "I see your point. I just can't bear to see her being treated so badly. Darren's always been rough around the edges, I mistrusted him from the very first time I met him."

Harold snuggled his wife down to the pillows once more, drawing cool sheets over their shoulders, and despaired as tears rolled from her cheek to his chest. Holding her close, he whispered, "Sophie's an intelligent girl, sweetheart, she'll not take the mistreatment forever. One day she'll come to her senses and leave Darren, but it's up to her to choose the right time, not us."

Innocent despite her age. "You really think she'll leave him?"

"One day, yes, of that I have no doubt."

Beryl closed her damp eyes, his warm reassurance comforting, and listened to his deepening breaths, which eventually lulled her to sleep.

Chapter 3
Broken BMW

I'd had a good chuckle after Beryl's tarot reading, hoping that meddling with her life in such a way would cause her distress, so when we met the following week I was stunned to find I had inadvertently helped her. I silently chastised myself, determined to find out more about the family for effective ammunition.

I didn't even have to try, because as soon as she sat at the table it was clear she needed to talk. Well, I wasn't about to stop her getting things off her chest, and she was grateful. I learned how their daughter's husband had been increasingly violent and how it affected Sophie's work as a solicitor, how much it upset Beryl and Harry, and how useless their son felt, knowing his beloved sister was being abused, but unable to do anything to stop it. Now I knew why she had accepted my advice so readily the previous week. And it seemed they weren't the only people with an intense dislike for the man. She told me that the day after she'd given Sophie the ultimatum, her son had received a call from his incredulous sister, explaining an unbelievable event that had happened at her cottage in the early hours of the morning.

As Beryl explained, I could picture the scene in my head, her account being so - and I hate to admit this - conscientious. I was soon lost in the relation, gasping intermittently at the extraordinary occurrences. I'll elaborate for you:

All was peaceful, the night sky clear of clouds and stars brightly shimmering in the late summer warmth that had the residents in the pretty village of Coleorton throwing off their covers in their sleep. Inside Iris Cottage, Darren and Sophie were no different, the duvet draping only their feet, eyes tightly shut, minds in separate dreamlands. A smash of shattering glass stirred them, but not enough to wake fully. The second thunderous crash had them both sitting in bed, looking at each other with questioning eyes.

"What was that?" Sophie wasn't sure if she had been dreaming.

Darren jumped off the bed without answering, racing to the window that overlooked the driveway, and tugged the curtain aside, straining to see. "I don't know, it's black out there."

Sophie stifled a yawn. "Maybe it was just a cat or something."

The ear-splitting sound of creasing metal rang out and Darren bolted to the door, throwing on his dressing gown. "Somebody's out there, I just saw a silhouette by the cars."

Sophie reached the bottom of the staircase as Darren darted through the front door, feet bare, fists clenched in anger. She hesitated, unsure, before running outside to join him. Standing in the safety of the rose covered porch, she watched silently as her husband, incredulous and almost crying, inspected the smashed windscreen, crumpled bonnet and indented driver's side door of his prided car. She had been horrified in the spring when Darren had bought the BMW, such flamboyancy while she was heavily debt-ridden, but now she felt nothing but compassion for him.

"How can this happen?" To himself, maybe nobody.

"Did you see anyone?" And instantly she surmised he would have given chase if he had, shoes or no shoes, and felt ridiculous for asking such a redundant question.

"Of course I bloody didn't." Shaking his fist, Darren glanced around and yelled, "Fucking wanker."

"Shush, Darren. Look, I'll go and call the police. Come back inside, there's nothing you can do out here."

He poured a vodka and Red Bull moments after returning inside, the first of many, and lit a cigarette, inhaling deeply. After a while he began to pace furiously, drinking excessively, smoking heavily, swearing copiously. A patrol car finally turned up after two hours and by that time Darren was seething; the police might not see it as an emergency but it certainly was to him.

Sophie invited the officer in and she sat on one of the cream-leather sofas, pen poised above her pad ready to take notes, but Darren continued to stomp back and forth, his face glowing crimson with anger and alcohol. "Have you seen what they've done to my car?" he spat, outraged. "I can't fucking believe it."

"My colleague is inspecting the damage right now, sir."

"I suppose that's a bloody woman too."

Sophie mouthed an apology to the irked policewoman, whose eyebrow was raised. "Do you have any idea who might have done this?"

"Of course I bloody don't."

"Any enemies, disgruntled employees, unpaid debts?"

Darren stilled and stared at her, astonished, and Sophie considered his head might explode with rage. The imagery brought a twitch to the sides of her mouth which she controlled masterfully. "Miss whatever-your-name-is…"

"PC Adams, sir."

He glared at her. "I have no idea who did this. I have no enemies, I'm a good bloke, everybody likes me." He often spouted about how wonderful he was and, unwilling to hear the lies again, Sophie headed for the door. "I'm self-employed with no employees and I'm financially solvent. What are you going to do about my car and the wanker who did this?"

Adams watched Sophie leave, having noted the bruises on her bare face, and knew the steaming man in front of her was definitely not a good bloke. She sighed.

Nobody had noticed PC Taylor enter the room with a scrap of paper in his hand. "I think you'll find that you *have* upset somebody somewhere, Mr Delaney, I found this note on the front seat of the car. I'm guessing it was thrown through the smashed windscreen."

Grey and black letters cut from a newspaper had been glued to a slip of paper: 'It'll be your legs next time'.

Despite Darren's puzzled expression, Taylor and Adams shared a knowing glance; it was possible this was an attempt at insurance fraud. A decent car left unlocked, hence no alarm; maybe he had vandalised his own car. And conveniently no witnesses, except his wife. "Your wife was in bed with you, sir?"

"Obviously."

"I'll take your statement here, and," she nodded to Taylor, "my colleague will speak with your wife."

Taylor found Sophie in the kitchen, glass in hand, leaning against the kitchen worktop with her head hanging low. He was struck instantly by her vulnerability, her sadness. She wore a flimsy, satin nightdress which showed heavy bruising on her wrists and the tops of her arms, and her face was discoloured and swollen. "Were you asleep when the car was vandalised?"

She nodded, surveying the floor tiles that were pleasantly cool against her bare feet.

"Is your husband in any kind of financial trouble?" He was close now, standing beside the sink.

Quickly. "No, not at all. Not unless he's run up debts behind my back."

"Of course, you may have reasons why you wouldn't want us to know…"

Too quick. "I'm the one with the debts, not him. He earns a good wage."

Taylor scribbled in his notebook, words Sophie wished she could see. Agitated, she set the glass down and reached for her cigarettes and lighter. "Maybe you feel you can't say anything in case there's any comeback."

She paused, questioning. "What do you mean?"

"Your face, your arms. You've had a little accident somewhere along the line, haven't you? Did your husband do that?"

Her cheeks reddened and she was defensive. "Now hold on a minute, Darren's a good husband, he'd never lay a finger on me, never."

"So how did you get those bruises?"

Sophie lit the cigarette and inhaled deeply, slowly breathing the smoke out as her unwelcome blushing subsided and concocting the feasible lie in her hesitance. "We have a shower over the bath. I slipped the other day and banged my face. It stunned me. Darren bruised my arms accidentally when he was trying to help me up, he was worried about me."

Taylor noticed her fidgeting, sure she was lying, but this avenue was dead for now. "Do you know of anybody with a grievance against Mr Delaney?"

Another long drag of odorous smoke and Sophie wondered if her parents were deranged enough to do something as vile as this… Of course they weren't, they were gentle souls. "No, I have no idea why anybody would be so vicious."

He sighed. "Okay, could you tell me exactly what happened?"

I had been trying not to laugh as Beryl told the tale - the image I had of Darren pacing was like something out of a slapstick comedy - but she was serious and I realised there was more to come. I offered to make tea and cleared some of the clutter on the sofa to one side. "Come and sit here, it's comfier than the chairs." I headed for the kitchen while she settled herself.

I dragged my chair to face her once the tea was made, explaining that I found it difficult to get up from the low settee, and I saw the once-over she gave my vastly overweight body. Politely she made no comment; damn the woman I hated for being so annoyingly pleasant.

"You see, Mary… can I call you Mary?" I nodded and she continued, her soft voice lulling me back to the unusual events of the past week. "Because I'd told Sophie not to be in touch until she," her hesitation showed how painful the decision to take my advice had been, "well, anyway, she called Harold. She's always been a daddy's girl and she knew he would talk, whereas I would put the phone down. Anyway, that's irrelevant. It seems Sophie had suspected she was pregnant the previous week when she took an instant and violent dislike to anything from the ocean. Fish of any kind has been a favourite food of hers for as long as I can remember, but the smell of it now, raw or cooked, made her retch. She'd not told anyone of her suspicions, worried in case it was a false alarm.

"But Sophie needed to know for herself and her gut feeling was right, the test was positive. She suspected Darren had a big battle with the insurance company ahead so decided not to tell him straight away in case it stressed him further. She hid the test in the back of the bathroom cabinet."

Beryl sipped her tea, eyeing me, questioning, and spoke timidly, as if she were asking a huge favour. "Look, before I go on, would you do the tarot reading. I mean, can you do one on Sophie, rather than me."

I mulled the question, unsure how to answer. Let's face it, I was doing this game as a money earner, there isn't a psychic bone in my body, so I said of course it was possible and we returned to the table. Once again I did the Celtic cross spread, the only one I had studied in depth, and prepared myself to make an educated guess at what it all meant.

I interpreted the cards to the best of the knowledge I had learned from the book. Obviously Beryl had told me about the pregnancy, and strangely the cards appeared to back that up, but there appeared to be warnings, something about heights. The images weren't clear, but Sophie was in danger somehow. I looked pleadingly at the woman I despised; maybe she knew something I didn't, but her face had paled, mouth hanging.

Bizarrely I felt empathy for her, she was so nice and kind, so gentle. Maybe I should stop hating her, after all, she did nothing wrong all those years ago, it was Harry and me who had the affair. All she did was remain loyal to him, which meant I couldn't have what I wanted. Maybe I should accept that my contempt for this woman was borne out of selfishness, that I had made her guilty by association. I swallowed hard, surprised at berating myself in such a way.

Her voice was strained as she pointed to the card at the top of the staff. "That card tells you how it's all going to end, doesn't it?"

I nodded, astounded by my new feelings for this woman. "Yes, it's the final outcome should you, well, Sophie, carry on…"

"Turn it." She was insistent, with no apparent interest in the cards before. "Please."

Fearing what the card would predict after seeing her reaction to the danger and warning cards, I felt a strange intuition that I needed to see the other cards first, it seemed imperative, and I told her so. Her expression became agonised so I hastened back to the cards. Moving slowly up the staff, I uncovered three cards that, in my experience, could only mean one thing. The Ace of Wands drawn with the Empress was a great combination, but add the Page of Pentacles too. That was pretty much failsafe. I smiled widely to relax her. "I think the baby's going to be bouncing and healthy."

But the tears coursing down her cheeks told me a different story. Guiding her back to the sofa, I helped her sit and shuffled my chair forward so I could hold her hand. "Beryl, come on, what's the matter?" I was confused. Maybe she didn't want Sophie to be expecting because it meant she would stay with Darren. I didn't know what to think.

But soon I knew why my reading had upset her so much. "Sophie's in hospital. She lost the baby."

I didn't know what to say. The silence in the room hung like a dark cloud for what seemed like an eternity. Several ideas of how to continue sprang to mind but none were befitting and I stayed seated, mind whirring but mouth closed, while Beryl sobbed quietly. Eventually I stood, unnoticed, and clambered through the cluttered living room to the kitchen. It was the only solution I could think of: the bottle of whisky that had stood in my cupboard for probably two years now with barely a drop touched. I poured two equal measures and took them through, passing one to Beryl, whose weeping had subsided. After a few sips she had composed herself enough to continue.

"Sophie wouldn't have called Harold unless she was desperate, she's a stubborn girl. From what he said later I guessed she was in turmoil and he was the only person who would understand. They're very close. She called him at work, I suppose because if she'd rung our home number I might have answered and rejected her again. Obviously he was pleased to hear from her, I mean, we love her - we love her so much - which is how this has all come about, really.

"She touched on the subject of me not wanting to talk to her and he explained how worried I was for her, but he said he could tell she really needed her mother by the way her voice dropped when he told her I was standing firm this time." Beryl stared at me with pleading eyes and I felt awful; it was difficult to remember why I was being so harsh on the broken woman before me. She grasped my hand firmly. "Please tell me I haven't done the wrong thing, Mary. I couldn't bear it if my actions led to her being in hospital."

Now, I rarely drink alcohol, there's no need, but on this occasion there was. I took both the empty glasses and refilled them, the trip to the kitchen giving me a little time to think things through. About why I detested Beryl so much, why it was important for me to destroy what she and Harry had. Then I remembered my babies, the babies Harry had implanted inside me, the pain of losing my cherubs, the fact that I was once a beautiful teenager with the whole world ahead of me and as a result of my children being stolen so cruelly, I became a fat, myopic, ugly blob with no feelings and a loveless life. I told myself resolutely that what Beryl was telling me was the information I needed to ruin that man. My barriers went back up and I returned to the room with the drinks, devoid of emotion once more.

Once I was seated again on the hard chair, Beryl continued. "Sophie told Harold about the baby and he was really pleased. He's such a gentle man, his family means the world to him."

The words grated on me, after all, if he was such a family man, why did he give my twins away so freely. Losing two beautiful children for what? To save face? Oh yes, the anger was well and truly back.

"She asked if I would change my mind about seeing her if he told me about the baby, and he said it probably wouldn't change anything unless she was rid of Darren. She spat a few words at him and slammed the phone down, which really isn't like her. The next we heard was that she was in hospital."

And Beryl proceeded to tell me what had happened:

Since Darren's car had been vandalised, he had used Sophie's car while she took the bus to work in Derby. She had only had a couple of clients that morning so had left earlier than usual and as she traipsed along the gravel driveway to her cottage, still deflated from the mishandled conversation with her father, Sophie was surprised to see her Fiesta parked outside. Darren wasn't due home for at least another hour, and she increased her pace, curious.

He wasn't in the living room or kitchen, and the bathroom door wasn't locked. "Darren?" Climbing the stairs, she wondered if he was at the local, or maybe in a drunken stupor on the bed. She hoped it was the former, not in the mood for walking on eggshells today. "Darren?"

She heard the chink of glass against glass from upstairs and sagged; he was awake and drinking. She prayed he was in a good mood as she tentatively stepped into the bedroom. Darren sat on the side of the bed with a full tumbler of brandy, scowling, glowering at the carpet. Her first instinct was to run - she'd had enough of the day already without his bad mood - but she said, "What's up, why are you home so early?"

"Bastards." His yellow-brown eyes shot vitriolic disgust at her.

She flinched, burning from his flames. "Who? What's happened?"

Darren gulped some brandy, rage bubbling. "I phoned the insurance company today and they told me

40

they're not paying out." Another swig. "I came straight home."

Darren and alcohol wasn't a good combination, but Darren and alcohol plus anger was dangerous. But it wasn't her he was angry with so she guessed she was safe and sat on the bed beside him. "That can't be right, why have they said that?"

"They said that after reading the police report they believe it was an inside job."

"What do you mean, an inside job?"

"Basically they think either I did it, or paid someone to do it." He downed the brandy and replenished the glass, and Sophie discreetly glanced at the bottle to see how close he was to passing out: very close, it was nearly empty. She breathed silently with relief. "Fucking bastard insurance bastards. I'd kill to see what the fucking pigs put on their notes. Bastards."

"Don't worry, I can testify that you were in bed with me when the noises woke us up. Nobody's asked for my story yet."

Wobbly, Darren stomped across the room, thunderous one way, thunderous back. "That's what I told them, but they said they won't accept your story because you're my wife."

Now she was as incredulous as he had probably been when he had heard. "That's ludicrous."

Instantly, he shoved her roughly on the chest and she fell to the floor. "Oh God, no," she pleaded, hands raised in self-defence.

He loomed over her, fists clenched and a cruel sneer on his face. "Maybe you arranged this, you're the bloody solicitor. Did you arrange for someone to do this just to spite me, knowing your story wouldn't back me up?"

"No, I wouldn't do that, you know that."

He grabbed her collar, the seam digging into the back of her neck, and pushed her brutally back on the floor. "You're a bitch, Sophie, you're a two-faced bitch."

She edged back, desperate to escape. Although she had been in this situation a hundred times she now had a special reason not to take a beating. "Darren, don't, you can't do this now, please."

He slugged half his drink, staggering about, trying to find the coordination to set the glass back down, which gave her the opportunity to clamber to her feet and dash to the staircase. But he snatched her, strong arm crooked around her neck from behind, squeezing, controlling. "Think you can run from me, do you, bitch."

She scratched his arms with her nails, sinking her teeth into his hand and his grip loosened with a growl of angry pain. In a swift movement, his other fist smashed into the side of her head, knocking her across the landing into the banister. Intense pain burned from her ribcage. Winded, she tried to speak, tell him about the baby, but no words came.

On her again, grasping hands viciously yanking her golden curls as he dragged her towards him, her resistance leaving clumps of torn hair between his fingers. But her dainty frame against his towering strength was useless. A fierce blow to her belly, again sending her crashing into the banister, and strong hands underneath her arms lifted her, her legs leaving the floor. She felt the banister on her back and realised

42

what he was doing. Her dripping blood hit the wooden stairs momentarily before her face and her mind blackened, silenced.

Beryl was struggling to relate the distressing story, but, remembering my Anna and Andrew, I adamantly kept my empathy in check. I oohed and aahed in all the right places, but not from the heart. "Darren called, said he'd found her at the bottom of the stairs when he got home from work. Of course, we had our suspicions as soon as he said she was hurt but, well, for the time being at least we had to take him at his word. We got to the hospital as quickly as we could.

"She was in the intensive care unit and there was no sign of Darren. The only sounds in the darkened room were the monitors beeping and the swishing of the ventilator. She was in a bad way and I started to cry. The nurse explained that she had been unresponsive when the ambulance had arrived and hadn't regained consciousness since.

"She explained that the bruising on her chest suggested she had broken ribs on the right hand side, but an X-ray was impossible until her condition stabilised. She said the ventilator was in place to ease the shock to her body, said she would breathe if it were removed, but the consultant wanted to keep it there for a day or so to give her body time to start healing."

The anguish in Beryl's red-rimmed eyes was replaced by reticence. "Do you have children, Mary?"

My jaw tightened, the anger for Harry beating me from inside, and it was hard not to grit my teeth when I replied. "I have five. Four sons and a daughter."

Her eyes dropped to the floor again, voice weak. "Then you'll understand how I felt at that moment."

Yes, I thought, but your daughter wasn't taken away like mine was. Again, I hated Beryl, wanted to smash her head in, kick her, beat her, see her blood spill, because she still had her daughter and I didn't.

"I sat on one side of the bed, Harold on the other, and we clutched her fingers; we couldn't hold her hands because she had a cannula in each wrist. The right side of her face was swollen and bruised dark blue and a deep cut on her forehead had been stitched. I was in a panic and looked at Harold for reassurance and, bless him, he insisted she had a strong enough character and constitution to recover from this.

"Then the nurse returned with Sophie's notes and told us she'd forgotten to mention that Sophie had lost her baby in the fall. I growled at Harold that Sophie wouldn't recover from *that* so easily, as if it were *his* fault."

Cool air swept through the door and Steve entered, a pained gasp at the sight of his sister, so helpless, peaceful, so hurt. With an arm around his shoulder, Harold guided his son's frozen statue to the seat he had left. Steve's eyes flitted between his mother, father and sister, watery and black, screwed with incomprehension beneath the frown. "What happened?" Creaky, barely there.

Harold answered, knowing Beryl's sobs would choke her words. "Darren said he found her at the bottom of the stairs when he got in from work. He got an ambulance straight away."

A flash of anger replaced the unspent tears. "Where is he? I want to talk to him."

"I don't know. He wasn't here when we arrived."

Steve stood, furious. "What the hell's he playing at, he should be here with his wife."

A dispirited sigh. "I know, but what can we do? You know what he's like." Harold pushed his son back onto the chair by his shoulders.

"Is she going to be okay?"

Throat parched, Beryl's voice cracked. "She'll be fine. They suspect rib fractures, but the rest is just bruising."

"But what about..." Steve gestured to the ventilator.

Harold waved, dismissive. "She's going to be fine, son, maybe a couple of weeks of rest. Peace and quiet."

"She was pregnant, Steve, she lost the baby," Beryl said bitterly.

"You think he did this, don't you, Mum?" He became agitated when his mother didn't respond and tenderly kissed his sister's unbruised cheek. "I can't stay, not right now, but I'll be back later. I've got something I have to do." He strode through the door, head high and shoulders back, and Beryl guessed her proud son needed some tears.

Harold took Beryl's free hand and caught her eye. "Do you think he did it?"

She nodded with vigour. "Yes, I do, and now you have to understand why I can't see her, why we can't see her. Because until she leaves him, this is going to keep happening. Or worse. I can't support my daughter's marriage to a man who may well kill her one day."

While the distraught parents tended their daughter, the atmosphere was sedate in the White Horse, Darren's local. It was predictably quiet, being a Monday, with just a few regulars, mainly older men. Most were divorced or widowed and visited the pub every night for company, but a few were there to escape their nagging wives. The walls were yellowed and floorboards stained, and the stale odour hung from hundreds of years of patrons smoking. It was a working-man's pub, through and through.

At thirty-three, Darren was easily the youngest in the bar, and had been drinking alone at a table, nodding hello occasionally to the other lonely drinkers as they came and went. He downed the dregs in his glass and strolled to the bar to order his sixth pint; he would have a few more before going home to a few shots of whisky. Jayne - not so attractive, but chatty enough with the punters to warrant her job - began to refill his glass without him asking; she knew him well. "No Sophie tonight?"

Darren perched on a barstool, the five pints freeing his tongue. "She's in hospital, went in this afternoon."

Their eyes met briefly while she pumped the amber liquid, pouring off the excess froth masterfully as the glass filled. "Oh? Nothing serious, I hope."

Darren checked his pocket for cigarettes and remembered the smoking ban. "She must have fallen down the stairs, I found her lying there when I got home from work. I called an ambulance straight away."

Astounded, she stopped pumping and stared at him. "She's in hospital from a fall and you're here." Immediately aware her judgement wasn't in the job description, she finished filling the glass, averting her eyes.

He held his hands in the air, questioning, an innocent wounded boy. "What could I do? There's no point me watching her sleep, she's in the right hands. I'll go and see her tomorrow." Passing her a handful of change, Darren took his drink outside to the smoking tent.

Half an hour passed and he was on his third cigarette, each lit from the previous stub; everybody chain-smoked now they couldn't light up inside. Old Ernie and his fourteen-year-old Jack Russell, Lucy, had accompanied him for the past two cigarettes, passing the time of day, commenting on the news, the weather - nothing substantial - but now he had gone inside for another Guinness, leaving Darren alone.

Darren heard the crack before he felt pain, sensing wetness on his collar; the blow had come from nowhere. He grasped the back of his head and he drew his hand back to see crimson red that appeared black in the scant moonlight. Before he could turn to see what was happening, another explosion knocked his head forward into the wooden slats of the table.

Hazily aware that he was under attack from an unknown assailant, he tried vainly to escape from the bench, hands up to shield his head, and the next blow crashed against his back, pain not registering now through his adrenaline filled fear. Struggling away, trying to defend himself, his attacker rained punch after punch to his face. Darren slumped prostrate on the ground and the kicks started.

Winded and in agony, his energy gone, Darren lay stilled on the cool concrete, awaiting the next strike.

Waiting. Waiting. Moments passed, a minute. Nothing. Somewhere - maybe in his head, maybe in the clouds - a faint voice rang out. "Jesus shit, it's Daz, he's bleeding. Somebody get an ambulance, quick."

Chapter 4
Darren's Comeuppance

It was proving to be a long night. Beryl had been here for hours and I was becoming tired, but I still wanted to know more about what had been happening in her life. For a start I was curious, it was a rollercoaster of a ride, but also the more she told me, the more ammunition I had for my own gain. It was clear how much Harry and Beryl doted on their daughter, and from what I could make out she was relatively wealthy. That was surely a double whammy. On the one hand I could use Sophie to get at her parents, and on the other, I could find a way to blackmail some of that cash out of her. The money I got from benefits and tarot reading paid the bills and fed me, but it would be amazing to move out of the shithole I lived in to somewhere more decent.

So, without resenting the cost of the alcohol, I passed Beryl a third glass of whisky, ready to listen again after her latest flood of tears. "We'd been there a few hours when the night staff said the police wanted to talk to us. I could see from Harold's eyes that he was thinking the same as me: they'd discovered Darren was responsible for the so-called accident. We'd both been sleeping, me with my head on Sophie's bed, him on a chair, so we were a bit woozy."

Harold glanced over his shoulder at the two uniformed officers and stood, unsure how to greet them. The nurse left the room and Harold glanced at his watch: 3.00 A.M.. "Mr Waller, please sit down again." The young policeman's blue-black hair reflected the dimmed lights as he quietly dragged two chairs up to the bemused Harold.

Officers Kanhai and Taylor sat, the former nodding at Sophie. "I understand this is your daughter, Sophie Delaney." Taylor briefly took in the patient he had already met before looking away. It was the first time his colleague had mentioned her name - he had been in the car when Kanhai had learned the details from the barmaid - and he despaired at seeing the woman he had an odd affection for so helpless and hurt. Harold nodded. "Could you confirm she's married to a," Kanhai consulted his notebook, "Mr Darren Delaney." Again, Harold confirmed without speaking. "I'm sorry to have to tell you this with your daughter, um..." Harold nodded his assent for the man to continue without further sympathies. "I'm afraid Mr Delaney has just been admitted here too, he's been severely attacked. He's conscious, but he's taken quite a, um, well, it was a violent attack."

Harold's jaw dropped, trying to work out how to deal with the news; his first reaction, suppressed, was to smile. Mouth opening and closing, he tried to uncover the correct words to use. Taylor drew strength and surveyed Sophie. "What happened to your daughter, Mr Waller?"

Harold shook his head slowly, unable to answer with his suspicions heightened, and Kanhai continued: "Obviously you don't want to leave your daughter's side at this time, however, she is Mr Delaney's next of kin. Do you have contact details of any of Mr Delaney's relations, even if just their names?"

Over Kanhai's shoulder, Harold noticed Steve approaching through the glass to the corridor and was relieved, but when his son saw the two officers, he turned and hastened away. Desperately controlling the expression on his face, Harold suddenly realised who had attacked his son-in-law. "Yes, of course, I can give you the names and a general area for his parents. We're not personally in touch, but I know whereabouts they live."

Kanhai smiled, positioning his pad and pen. "Oh, er, by the way," he gave Harold his full attention once more, "I don't suppose you have any idea who may have attacked Darren, do you?"

"No." Harold breathed deeply and relaxed, before furnishing the constables with what he could remember of Maureen and Bob's details.

Taylor took Harold to one side as he and Kanhai stood to leave. "Could you please let me know when Sophie wakes up, Mr Waller? She's a friend of a friend and I just want to know that she's okay."

After the policemen had gone, Harold fought his tiredness to keep his eyes on the door, waiting hopefully for Steve to return. Presently his son appeared, tentatively checking the coast was clear, and Harold was relieved Beryl had fallen asleep again because he wanted to protect her from the truth he knew. Steve entered the room shiftily, tiptoeing, and joined his father, sitting beside him in the chair Taylor had evacuated. "What did the police want, Dad?"

Harold shook his head. Every bone in his body wanted to congratulate and thank Steve for defending his sister, but on the other hand he had always maintained that disputes should be settled without violence. He could think of nothing that wouldn't sound hypocritical. "They don't suspect you, son."

Steve's jaw dropped and, concerned, he growled quietly, "How did you know it was me?" His eyes wandered to his sister, serene in her comatose state. "He did this, Dad, you know that as well as I do. But this time it's not just her, it's her baby too. He deserved it. He deserved more."

"Maybe so, but you don't deserve to be imprisoned for assault for protecting your sister, and that's what will happen if the truth ever gets out. So let it go and don't dare say anything to your mother. I won't say a word and we'll pretend this never happened. Anyway, I can't imagine Sophie will stay with him after this. If it was down to him - which I hasten to add we don't know for certain - then the police will discover the truth. Hopefully this will be the end of the matter."

The police had taken a while to trace Bob and Maureen Delaney from the scant details Harold Waller had given, and the sun was rising as they reached Derby to see their son, who, to their relief, was sitting in bed eating toast. His face was blackened and swollen with a few minor cuts and his head was bandaged, but he seemed in good form, smiling as they hurried towards him. Bob was stunned. "Bloody hell, son, you don't do things by halves, do you?"

Darren put his half-eaten toast on the plate and took his mother's outstretched hand. "It hurts, Mam, it bloody hurts."

Gently stroking his forehead, his cheek, smoothing the covers, straightening the water jug. "I'm sure it does, baby, I'm sure it does. Have they given you painkillers?" She yelled across the ward. "Nurse, my son needs morphine, he's in tremendous pain. Nurse."

"Mam, stop shouting, everyone's looking." Darren indicated the armchair beside the bed, while Bob drew up a plastic chair. Maureen sat on the edge of the seat, leaning over the bed as she made sure the sheets were perfectly arranged.

"Baby, who did this to you? The police say they don't know, which is ridiculous, I say, they get paid to do nothing. They should have him behind bars by now. What we pay taxes for, I just don't know."

"Mam, it's only just happened and nobody saw anything. I'm sure they're doing their best." Darren winced, not so much in pain but enjoying the motherly sympathy curling around him.

From the blue, Maureen said, "Move to Mallorca with us, Darren." Bob stared at his wife, nonplussed. "You can't stay in a country where things like this happen, that's why we're moving abroad, the crime, the violence. Just think of it, baby, sun every day. You've got a good trade, you'll find work. We've still got the profit from the sale of your flat in our investment account and we'd double it so you could buy a nice place, help you out in any way you needed. What do you say, baby?"

Darren laughed as hard as his swollen mouth would allow, while Bob reeled from the unexpected suggestion. "Mam, I can't just give up everything here, not just like that."

"Yes you could, of course you could, we'd help you in any way, with the documents, moving, money, we'd help. Wouldn't we, Bob?"

Bob's head was spinning; he was used to Maureen's determination to organise everybody, everything, but still he was gobsmacked. He nodded, forcing a smile, while considering how welcome a glass or two of La Motte Shiraz would be at this moment.

Maureen's jaw tensed, thin lips pursing. "We would even let your wife come if that was what you wanted." Strained, through clenched teeth. She glanced around the ward. "Hold on a minute, talking of that woman, where is she? She should be at your bedside right now. How dare she not be here when you need her, baby. What is that woman like."

Darren held her hand, interlinking his fingers with hers, her perfect pink manicure offsetting the ochre nicotine stains on his hands. "She's here, Mam, she just went upstairs for a bit."

Maureen tutted her disgust. "I should give her a piece of my mind."

Bob was fond of his daughter-in-law of two years, she was pretty enough - would probably make a good mother one day if she would just lose the silly job and concentrate on her man instead - but no woman was good enough for Maureen's son. Right now, it was time to diffuse the situation. "So, Daz, what do you think of your mam's suggestion then?"

Darren thought for a minute, nodding, a light smile. "You know, I think it would be good. It'd be good to be near you guys and I definitely like the idea of all-year sunshine. You reckon I'd be able to find work, Dad?"

"Of course. Carpentry, woodwork, you'd get plenty of work out there, and like your mam says we'd help you with everything. Run it by Sophie when you see her. It's about time she stopped that career lark and gave us a grandchild. I mean," he guffawed, "after all, there won't be much call for an English solicitor in Mallorca, will there, so she'd have to look after you and a few kids instead."

Maureen straightened, hands neat in the centre of her lap, and she smiled sweetly, mission accomplished. She would have to put up with *that woman*, but at least her darling son and his babies would be nearby.

Gasping, Harold jumped up and patted Beryl's shoulder. "Sweetheart, wake up." Beryl stirred, sitting upright as she remembered where she was. "Sophie's awake." Fumbling, overexcited, he pressed the assistance button a few times. "Nurse."

Sophie's wide eyes were deep brown puddles in scared whiteness. Her weak hand rose to her throat, tugging lamely at the ventilator. A nurse opened the door and shouted out for assistance, running over, pushing Harold aside. Taking Sophie's hand, calm and reassuring, she said, "Hello, Sophie, calm down, love, I know it's awkward to breathe, just let the machine do it for you until the doctor comes. Just relax, love, it's okay."

Gossip was rife at nurses' stations, the canteen, sneaked cigarette breaks: the tale of the tragic couple who had both ended up in hospital on the same night for completely different reasons. They hastily arranged for them to have a private room, the least they could do in the sad circumstances. A porter wheeled Darren's bed into the small room, away from the coughing and spluttering, wheezing and grunting of the previous ward, which pleased him immensely.

Meanwhile, a consultant discharged Sophie from intensive care. The ventilating tube had been removed, leaving her throat sore and grazed, her voice husky, and the only drip still attached was to rehydrate her. Harold and Beryl, hand in hand, waited nearby, relieved and grateful. "We're transferring you to a ward now Sophie, and they'll take you for an X-ray to check that the ribs we suspect are broken won't cause any further problems."

Sophie nodded, her parents beaming warmly. The consultant moved to the next patient, while a nurse plumped her pillows and smoothed the covers. "We've got a treat for you too; just wait until you see who's waiting for you." Harold's smile waned when he realised the horror Sophie was about to face; he hadn't told her or his wife about the attack on Darren. He excused himself, searching his trouser pockets for the phone number Taylor had given him.

He only suspected Darren had lied about finding Sophie at the bottom of the stairs, and blustered through the difficult conversation, trying not to incriminate a man who was possibly innocent, and the result was nonsensical gibberish. All Taylor understood was that Sophie had woken and was going to be fine. Had he realised she was about to share a room with her husband, he would have halted the transfer immediately.

It was too late, however. When Harold returned, Sophie was gone, her bed replaced with a fresh one ready for the next patient. He dragged his fingers through his hair, hunting for someone who could tell him which ward his daughter had been moved to.

The doors burst open and a porter's back bumped through, dragging a bed into the room. Darren had relished the quiet and his heart sank, wondering how they would fit another bed in such a small space. But then he saw Sophie and grinned, crinkling the bruising and stretching the cuts.

Beryl recoiled in horror on seeing Darren, hand clutching her heart, and left, unable to be near the man she loathed. When Harold arrived, clearly having knowledge about her son-in-law's admission, she demanded they return to Littleover.

PC Taylor, who in retrospect had deciphered Harold's call to mean he wasn't the only person to suspect Darren had caused Sophie's injuries, was eager to question her, find the truth, and he visited during his lunchbreak. He too was shocked to find the abuser and abused sharing a room, man and wife, in sickness and in health. She would never admit to anything in Darren's presence so, his break wasted, Taylor headed back to work.

Darren devoured his dinner greedily, wishing for more, but Sophie had no appetite, sadly pushing the food around her plate. She was so confused. She loved Darren, had done for the past four years, and their wedding twenty-three months before had been the most wonderful and exciting day of her life. But she was scared of him now, terrified of what he was capable of.

He had hit her before, in fact she was used to it, but it had only been a punch here, a shove there, a bit of wrestling. This attack was different, more sinister. One she had never anticipated and never wanted to repeat. If only he would admit he drank too much; he was lovely on the rare occasions he was sober. She would have to try and talk to him somehow, especially now a baby was on the way.

Nobody had mentioned the miscarriage.

Darren scraped the last forkful together and ate hungrily, turning the television down while he chewed. "You know we were planning to move somewhere smaller and cheaper when your house sells, Soph?" She nodded, unable to make eye contact with the tyrant she loved so dearly. "How do you fancy moving to Mallorca?"

Now she stared at him, mouth ajar, words absent, and laughter lines crawled from the corners of his snake eyes as he chuckled at her reaction. And his words tumbled, gushing the offers his mother had made, his mind already decided.

But she had been beaten. He had almost killed her. Her anguish grew, and the timid shell she found herself locked inside didn't know how to say no.

Beryl had talked everything off her chest during the four hours she had been at my flat, leaving her more cheerful than when she had arrived. By cutting dead my emotions, building a brick wall between my heart and my head, her story was now just that: a story. Not a girl in hospital having suffered domestic violence, but a girl in hospital who I was going to befriend for my own benefit. Not a mother who was distraught at her child's injuries, but a woman who stole the man I'd wanted thirty years before. Not a son who had defended his sister, but a man I could now bribe and manipulate.

Beryl had called Harry on her mobile to ask him to collect her and I watched through the window after her departure to see if I could catch a glimpse of him, but, being on the fourth floor, all I saw was the roof of their car.

My revenge for him could wait; I needed some sleep in order to be up bright and early tomorrow. Now the fun was really about to begin.

Chapter 5
The Stalking Begins

Four days had passed since Sophie and Darren had individually ended up in hospital, and as their home was so far away, Maureen and Bob hadn't visited again, but had kept in contact by phone. Maureen was annoyed that her son's attacker hadn't been caught and she wasn't the type of person to let things go. For the fifth time she dialled the number Darren had given her for the officers who were supposed to be finding the beast, and this time she couldn't be bothered to be polite any more; the whole debacle had become tiresome.

After stubbornly refusing to accept excuses, Maureen was finally put through to Kanhai, who listened to her angry rant for a while, unable to get a word in edgeways - did the woman never breathe? "It's been four days since my Darren was beaten up and I still haven't heard anything. You should have found who did it by now and have them behind bars."

At last there was a break in the verbal spillage and Kanhai pacified her diplomatically. He'd not so much forgotten the event, but had other more pressing tasks to take care of. However, her call brought Darren Delaney to the forefront of his mind, and as he and Taylor approached their patrol car, he mentioned Maureen's call. Taylor stopped abruptly and Kanhai, concerned, asked, "What's up?"

Taylor shook his head, unsure whether to voice his thoughts or not, and eventually shrugged, slipping into the passenger seat. Chugging the engine to life, Kanhai drove slowly from the car park.

Patrolling the villages and countryside, Sophie Delaney's battered face and body was on Taylor's mind. He felt protective towards her, but annoyed by her pig-headed stupidity for defending the man who treated her so badly. Of course, that was supposition; there was no proof Darren had laid a finger on her. But he had to do something, one way or the other.

So when they stopped for lunch, he confided his fears to his colleague amid sips of hot coffee. Kanhai listened keenly. "Well, that would make sense, especially the timing. Are either of them out of hospital yet, do you know?"

Taylor shook his head. "I don't know. I went in to see her the day after her so-called fall, only to find they'd put her in the same room as him. I couldn't do anything about it, I mean, I can't incriminate him with no facts, so I just left without talking to her."

"Want to go there now?"

Grateful, Taylor shoved the last of his sandwich in his mouth and they returned to the car, heading towards Derby.

The consultant had barely uttered the words, yet Darren was already packing his belongings, ready to go home. He detested hospitals - vile places that stank of disinfectant, where people came to die - and he couldn't wait to have a bath, change into clean clothes and have a drink or ten at the local to bask in the sympathy he would no doubt receive.

Sophie needed to stay because although her injuries were healing well, the trauma she had taken to the side of her head was still a concern. She didn't mind though; distance from her husband was what she needed right now. "Do you want me to chase the estate agents when I get back, ask them to drop the house price or something?"

Sophie choked on her tea. "What? Why?"

Unfazed by her reaction, Darren continued to throw his array of hair and skin products into the holdall. "If we're going to move abroad, we may as well cut our losses here and get out as soon as possible." Darren moved the Interflora flowers his mam had sent him to Sophie's bedside cupboard.

Placing her empty mug on the table, she spoke clearly and calmly: "Darren, I don't know that I want to move abroad, we haven't decided. We haven't even discussed it."

"Of course we have. We'll only be downsizing if we stay here and that's not good if we want kids. Following Mam and Dad is the best option."

Sophie gulped back her threatening tears at the mention of children, unable to face a barrage of questions. A nurse had told her about the miscarriage and it had taken so much strength to hide her emotions from Darren, not wanting him to feel guilty; it was her cross to bear. Pulling herself together, she controlled the waver in her voice. "We don't know anything about schooling, documentation, house prices, and what would I do for work?"

Darren sneered, rolling his eyes. "I told you, Mam and Dad will help us with everything. Come on, Soph, they wouldn't consider me bringing up a family out there if it wasn't the best place to do it. And as for somewhere to live, we'll have the money from the sale of your place, plus the money from mine..."

She couldn't help herself. "If you'd ever shown any of the money from the sale of yours, I wouldn't have to be selling mine."

Silence echoed ominously, Darren's expression darkening, eyes narrowing, lips twisting. Menacing, his face close enough for her to feel his hot breath, he said, "So that's why you had my car smashed in, is it? Money. It's all boils down to money with you, doesn't it? I buy all your drinks in the pub, remember. I buy the majority of the booze you throw down your throat at home. If you fancy a curry or a Chinese, who gets it? Me. And you want to steal the money from my flat on top of that as well, you greedy bitch."

Sophie had subconsciously raised her arms defensively. "Darren, that's not what…"

"Yes, it is." He grabbed her arm and the pain from her broken ribs made her wince. "Money's all you care about. Well, fuck you, bitch, you'll never get your hands on any of mine, or my pension. In fact, maybe I should leave you and go to Mallorca on my own…"

"I think it would be a good idea to leave her alone right now, don't you, Mr Delaney?" Darren jumped, and Sophie, heart thundering wildly, released her pent-up breath as Taylor and Kanhai entered the room. "You probably won't remember us, Mr Delaney, you were a bit dazed when we saw you, but we're the officers who are investigating your assault."

In a beat, Darren had morphed into the good bloke everybody knew and loved, smiling widely, striding around the bed with his hand extended. "Have you found out who attacked me then?"

Kanhai shook his hand. "No, we're here to ask you some questions about the events leading up to it."

"Of course." Darren eyed Taylor quizzically. "Don't I know you from somewhere?"

Distaste riding high, Taylor resisted the temptation to punch the smarmy man before him. "It's possible you may remember me from A and E the other night. I need to ask Mrs Delaney some questions, Officer Kanhai will talk to you."

Darren's face twisted. "That's where I know you from: the night my car was done in. You're the bloke who came out with that dippy blonde copper. You went into the kitchen with my wife. That's what this is, isn't it, you fancy her and you're trying to get alone with her."

Kanhai stepped between the two. "Mr Delaney, you're not doing yourself any favours. If it's preferable, I'll talk to your wife while Officer Taylor takes your statement. There's nothing underhand going on."

Darren raised his hands, submissive. "Fine. Okay. I hold my hands up, I overreacted. I'm sorry, it must be the bang on the head. Look, she was in hospital, she wasn't even there, so there's no need to talk to her. I'll tell you what you want to know and we'll leave it at that."

I had fallen asleep as soon as my head hit the pillow after Beryl had left the night before, the whisky having relaxed me. I won't deny that I had a headache when I awoke, but a few mugs of tea soon sorted that out. I opened the phone book and began making calls to all the solicitors in Derby, asking each if Sophie Delaney worked for them. Many 'no's later, I dialled Hodgekinson, Neville and Barton and a pleasant voice gave me the yes I had been waiting for.

"I thought so, I just wanted to check I had the right number. Can I make an appointment with her, please?"

"Mrs Delaney is on leave at present, but I can arrange for you to see a colleague?"

Of course I knew she wasn't there, but the bluff had to be believable. "Oh, er, well, Mrs Delaney has come highly recommended by a good friend of mine. When do you think she'll be back in the office?"

"We have no idea at present. I can assure you our other solicitors are very good."

"No." I realised I had said it far too quickly and took a deep breath. "No, my friend specifically named Mrs Delaney. You see, I want a divorce and…"

"Well, may I stop you there, because Mrs Delaney doesn't deal with divorces, she's our conveyancing solicitor."

I was thinking on my feet here; I had to get into those offices. "Yes, I know, but if you'd heard me through, I also need somebody to arrange the purchase of a house I'm desperate to get, somebody who can get me through some awkward problems."

Her tone softened. "Ah, I see. Well, in that case, perhaps you could leave your number and I'll get her secretary to give you a call to arrange an appointment for when Mrs Delaney returns."

I was getting there, but not quite enough. "Well, if I could see somebody else about the divorce today, I can give you my number in person."

She certainly wasn't the friendliest of receptionists by any means, but finally I persuaded her to let me see a Mr Gordon that afternoon. I had never been to the offices and was clutching at straws, but I would make it up as I went along.

I finished my tea, had a quick wash in cold water and put my smartest clothes on. A quick glance in the mirror I tried to avoid showed me I was still scruffy regardless, with rolls of fat spilling over the waistband and messy grey hair reluctant to stay in place. I sighed at the brief memory of when I had been pretty and desirable, days long gone.

I decided to make the most of the bus ticket to town and buy some necessities while there, jotting a shopping list on a pad before leaving, and locked up just in time to get to the bus stop.

Hodgekinson, Neville and Barton Solicitors was on the outskirts of the town centre, occupying an imposing building that must have been a couple of hundred years old, with tiny windows at the top to what once would have been the servants' rooms. With a bulging carrier bag of groceries in my hand, I awkwardly pulled the door open, the sticky heat of the building hitting me. The receptionist's overly powdered face broke into a practised smile that didn't reach her eyes.

I explained who I was, and Barbara - displayed on a nametag - remembered my call. She told me to take a seat but I remained standing. "Just out of interest, where is Mrs Delaney's office?"

She frowned, pointing to a door nearby. Puffing, out of breath, I dropped the bag on the laminated floor and leaned heavily against the desk. She enquired if I was okay, nonplussed, and I nodded, explaining I was a little asthmatic. It wasn't a lie, but the 'attack' I was having right now was an act. I laboriously lifted the carrier and shuffled to a seat in the waiting area, wheezing loudly.

After ten minutes, an affable man bounced down the stairs into the reception area and called my name. I stood, collecting my bag, breathing heavily, and walked towards him. Concerned, he asked, "Are you alright, Mrs Miller?"

"Just a touch of asthma, that's all, I forgot my inhaler. I just hope I can manage those stairs without it getting worse. Unless you have a downstairs office we could use?"

Mr Gordon glanced expectantly at Barbara, who issued me a filthy glare. "My colleague isn't in today, I'm sure we could talk in her office. Have you got the keys, Barbara?"

My plan worked, because now I was in Sophie's office. Mr Gordon took her chair and I sat on the other side of the desk, the afternoon sun flooding through a huge, frosted window behind me. It was a pleasant and feminine room, with thriving plants dotted around, framed certificates on the walls, a neat and tidy desk and a photo of a man who I presumed must be Darren.

He asked a few preliminary questions, writing notes on a pad with a fountain pen, and I explained that my husband and I been separated for years - I guessed at ten - but a divorce had never seemed necessary. He chuckled, stating that the court would have no problem granting a divorce. I told him I had no idea where Kev was nowadays and his optimistic grin waned.

Bored of the timewasting, I decided to start the next part of my plan and began to wheeze again. Concerned once more, he suggested getting me a glass of water and picked up the phone. Panicking, I stopped him before he could dial. "Oh no, don't worry that poor receptionist, she had enough trouble with me before. You pop and get it, love, save her the bother."

He shrugged and left the room, bemused. Wasting no time, I delved into Sophie's top drawer, searching for anything that would give me some of her personal details. I swiftly slid the address book, a diary and a repeat prescription into my carrier bag and slipped back to my seat just as Mr Gordon returned.

The rest of the appointment was redundant to me, my motive accomplished, but I went through the motions to avoid raising suspicion. Getting a divorce made no difference to me because I had been lying when I said I didn't know where Kev was. I was the one who had disposed of his body in a skip, useless piece of rubbish that he was.

I had taken the bus from the town centre to the hospital and now, as I walked towards the helpdesk, I regretted having bought so much shopping; dragging the cumbersome carrier bag around was tiresome. The smiling woman asked if she could help and I dropped the bag wearily on the floor, asking which room Sophie Delaney was in.

I retrieved the bag, arm aching, and made my way through the corridors to the ward, where a nurse showed me to Sophie's room. Now it was time for fun and games at Harry and Beryl's detriment.

Sophie regarded me blankly as I approached her bed, the overhead television chattering to itself, and I thankfully dropped the bag again, slumping onto the chair by her bed. Curious, she frowned. "Can I help you?" Her voice was soft and well-spoken, just like her father. I wasn't able to speak at first; coming face to face with the spawn of the man I would love until the day I died was bizarre.

She wasn't conventionally beautiful, but there was a glow, an aura, about her. The bruising and scabs were still apparent, but something in her eyes - deep pools of brown - exposed a gentle soul. Her hair was long with corkscrew golden curls that I guessed had come from a bottle, judging by the root growth. It was difficult to believe that this strong-featured woman could have been borne by the timid and tiny Beryl. But then again, Harry was her father and he had been a striking man when I had known him.

She didn't know me from Adam, this fat piece of scruffy trash sitting beside her when she was vulnerable and in hospital, and was understandably getting annoyed. I have to be honest: the inclination to reach out and hug her, hug the product of my Harry's loins, was overwhelming. It was confusing, because I was there purely to hurt her, which would in turn hurt him. And hurt Beryl. What was I supposed to say?

Sophie grasped the control pad, finger hovering over the assistance button. "Look, I think you should be in another ward, let me call the nurses to help you."

I didn't want the staff to remove me and all I could come up with was the truth: "Sophie, I know your parents, I mean, I know Beryl."

She relaxed, smiling lightly. "Why didn't you just say?"

My heart thudded. Her resemblance to Harry was spectacular - her expressions and mannerisms, the tone of her voice - which should have made me hate her, but instead I felt fondness. Love, if that's possible. I struggled to breath, claustrophobic, sweaty but cold, and stood, forgetting the carrier bag, even though it held the items I had so cleverly stolen from Sophie's desk.

Then words tumbled out and there was nothing I could do to stop them. "Sophie, you need to know this: you haven't lost your baby. It's still there, I know it is."

Where the hell had that come from? I was the biggest fake tarot reader in the world and now I was believing my own crap.

Her face paled, puppy dog eyes welling with tears, and I had achieved my desire to hurt her, but believe me, it hadn't been planned that way; the compulsion to utter those words had been overwhelming. My own eyes were watering, the thick lenses of my unflattering glasses hiding my emotion from the world, and I wondered if I was indeed truly evil.

And she confirmed my worries. "For God's sake, how could you say such a thing, such a cruel thing. Go away. Just go away."

I wanted to, really I did, but the words were spilling and I couldn't stop them. "You are surrounded by a deep, deep red, which tells me you are nervous, anxious, and that danger and anger surround you."

Where was this garbage coming from?

"The edges are greying, a dirty, nasty grey, which suggests fear and insecurity. The only saving grace about you at the moment is the child you're carrying," Sophie's tears were unstoppable now, "the small flecks of orange show it's healthy and strong."

"You bitch. You vicious bitch. Why are you doing this to me? Just get out of here, get away from me."

I wanted to go, get away from the weirdness, but I took a deep breath and spoke louder; it seemed imperative that Sophie heard what I had to say. "You have to get away from the dark forces that surround you, if not for your sake, then for your unborn child's."

She was screaming now, hands over her ears, desperately trying to block out the words that were breaking her heart. "Get out of here."

I grabbed my bags and hurried to the door, just as a nurse approached to see what the noise was about. I had no idea what had just happened and was as scared as Sophie, as angry as Sophie, because for once I had lost control. Suddenly, I had to get away from her.

The words wouldn't leave her head, no matter how much she tried to block them out. Such cruelty. And who was that awful woman? She had mentioned she knew her mum, but hadn't given a name. Tossing and turning in the stuffy heat of the hospital room, the night seemed to last for weeks.

If only the woman had been right about the baby.

Tears flowed, so many, pooling onto the pillow, the thought of her lost child unbearable. What if it were true, though? Could it be true? Sophie chastised herself, certain the consultant couldn't be mistaken about something as grave as miscarriage, and anyway, a scan had confirmed it. In the early hours, Sophie eventually drifted into a fitful sleep, but when the birds began to sing and the sun crept over the horizon, she awoke again and instantly remembered the dreadful woman. It seemed ridiculous, but she had to know the truth and she pressed the button to call for a nurse.

"Is everything alright, Sophie?" Nurse Messaoud entered, wiping the toast crumbs on her chubby fingers onto her uniform.

"I know this sounds silly, but is it possible I could still be pregnant?"

The nurse flicked through the notes at the end of the bed and answered in her lilting Jamaican accent. "According to your notes, my love, you had a heavy bleed, and when the scanner was passed across your belly they found no trace of pregnancy."

Sophie, upstanding, staid and professional, was on the brink of losing her credibility. "I want another scan."

The process had involved much huffing and puffing, and if it hadn't been for their professionalism, Sophie was sure the medical team would have been rolling their eyes and patronising her. But her tenacity had succeeded and she was lying on a trolley in the gynaecology department with a sonographer squeezing cold gel onto her abdomen. She moved the scanner slowly over the area, thorough, but eventually stopped and wiped the gel off. "I can't see anything in the womb."

On top of the empty grieving, Sophie felt like an idiot for even considering believing the vicious woman and her false hope, and she slowly sat, mindful of her healing ribs, head sagging with embarrassment. "I'm sorry for wasting your time." Pitiful.

The sonographer took Sophie's notes and scanned them briefly. "It says you had only just found you were pregnant when the accident happened. Do you have a rough idea of how far gone you would have been?"

"It would have been about four, maybe five, weeks. I don't have regular periods so it's impossible to pinpoint it."

"Look, I'm going to try one more thing. I want you to go and empty your bladder, then wait outside and I'll call you."

Ten minutes later Sophie was back on the trolley, shocked at the degradation of the internal ultrasound, but the humiliation was worth it when she heard the words she had not expected. "There it is." The sonographer angled the screen towards Sophie, finger detailing the outline. "That, you see, between there and there. That's a pregnancy sac, and it appears to be intact. I can't tell this early the exact gestation date, but I can tell you that either the bleed didn't disrupt the pregnancy, or you were carrying fraternal twins and only lost one. Congratulations, Mrs Delaney, you're going to be a mum."

Chapter 6
Taylor's Infatuation

I had no idea what had come over me when I'd visited Sophie in hospital, I don't think I've ever behaved so irrationally, and when Beryl told me at her next session that she was going to be a grandmother after all, it frightened me. Was it a big coincidence, or could I actually have some kind of psychic ability? All that rubbish I had spouted about auras, I mean, I know I advertise myself as seeing them to get the clients in, but I make it all up, just saying what the troubled people - because they are always troubled - want to hear. I had seen no colours when I saw Sophie, but the words had come out as if I had. I just didn't know what to think.

For the first time in thirty years, I dug out the only photo of Anna and Andrew I possessed, framing it, displaying it beside the kettle in the kitchen. I had to, I had to remember why I was trying to hurt this family, and a visual reminder was the only way. But the confusion of that day stayed with me, and when Hodgekinson, Neville and Barton rang to say that Sophie was returning to work and did I still want to see her, I said no. It was the same story with the divorce; I told them I didn't want to go through with it any more.

Likewise, even though I had read Sophie's diary and address book from cover to cover, any thoughts of using the details to my advantage had been quelled. I continued to do the 'readings' for Beryl, every fortnight now, and I think she kind of considers me a friend in a way, at least she is always open about what is happening in her life. I still wanted to punish her for my lifelong pain, but couldn't bring myself to do anything about it. In short, I was scared of the intensity I had felt in Sophie's presence.

The weeks turned into months, and October had arrived before I felt strong enough to put the visit with Sophie to one side, relegate it to mere coincidence, and remember that I had a plan I wanted to carry out.

Sophie had not mentioned the miscarriage to Darren, and now she had found it was a misdiagnosis, it was irrelevant. My visit to the hospital had also been relegated to the back of her mind.

Darren had been thrilled when she had told him the happy news after leaving the hospital, and hadn't laid a finger on her since, treating her like a precious jewel, worshipping her body - the vessel that was bringing the fruit of his loins into the world.

Likewise, his parents were delighted, boastful, convinced they were going to have a grandson.

They hadn't made a decision to move abroad, it had simply become an accepted fact. Darren and his parents had devised a plan, and as she intended to put her career on hold for a few years to be a stay-at-home mum, Mallorca or England didn't seem to make much difference now her parents refused to speak to her.

A month before Maureen and Bob were due to relocate, they suggested their son and Sophie holiday with them after the move, give them a chance to survey the area and house prices, and Sophie eagerly dropped the price of her house, which brought renewed interest. Teething problems and angst in the past, life was wonderful.

With such a tumultuous personal life, Sophie had lost enthusiasm for her job. She continued to provide a competent service, but her heart lay with impending parenthood and happy families now. After a lengthy and tedious day at work, Sophie was grateful to be home at last. She stepped through doorway of her delightful cottage and a delicious aroma wafted from the kitchen.

Darren called her through and she dropped her bags on the sofa, hanging her coat on the hook. "I've made us some minestrone soup, thought it might warm us up a bit." Sophie had never known him to cook before, in fact she wasn't aware he even knew how, and she pecked him on the cheek, surprised.

He busily sliced and buttered fresh, crusty bread and dished out the chunky, steaming broth into waiting bowls. "Is there anything I can do?" she asked, bemused.

"Just go and sit yourself down in the dining room, I'll bring these through in a minute."

They rarely used the room and she was astonished to find the normally bare beech table draped with their best tablecloth and cutlery, an open bottle of Chianti and two burning candles in the centre. She sat by the drawn curtains of the bay window and her brow furrowed. "Have I forgotten an important date or something?"

Darren chuckled as he brought the deliciously tempting soup through. "No, I just thought I'd treat you, Soph. Eat up, it's full of fresh ingredients that'll be good for my boy in there. I'll just go and fetch the bread."

The meal was exquisite, puffy wild rice and diced vegetables floating in a thick and spicy tomato sea, and she wondered if she had died and gone to heaven.

Darren cooking was amazing in itself, such a romantic gesture, and she resolved that after the meal she would have a relaxing bath and don an alluring nightdress, make herself beautiful for him.

But later, snuggling up on the sofa, hair fresh and perfume subtle, Sophie's ardour had disappeared. Maybe it was her hormones, maybe this happened to all pregnant women. Once the lights were out, she gently rejected his advances, claiming tiredness as an excuse, and hoped this phase wouldn't go on for too long. The small glass of Chianti had relaxed her, the only alcohol she'd had since discovering the pregnancy, and Darren had followed the rest of the bottle with a few brandies; they fell asleep quickly.

Hours passed, the dead of night, and a storm began to rage outside. Sleeping deeply, the warm winter duvet tucked closely around her shoulders to ward off the chilly night, beads of sweat formed on Sophie's brow and she threw off the covers, murmuring, moaning.

Darren rolled over, concerned. "Soph?" Lightning cracked the clouds, a belt of thunder booming, but she remained unconscious. Leaning over, he gently shook her shoulder, but her thrashing and muttering continued. "Soph, you're having a nightmare, wake up."

Lashing out, she struck him painfully on the cheekbone and he recoiled, stunned. This time her words rang clear: "You bastard, Darren, you killed my baby." Instantly, she calmed, a weak hand tugging the covers up as her breathing settled to a gentle purr. Unnerved by the intensity of the statement, Darren crept from the bed and shrugged into his dressing-gown and slippers, tiptoeing down the stairs. He needed a stiff drink.

Darren had taken a day off to meet with his parents in order to plan the arrangements and documents he and Sophie would need to move to Mallorca. Sophie quietly dressed for work and, having a few minutes to spare, brought a mug of tea upstairs, placing it on the bedside cabinet. "Are you awake, Darren?"

He shrugged up the bed, resting against the pillows, and Sophie gasped. "Your face looks sore, it's all red on one side."

"That's because…" He remembered her nightmare well, but was it worth stressing her over something out of her control? "I guess I must have been lying on that side." He pulled her close and brushed a kiss on her nose. "What time do you think you'll be home today, you were quite late yesterday?"

Sophie winked mischievously. "Why, are you planning to cook for me again?"

"Sure, I will if you want."

Normally he would have told her to stop being ridiculous and she was gobsmacked. What was wrong with him? "I was just kidding; I don't expect you to cook. My last client's due at three, so I'll sort that out, do a bit of paperwork, then get myself home for about five. Say hi to your mum and dad from me and the baby."

Darren smiled and patted her belly. "Will do. Love you both."

Sophie smiled and headed from the room, leaving Darren confused; for the first time in their relationship she hadn't returned his affection.

I had consistently advised Beryl to stay away from Sophie as long as she was with Darren, and it surprised me that she willingly accepted the suggestion. It certainly wasn't causing her the pain I wanted it to. But this cold October night, she told me that her son, Steve, had visited Sophie and been shocked that she and Darren were planning to move abroad. Without devising a plan, I phoned Hodgekinson, Neville and Barton and made an appointment to see her the next day.

With the weather cooling rapidly as autumn replaced summer, I'd been delighted to find a ridiculously cheap outfit in Evans: a pair of leggings and a light summer shirt. Unable to afford to heat my flat to a comfortable temperature, I had become toughened to the cold over the years, so while everybody else wore coats and gloves, an antiqued cardigan over my new clothes kept me warm enough. I twirled in front of the neglected mirror, admiring my unusually smart appearance.

I caught the bus just in time, and as we passed the exhaust-blackened city buildings, I wondered how Sophie would react when she saw me again. It would be a shock, for sure.

Barbara recognised me as I entered and her usual welcoming face didn't appear. She rang Sophie's office to tell her I had arrived and I took a seat, skimming through a mindless magazine. When Sophie finally opened her door, the wide smile on her face waned and she paled. "You."

"Yes, I need to see you."

Furious, Sophie marched towards me and I was surprised to note we were the same height; she had looked taller in hospital. To my embarrassment, she pointed at the door and shouted, "Get out of here and stay away from me. I don't ever want to see you again. Get out now or I'll call the police." Her hand settled gently on her tummy, which concerned me, so I backed away without argument, but I had no intention of going home yet.

I hastened from the building, unaware that Sophie was watching my bulky body waddle away, that she breathed a sigh of relief. But I had prepared myself to meet with her and wasn't going to let the chance pass.

The October sun was bright, although it issued no warmth, and it cast a stunning orange glow across the sky as it neared the horizon, giving me something to focus on during my tiresome wait on a nearby bench. Three hours later, Sophie finally left the building.

She looked tired and I imagined that balancing the tiredness of pregnancy with a high level job must be difficult. Relieved the lengthy wait was over, I addressed her as she passed. "How's the pregnancy going, Sophie? Beryl told me about it."

Her face filled with horror and her head dropped down, eyes on the pavement as she hastened away, ignoring me as I did my utmost to keep up with her. Frustration raged inside me and the bizarre compulsion to warn her about god knows what swamped me again. "You've got to listen to me, Sophie, you know I was right about everything I said. I'm only here to protect you."

Unexpectedly, she stopped abruptly and turned, sneering with venom. "Look, I don't know who you are or what you want, but just leave me alone. I don't owe you anything and you're scaring me. Just go away."

I was unperturbed by the harsh words, the urge to speak to her was intense. "Just come and have a drink with me, one coffee and I promise you won't see me again."

"I said get lost."

Begging wasn't my usual style, but, "Please Sophie, I'm as scared about this as you, it's weird, but really, if you talk to me now, I'll keep away from you after that."

Growling, Sophie glared into my soul, her deep brown eyes the spit of her father's. "For good?" Her resolve was weakening.

"Yes." Relieved, I clasped Sophie's elbow, her woollen coat rough on my hand. "Now, come on."

She shrugged my hand away with distaste. "I'll have a coffee with you and that's it." Reluctantly, she followed me around the corner to a small, featureless café, which sat on a one-way street running parallel to Friar Gate. We entered and the overly warm air was stifling. I swept the cardigan from my shoulders and she unbuttoned her coat, and we sat at a table beside the window. Sophie requested two coffees and I added a tempting slice of carrot cake.

Silent minutes passed, and when the waitress brought our order over, my whispered 'thank you' barely broke the quiescence. Eventually, Sophie bored of watching through the window and turned to me, hostile. "How did you know?"

"Know what?"

"Don't be difficult, I can always leave."

"I don't know, I just did." Keeping Beryl's confidence, I didn't mention the oddly predictive tarot reading. "Is it going well."

She subconsciously stroked her belly, protective. "Yes."

"Beryl told me you're moving abroad."

"I'm surprised she even remembers who I am, it's been that long since I saw her."

I sipped my coffee, the cake tempting but uneaten, guilty for the pain I detected in her voice. Sophie impatiently tapped her foot against the table leg, fiddling with the strap of her handbag, and it was clear she would rather be anywhere but here with me. I realised that if I didn't talk soon she would leave, and I didn't want that. "Sophie, that day in hospital."

She swallowed, her voice a gentle breeze, "You put me through hell that day, but I wouldn't have asked for the scan if you hadn't said what you did, so I guess I should be thanking you."

My cheeks glowed with the cautious gratitude. "It was scary for me too. Those words, they came from nowhere. How are things at home now?"

Sophie almost answered, but her face twisted as the words registered. "What do you mean, at home now?" I shifted, averting my eyes and shoving a large forkful of cake into my mouth, aware I'd said too much. I tried to act nonchalant to dispel the tension but it didn't work. "What do you know about my home life?" I forced another huge chunk of cake into my already full mouth, and Sophie seethed. "Are you some kind of a stalker? You know nothing about my home, my family, my life." Standing abruptly, collecting her coat and briefcase. "Just get lost, Mrs Miller, get away from me and stay out of my life. If you come near me again, I'll contact the police and have you arrested for harassment." She stormed out, awkwardly shrugging her coat on as the door slammed behind her.

I was still chewing, but it didn't stop my smile. Shoving the last of the carrot cake into my mouth, I finished the dregs of my coffee and hers and slipped into my cardigan, leaving a couple of pounds on the table in payment.

Reaching across the table for Sophie's forgotten handbag, I hooked it over my shoulder. Now she would have to see me again.

Sophie Delaney had been on Taylor's mind for a couple of months, and he had considered researching her a little, find out where she worked, maybe, to check all was well, but wasn't sure it would be ethical. As he sipped his cocoa, welcome after the freezing foot patrol through the streets of Coalville, he had to concede that no news was probably good news. She hadn't been hospitalised again, that he knew of anyway, and she hadn't called the emergency services. Professionally, he wanted his preoccupation with her to stop, but she was firmly rooted in his mind and the compulsion to see her was intense.

Off duty but still uniformed, he knocked on the door of Iris Cottage and Sophie answered, bewildered, moving aside to let him enter. "I just thought I'd give you a follow up call to check that you and Mr Delaney have both recovered, and to make sure there's been no more vandalism."

The explanation didn't ring true, but Sophie was too tired to care. "We're fine, everything's fine."

Taylor removed his cap, fidgeting. "Good. Good."

There was no need for elaboration, but the silence was awkward. "In fact," she patted her belly, "we've found that I didn't lose the baby after all, I'm going to be a mum."

The words cut through Taylor like a knife, an invisible hand reaching inside his body and scraping out his heart. Shocked, he realised he had feelings for her, and suddenly his preoccupation made sense.

She was oblivious to his pain. "Oh, and we've decided to move to Mallorca once the house sells. Darren's parents are going to help us out."

Taylor couldn't breathe, his chest constricted and the atmosphere dense; he had to get out of there, get away. Go to the pub, find some girl to shag, something - anything - to forget his futile obsession with a married woman. He tugged the door open, slamming it behind him, leaving Sophie wide-eyed with confusion.

"What do you mean you didn't lose the baby after all?"

The tone of his voice brought back memories from less happy days and she turned, filled with consternation. "Darren, I…"

"Answer me."

The angry demand shuddered through her and her hand rested on her tummy, protective. She swallowed, mustering courage. "I found out I was pregnant the day I had the accident, but the doctors told me I'd lost the baby. Then Mrs Miller said I was still pregnant."

"Who is Mrs Miller?"

"She's just some weird biddy who seems to think she can tell the future or something. I asked them to scan me again, so they did and found I hadn't lost the baby after all."

"Why didn't you tell me you were pregnant when you found out?" His voice was a low growl.

"I was going to, but..." The crack on her cheek knocked her into the doorframe and he grappled for her neck, throwing her on the floor; she could taste blood on her tongue. "Darren, no. The baby."

Scowling, he strode to the kitchen, dusting off his hands. "Dinner's nearly ready, put the telly on." Desperate not to cry and infuriate him further, she swallowed her tears, yearning for a brandy to block out the emotional pain. Pulling herself up, she switched on the *News at Six*.

Chapter 7
Anna

Beryl arrived for her fortnightly session that evening and I did the usual fake reading, telling her what she wanted to hear, but she remained seated when I had finished. I asked if everything was alright and she looked at me, timid. "Actually, I wanted to ask you a favour."

I nodded, tidying the cards, replacing them in their blue silk sheath. "Go on."

"Well, you know Harold usually picks me up, it's just he's going to be delayed this evening, he's at a meeting. I hope you don't mind me asking, but can I stay here for an hour or so?"

It was such a silly request to be embarrassed about and I couldn't help smiling as I told her it was no problem, offering her a mug of tea. We chatted for a while and I asked if she had seen Sophie, despite knowing she hadn't. She told me she was keeping a distance, but admitted that Steve had kept her updated with Sophie's situation.

"I assume Darren's been behaving himself."

She nodded, sipping the tea. "It appears so, I think the pregnancy's made quite a difference. Steve says he's being very attentive and that they seem to be happy. Maybe trying for a baby was getting to him and that's why he was behaving like that."

"Oh, I don't know," I said indignantly, "a leopard doesn't change its spots." Beryl was wilting and I couldn't have that.

"I hear what you're saying, but to be honest with you, it's so hard not to see her. Not just for me, but for

Harold too. We miss her so much. I mean, she turned thirty-one a few weeks ago and we sat at home all evening, wishing we could be with her, give her presents, cards. A cake. The world seems so empty without my little girl." I knew that feeling only too well, picturing the tatty photo of my twins. "I might go and see her, see how she's getting on."

Beryl left soon after and I lay in bed, mulling the conversation, when a horrifying thought occurred to me. I ran to the living room and grabbed Sophie's diary, scouring the pages while my heart beat wildly in my chest. The words I had been looking for glared at me and I gasped, woozy, dizzy. The world darkened to black as I slumped, unconscious, to the floor.

Running late after an extra ten minutes in bed, Sophie shrugged her coat over her suit, the button of her skirt straining with the growing baby bump. She grabbed her briefcase, searching for her handbag. "Shit, I must have left it at the café."

Glancing at her new diary - she had no idea what had happened to the last one - her first appointment wasn't until mid-morning, which gave her time to nip back in the hope someone had handed it in.

The cashier shrugged indifferently, briefly looking under the counter. "Nope. Nothing."

Like any woman, Sophie's life was in that bag, and the mere thought of replacing everything, cancelling her cards... "Are you sure?"

The girl huffed, rolling her eyes, and half-heartedly rooted about under the till. "Nope. As I said."

Muttering under her breath as she walked away, Sophie yanked the door wide, contemplating the nightmare ahead, when, "'S'cuse me, miss." The girl who had served her the previous day waved eagerly and Sophie stopped, waiting while the waitress came over. She held out a scrap of paper. "The woman you was sat with yesterday said she was taking your bag for safekeeping. Said to give you this."

Sophie bristled, wishing she hadn't left so abruptly as she unfolded Mary's address. She briefly considered forgetting the bag, but common sense disregarded the stubbornness and she reluctantly accepted she would have to visit the dreaded woman on her way home.

A graffiti-peppered building loomed underneath dark clouds, flaking paint on the windowsills exposing rotting wood and black rubbish bags spilling from the entrance, and Sophie checked the address on the scrap of paper to make sure it was the right place, appalled. The entry system had been vandalised and the door was wedged open with a flattened tin can. Impeccably dressed and fully made-up, Sophie felt conspicuous and a twinge of fear ran the length of her spine. She stepped tentatively into the hall and climbed the concrete steps to the fourth level, pushing open a blue door onto a lengthy balcony. Number thirteen was the fourth door along and she glanced around before tapping lightly with the knocker.

I guessed it was Sophie, but checked through the peephole out of habit. "You've come for your handbag." She nodded, uncomfortable. I indicated the living room and she hesitated, awkward. "Come on then, don't stand in the rain." I saw her distaste as she surveyed the clutter that covered every piece of furniture and most of the threadbare carpet, a look I had seen on Beryl's face; like mother, like daughter. "Cup of tea?"

She shook her head, with a fleeting tell of horror. "I'll just take my bag and go, thanks."

I bristled, annoyed by her rudeness, and pigheadedly resolved to make her stay as long as was possible. "If you're sure," I said curtly, and rummaged behind the door, buying time. Eventually, I 'found' the bag and she snatched it from my hands, smiling weakly, and before I could stop her, she had let herself out. Through the bathroom window, I watched her holding the bag at arm's length with a grimace while she rummaged in her briefcase for a carrier bag to place it in. The realisation that she found me repulsive hurt like a dagger now, because I had an idea - a hunch - and, believe it or not, she had a special place in my heart. Under other circumstances, I would voice my thoughts gently, but bad manners had never settled well with me and I wanted retribution.

I glanced at my watch; the bus into town was due in ten minutes so I had to get a move on. This time, it was unimportant to wear my smart clothes, not that they were holding out too well with me being such a messy eater; timing mattered more. I grabbed my spare cardigan, a drab, olive affair that had seen better years bought second hand from Oxfam, and my fingerless gloves, and trotted to the ground floor as fast as my bulk would allow.

It took an hour for the staff at Royal Oak House to supply me with the information - more accurately, lack of information - that confirmed my suspicions, and another hour for me to recover from the shock.

The sun was setting as I approached Hodgekinson, Neville and Barton's offices, and I was unsure whether to go inside and ask for Sophie directly, or wait until she made her way home, but she stepped through the door at four-thirty, resolving the quandary.

I followed discreetly at a distance to a small car park, where she unlocked her Fiesta and climbed in, throwing her bags onto the passenger seat. Turning the ignition, clutch down and reverse gear, she checked her rear view mirror and... I saw her wide eyes in the mirror, sensing her fear through the glass. But I wasn't about to move from behind the car.

I suspected Sophie's knee-jerk reaction would be to reverse into me, to be done with me for good, but she restrained herself and my baited breath floated out on a cloud of relief as the reverse lights died. Slowly, aware she may drive off if I moved too far, I inched towards the passenger side. Sophie revved the engine, probably to scare me, but instead I scuttled behind the boot again, firmly blocking her exit.

Minutes dragged as our stubborn impasse continued and I realised she was as headstrong as me. Almost. She killed the engine and stepped from the car, leaving the door wide open as a precaution. "What do you want this time?" Strained, through gritted teeth.

"I need to talk to you, Anna." Her brow furrowed, confused, but she didn't speak; I guess she didn't want to encourage my craziness. "Your birth name is Anna Sophia Bryce. Sophie, I am your mother. You must know from your birth certificate that you were adopted." She stared at me blankly, incomprehensive. "I've been to the registry office, there is no birth certificate for your so-called birth name on your date of birth. I had a child whom I named Anna Sophia Bryce on the day you were born."

Sophie's eyes crinkled, aggressive, baring her teeth, and I wondered what I had expected. A hug? I felt so bad for her, she must have been sick and tired of me following her about and now I had dropped this bombshell on her. But what else could I do, she was my long-lost child? I - *me* - wanted a cuddle.

In an instant she jumped into the car, restarted the engine and slammed into reverse. I couldn't move quickly enough and she knocked me to the ground before wheel-spinning away.

Maybe I'm naïve, but I hadn't expected such hostility, and, shocked, I squirmed on the wet tarmac until I could heave my fat body up, rubbing my bruised thighs and shoulder and dusting down my clothes.

Indignant, I seethed; so what if the sensitive news had been a surprise, there was no excuse for violence. Swearing under my breath, I imprinted the registration number of Sophie's car to memory. Tomorrow - or whenever, it didn't matter how long it took - I would be waiting in a taxi to follow Sophie home. Once I had her address, she wouldn't be able to ignore me.

Truth is, I had no idea how much I had upset her.

Ignoring speed signs, Sophie hurtled through the country lanes, but still the journey seemed to take an eternity, and when she skidded into her driveway, she was relieved to find Darren's BMW parked in front of the cottage. They may have had their problems, physical affection having taken a back seat to the pregnancy, but she needed him more than ever right now.

Forgetting her bags, she jumped out and ran to the door, fumbling for the key, desperate to retreat to her comfort zone. "Darren?"

She tried to control her breathing, wiping sweat from her hands, and her heart ached when no response came. Either he was at the pub, or drunkenly asleep on the bed. Afraid of his temper if she were to awake him, she crept up the stairs and found him snoring loudly under the covers, inebriated, the dregs of his poison in a tumbler beside the bed.

Alone and devastated, her mind in chaos, she headed to the kitchen and switched on the kettle, throwing a teabag into a mug she took from the draining board. Tears threatened and she locked them inside, but frustration faltered her resolve; she took the cooking brandy from a wall cupboard and poured a large measure, downing it, shuddering with the bitter aftertaste. Tears of remorse broke the floodgates and she patted her tummy, whispering, "Sorry, baby, I need this today."

The child inside her, almost fully formed, whose heart was already beating…

She poured another drink and replaced the bottle. "This will be my last, I promise."

Sophie headed for the living room and sat heavily, staring at the phone. Should she call the parents who had demanded she leave her husband if she wanted a relationship with them? Alternatively, she could call the police.

Minutes ticked by with only Darren's regular snoring breaking the silence, a distant rumble behind the closed door, while Sophie ran through the latest altercation with that damned woman and her cruel lies.

Of course she wasn't her mother; Beryl Waller was. The crazy bitch should be locked away in an asylum, not a crummy council flat.

Unsettled regardless, Sophie opened the sideboard and searched for the photo album her parents had given her on her wedding day. She flicked through until she found the picture: Mum, Dad, Steve aged twelve and she at six.

Steve was the spit of Beryl: dark eyes that appeared black and olive skin, straight ebony hair reflecting metallic blue in the summer sunshine of that happy day all those years ago. Then Sophie and Harold with pale skin and chocolate brown eyes, chestnut curls tinged with the auburn she detested enough to have her hair coloured blonde quarterly. A handsome family with no room for intruders.

Mary Miller was clearly a nutcase.

Sophie grasped the phone book and found the number of the police Station.

Chapter 8
Enough is Enough

Taylor plodded through the tedious paperwork that took up so much of the time better used policing the streets and reducing crime. Mindless, lost, until his colleague's voice broke the spell. "Leon," on his feet, walking, "Leon."

Peeved, Kanhai pointed to the phone in his hand, mouthing 'on the phone', but Taylor was insistent. "Mrs Delaney, could you hold on a minute, please." Hand over the mouthpiece. "What?"

"Is that Sophie Delaney?"

"Yes."

Taylor's heart hammered in his chest and it pissed him off, wishing he could lose his absurd preoccupation with her. "I want to come too if you have to go out and see her, okay?"

Kanhai rolled his eyes and uncovered the receiver. "Sorry about that. Where were we?"

Sophie had been waiting at the window since the call and was relieved to see a familiar face when Taylor climbed from the patrol car. While Darren rasped and grunted upstairs, Taylor and Kanhai followed Sophie to the kitchen, where she filled the kettle, describing Mary Miller and her harassment. Eyes dropping, ashamed, "I reversed into her deliberately, she's probably been on the phone to you herself."

While Kanhai took notes, Taylor was bewitched by her glistening eyes, puddles of velvet that ached with vulnerability and sadness. He heard no words, only the thudding in his chest.

94

"Have you spoken to your mother about this woman's claims?"

Buying time to avoid the embarrassment of explaining her parents no longer talked to her, Sophie passed a mug each to the policemen and they followed her to the living room. "Why would I? I mean, they're just the words of a crazy woman."

"Would you mind if we had a word with your mother?"

"Yes, I would," shocked by her own ferocity, "that woman is already trying to destroy my life with her weird auras and spooky predictions, I certainly don't want my mum upset by her too."

Footsteps thundered on the stairs and Darren stood at the door, head cocked, glaring at Sophie. "What are they doing here?"

"I'll tell you about it after they've gone." Nervous, Sophie was reassured by the police presence.

He snatched his jacket from the coat rack by the front door. "Well, seeing as you seem to have more time for the pigs than for getting my dinner, I'm going to the pub. Don't put yourself out by cooking, will you, I'll get something from the bar." The front door slammed and the sound of his stumbling footsteps on gravel diminished.

She was humiliated. "I'm really sorry about that, I guess he's had a bad day at work."

"You know that if he ever hurts you, or is going to hurt you, dial nine-nine-nine. I had your number listed as a priority."

Sophie swallowed hard, staring at the wall until she found the strength to lie. "Darren doesn't hurt me, never has and never will. He's not that kind of person, so stop insinuating he is. I insist my number is taken off priority, whatever that is."

Kanhai tucked his pad into the chest pocket of his uniform. "Okay, I think we have enough details to go on here. We'll pop over to Mrs Miller now and tell her to leave you alone."

The first I knew about Sophie involving the police was when the two handsome young men turned up on my doorstep. I quickly cleared piles of wool, clothes, newspapers, magazines, puzzle books and more so the officers could sit. Like most people who visit me, they politely declined a cup of tea; I guess the clutter makes me look dirty, but it sure saves on teabags and washing-up. Kanhai questioned me, while Taylor looked on with distaste.

I gave them my birth date and noted the disbelief; hell, I know I'm not well kept, but fancy creams and hairdressers are expensive. Aged only forty-six, I looked nearer sixty.

They stepped to the hall with the excuse of checking my background, but I was sure they were sharing a joke at my expense and felt acutely self-conscious. Yes, I'd let my hair go grey, and yes, it was thinning at the top, and I knew the thick-rimmed glasses with bottle-bottom lenses made my blue-grey eyes seem tiny. So what if I was overweight; exercise wasn't a hobby. My insides churned with shame as I stroked the deep wrinkles and lumps of errant rosacea on my face. Taylor, who was plainly besotted with Sophie - the faraway look when her name was mentioned made that obvious - must have found the idea of such a fat and ugly flump producing the effortlessly beautiful Sophie laughable.

They returned, having found nothing untoward, and Kanhai stressed that I would be charged with harassment if I didn't leave Sophie alone.

"She is my child. I had an affair with Sophie's father when I was fourteen and had twins at fifteen, a boy I named Andrew and a girl, Anna, and the babies were adopted against my wishes. I've searched for my children for thirty-one years and have finally found Sophie. Harold and Beryl are obviously using her middle name, Sophia. I haven't found Andrew."

"Mrs Miller, I'm warning you: don't approach Mrs Delaney again."

They closed the door behind them, but I still heard Kanhai say 'mad as a hatter' through the thin wood. I'd been called that many a time before, but that didn't stop it hurting.

I waited by the window until I saw the officers drive away, furious and humiliated. And alone, as always, with nothing to do other than think. I paced the flat, wondering how to overcome this new problem.

If I saw Sophie again, I would be arrested, but she was my daughter, the precious baby I had been searching for.

And worse, not only did Beryl have the man I wanted, she also had my child. She had watched my chubby newborn grow into the stunning creature she now was. I had wanted to hurt her emotionally before, but now I detested her with such a passion for the life she had stolen from me, I was capable of anything.

Sophie had considered a stroll to the pub, but the idea of sitting with a bunch of boring drunken men while sipping soda water was unappealing. Her appetite non-existent, she'd had cheese and crackers for the baby's sake, which broke the monotonous evening only briefly.

At ten, she switched off the television and snuggled into bed, but after half an hour of her mind screaming, the obliterating brandy became tempting. She knew she shouldn't, but...

It only served to enhance her confusion and questions battered her like stormy rain on glass. Her inhibitions drowned, she dialled a number. "Mum, it's me."

Curt, unfriendly. "Have you left Darren?"

"Don't do this, please. Of course I haven't."

"Then there's nothing more to say. Goodbye."

"Don't hang up, this is important." The reluctant sigh brought her mother's uptight expression to her mind - raised eyebrows and pinched lips - and she swigged her Dutch courage with a grimace. "Did you give birth to me?"

Beryl gasped. "What kind of silly question is that?"

"Why have you never shown me my birth certificate?" Sophie had never questioned her mother's insistence to organise her passport, or her offer to take the certificate to the registry office to save her time before she married.

"I've got it in safekeeping here, you're welcome to see it any time you like. Now, have you finished with this ridiculous conversation?" Defensive, bordering on angry.

"No, I haven't, and if you cut this call I'll be on your doorstep in minutes, because I want answers. The truth. Have you heard of a woman named Mrs Miller?"

"Never heard the name in my life. I can see what's happening here: you're drunk. You never used to drink before you met that man, and it's about time you thought about your baby instead of being a paranoid alcoholic."

Sophie reeled as she heard the dial tone and slammed the receiver into its cradle, swearing, refilling the glass, no longer caring that Darren would smell it on her breath. Returning the photographs of the once happy family to the sideboard, Sophie took her glass upstairs and flopped on the bed, hugging herself under the warm duvet for comfort. Enough was enough and she was at the end of her rope; when Darren got home she would suggest moving abroad immediately. Maureen and Bob wouldn't mind helping them until they got back on their feet.

They had gone to bed, but Beryl's tossing and turning had kept Harold awake. He tried to coax out of her who had been on the phone, but she wouldn't tell him. He was a calm man, rarely losing his temper, but he had work in the morning and it was already two o'clock. "For heaven's sake, Beryl, either tell me what's upset you, or go to sleep." She turned her back, annoying him further. "I've had enough of this, I'm going to dial one-four-seven-one and call them back."

She sat instantly. "She knows."

"Who, for god's sake," he wriggled up the bed, "who knows what?"

"Sophie. She knows we adopted her." He had never heard Beryl shout and it shocked him as much as the revelation. He slumped against the headboard, wallowing in the silence that seemed to last for hours. Eventually, "How?"

She climbed from the bed, shrugging on her dressing gown. "I'm going to get a cocoa; do you want one?"

"Make it a nightcap." If there was ever a time to have a drink, this was it.

She soon returned, composed now, and handed him port in fine crystal, slipping back under the covers. They both sipped, neither knowing what to say, until Harold found his voice. "Did she say how she found out?"

"No, but she mentioned a Mrs Miller. Do you have any idea who that could be?"

He thought for a while and shook his head. "No."

"Apart from us, our Steve's the only other person who knows. Sure he wouldn't…"

"No, Steve would never do that."

Hands raised in frustration, her voice rose. "But it can't be anyone else."

Despite the unsociable hour, Harold snatched the phone and punched the buttons. "Then I'll ask him."

Steve, however, was as nonplussed as his parents at the news.

They had protected Sophie all her life, but now the secret was out, they had to find a way to deal with the inevitable repercussions.

Darren had staggered home from the White Horse just before midnight, reeking of stale cigarettes and beer, but regardless of his drunken state, Sophie had excitedly put the question to him. They had stayed up half the night discussing their imminent move, the two officers from earlier forgotten.

The alarm buzzed at seven and Darren pulled a pillow over his head, groaning. Sophie slipped from the bed, loosely tying her dressing gown over her belly. "Do you want a cup of tea?" Her own head didn't feel too wonderful and she guiltily recalled the brandy the night before.

"More sleep, that's what I want. I think I'm going to pull a sickie today, I feel like shit."

Sophie moved his pillow aside, full of consternation. "You said you were going to take today off anyway. Don't you remember what we talked about last night?"

Brow furrowed, Darren pulled himself up onto his elbows, trying to remember, but the previous evening was a blank. He gave up. "No. Remind me."

Sophie sat beside him, stroking his hair. "You were going to speak to your parents about us moving to Mallorca at the same time as them, ask if they'd mind putting us up until we get ourselves sorted out."

Darren scrabbled up the bed, plumping the pillows behind his back. "I remember now: the cops were here. Why were the pigs here?"

"I told you last night about that weird woman, Mrs Miller, the one who's stalking me. That's why I want to get away from this place. She won't stop hassling me, follows me wherever I go, keeps turning up at work. Remember that yesterday she said she was my mother?"

Darren laughed. "You what? That's insane."

"It's not funny, Darren, she's beginning to scare me. I just want to get away from here, away from work, away from my parents and Steve. I want to get away from everything, bring this baby up with no problems or drama. Please try and persuade your parents. If they say yes, I'll hand my notice in straight away."

"What about this place? You don't have a buyer yet." Now fully awake, Darren's mind whirled.

"The estate agent can show people around. It'll sell one day, maybe if we reduce the price even more. Perhaps we could leave the furniture and rent it out, I don't know. I don't care. Please, Darren."

"Okay, I'll call my mam today. Now get your arse downstairs and get me that mug of tea, woman." Sophie chuckled as she trotted down the stairs.

Chapter 9
Andrew

Sophie's day had again been stressful and she couldn't wait to get home to the cottage she loved, yet wanted to leave. She dropped pens and pencils back into the jar and tidied the paperwork on her desk, and was putting her coat on when the phone rang. "Soph, it's me."

"I thought you'd forgotten me." She perched on her chair, listening eagerly.

"Mam and Dad have been out all day and their mobiles were turned off. I've only just spoken to them."

"And?" Sophie held her breath, nerves ragged, wondering if her heart was still beating.

"It's good news, love. That underbuild they said they were having done, well, it's got a bedroom, an en-suite and a kitchenette. They said we can live there for as long as it takes. Mam said she didn't know why she hadn't thought of it before."

Sophie punched the air, expelling her pent breath. "Yes."

"You do realise it's only three weeks away, though. There's a lot to arrange if we're really going through with this. Do you think you're up to it, what with the baby and everything? And don't you have to give two months' notice?"

"Oh, stuff work, I'll get around that. I'll go and see Mr Barton now, I'm sure he'll understand."

"But what about the flights, removals, all the rest of the things that'll need doing?"

"Organisation is one of my strong points. In three weeks we'll be packed and ready to go." They resolved to discuss the arrangements later over a takeaway, and after she had hung up, a beaming smile on her face, Sophie locked her office and climbed the stairs to find her boss.

She knocked and waited.

"Come."

Opening the door. "Mr Barton, I…"

"Ah, Sophie, I'm glad you're here, I've been meaning to talk to you."

Sophie didn't have time or patience for an irrelevant discussion with the bad-tempered man she couldn't bear. "Mr Barton, I'm handing in my notice."

Today I intended to find out where Sophie lived, regardless of the threat of being charged with harassment, and waited in a taxi for Sophie to leave work, having given the driver a few believable lies. He duly followed her car until it pulled into gated driveway and I instructed him to drop me off. My imagination had been certain Sophie was a Derby dweller, an easy distance from her workplace, but in reality the journey was long, and after paying the driver fifteen pounds, I didn't have enough money to get back. I swore inwardly and resolved to worry about that later. At least now I knew her address.

The rambling cottage was charming, with ivy clinging to the walls and the final few blooms of fragrant jasmine covering the porch. I was jealous; life had been unfair to me and luck wasn't in my dictionary. Things would have been different if Beryl hadn't been in my way. Avoiding the noisy gravel, I padded along the borders, dodging shrubs and trying not to snag my old jumper on the rose bushes. I slowed as I neared the house, stepping as quietly as possible.

My stealth, however, was in vain. The front door opened and a tall, well-built man carried a bag of rubbish towards the bin. I immediately stilled, but autumn leaves crackled underfoot and the man stopped walking and scoured the area. "Who's that? Who's there?" And he looked directly at me; the moon must have reflected on my glasses and I wished I had discarded the damned things. I didn't move - breathe - but he wasn't about to give up. I swore under my breath, seeing no other solution but to show myself; he would find me one way or another now.

Racking my brain for a feasible excuse, I shifted onto the gravel. "Hello."

Dropping the rubbish in the bin. "Who are you?"

"I, er..." He was becoming impatient with my hapless dithering, but words, for once, had escaped me. To turn and leave would have been the safest option but I only had five pounds left, not enough for a taxi... unless there was a bus. "Are you Mr Delaney?" Why did I say that? I could have excused myself as a Jehovah's Witness or something. Smart ideas always appear in retrospect.

Darren was trying to place my face. "Who wants to know?"

Truth it was, then: "My name is Mary Miller. I'm your wife's birth mother."

Darren's eyes twinkled, hands rubbing with glee, and his grin was devious. He reached into his trouser pocket for his well-stocked wallet, whispering, "Look, you can't come in, Soph would go mad." He handed me a twenty-pound note and my eyes boggled. "There's a pub around the corner, the White Horse. Go to the lounge bar, it won't be busy, get yourself a drink and I'll meet you there in five minutes."

Laughter lines crinkled beneath my bottle-bottoms and I snatched the money and toddled up the drive as he closed the door softly behind me.

Sophie was about to pour some baked beans into a microwaveable bowl, but Darren took the tin from her hand and pushed the lid down, placing it in the fridge. "Tell you what, Soph, I'll nip to Swadlincote and get a takeaway; I fancy a Chinese tonight." He snatched his car keys from the worktop.

"But that'll take ages, we need to discuss the move."

Smiling mischievously, he shrugged. "It won't take long. You find a pad and pen so we can take notes while we're eating. You want the usual?"

Resigned, Sophie nodded. When she heard the front door close, she took the menu from the drawer and rang the usual order through, reasoning it would at least save him the waiting time.

Easing his BMW into one of the many empty spaces, Darren jumped out and hastened to the lounge bar. Normally he drank in the games room with the other regulars, but tonight he wanted a bit of peace and quiet to talk to me. As demurely as one with such bulk could, I was seated in the corner, toying with the half-pint of cider I had nervously purchased from the bar. Darren collected a lager and joined me. "I can't stop long, Soph will get suspicious. Now, what's all this about you being her birth mother?"

I fidgeted anxiously with my glass, despite his apparent friendliness. "I am. I gave birth to twins on the thirtieth of August, nineteen eighty, a girl, Anna Sophia Bryce, and my son, Andrew Stuart Bryce. Bryce was my maiden name." I explained my affair with a married man - without mentioning Harry - and how my parents had signed my babies away without my knowledge or consent. How I had searched for them tirelessly ever since - not quite the truth, but it elicited more sympathy.

Darren nodded thoughtfully. Sophie's middle name was Anna - coincidence? - but she bore no resemblance to the woman who sat before him. Sure she was a mentally unstable crank, he played along anyway, mindful of squeezing some easy money from her desperation. "So what makes you think my Soph is your daughter?"

"Years of searching. I gave up with the registries in the end, guessing their names had been changed by their new parents, but I had no idea which adoption agency had organised it all. By chance, Beryl came to see me in my capacity as a tarot reader."

Darren laughed, downing his pint, and motioned to my full glass. "Can I get you another?"

"No, thank you, I'm not a drinker normally." I sipped the cider as he took his glass for a refill. I may be hideous and pathetic, but I'm bright as a spark, and it was obvious he didn't believe a word. I was curious to why he had asked to meet up.

"So who was the father, then?"

If he was playing games, then so would I, and meddling was my speciality. "His name is Harold Jacob Waller."

Hearing his father-in-law's name, Darren spat his beer into the glass and gave me his full concentration. "Go on."

"He was a lot older than me and married with a child, a son, can't remember his name." Of course I remembered his name, I simply wanted some interaction.

"Steve?"

"Yes, that's right. I was a keen student, a real bookworm, and I wanted to go to college, so when Birmingham held an open day I jumped at the chance. The moment I laid eyes on Harry, I knew I had to get to know him better, he was gorgeous."

Eyebrow raised, Darren tried to picture Sophie's weedy father as a handsome, young man but it was hard. Harold had a full head of hair, but it was mad-professor grey, and he was hunched, timid, with myopic eyes and a monotonous voice. Gorgeous? Just not happening.

"I did all the chasing, told him I was eighteen so my age wouldn't frighten him, and he tried again and again to fend me off, but I was persistent. Eventually we made love, but weeks later I realised I was pregnant. I was terrified."

"The dirty old bugger, I'd never have thought he was capable." Engrossed in the story, Darren had forgotten the time.

"I thought we were in love - daft, stupid child that I was - but he dropped me like a ton of bricks. I never heard from him again, not once. I searched for my children for years, but heard nothing. Then, after reading the cards for Beryl for a few months, I found that Sophie and my twins shared a birthday. Curious, I contacted the registry office for her birth certificate; there wasn't one. So the educated conclusion is that Harry and Beryl had adopted my Anna." My throat tightened. "I don't understand why only her, not her twin brother. I still have to find him."

Darren glanced at his watch and gasped. "Shit, I've lost track of time. Look, I want to continue this conversation sometime, it's got to be soon because we're moving to Mallorca in three weeks, but I have to get going otherwise Soph will be tearing her hair out."

I gripped his arm tight, eyes pleading with emotion I wished I could hide. "Please try and get her to see me, Darren, promise me you will." I sounded, and felt, desperate.

"I'll see what I can do." Darren stood, car keys in hand, eager to leave, but I held his arm long enough to scribble my address on a scrap of paper from my bag. Handing it to him, he said, "Derby! How are you getting home?"

Of course, I had the change from his twenty-pound note in my purse, but playing the sympathy card every now and then doesn't hurt anyone; I'd seen his thick wallet and I was broke. As always. So I mustered a sorrowful expression, my voice quiet and blue. "I don't know. I'm not familiar with the buses around here."

Needlessly glancing at his watch again, Darren sighed. "I'll drive you back if you'll direct me to a Chinese takeaway once we get there."

I mulled the conversation for a while after he left, and how the violent man I had heard about and seen evidence of didn't tally with the generous and kind spirit I had kept company with. He didn't seem aggressive at all. Now, I've been on the receiving end of a few fists in my time and I know how difficult I can be, so in my humble opinion, Sophie must have done something to deserve it.

Two plates and a serving spoon had been waiting on the worktop for an hour and Sophie was worried. She picked up the receiver on the first ring, hoping to hear Darren's voice, but, "Mrs Delaney?"

"Yes, can I help you?"

"You order Chinese takeaway. When you pick up, please?"

Sophie paled, an ominous chill running through her. "But my husband left ages ago." The front door slammed and she cut the call, meeting Darren in the hallway. "Where have you been? I've been worried sick. The takeaway has just called…"

"I decided to get the food from Derby for a change."

Sophie followed him to the kitchen, annoyed and confused, and watched him empty the white plastic bag onto the side. "But I ordered our usual by phone to save time. They've just called asking where you were."

"That's not my fault, I didn't ask you to." A slight whiff of alcohol mingled with the tempting takeaway. "Come on, let's dish up before it gets cold."

"But Darren, Derby's miles away, why go there when we always go to Swadlincote."

Darren slammed the spoon on the side. "I just did, okay. End of conversation." Afraid of his fraying temper, Sophie reluctantly let the subject drop.

Twelve weeks pregnant and about to emigrate, Sophie felt no guilt when she called in sick after her antenatal appointment at Belton Surgery. Her time was better spent at home, packing, arranging, preparing for the move. The doorbell chimed and she trotted to the hall,

110

surprised to see Officer Taylor. "I was in the area and thought I'd check that you haven't had any more bother from Mary Miller." Actually, he had taken a detour of twelve miles. He knew he shouldn't have, but he couldn't get her off his mind.

And later, over sumptuous roast beef and trimmings, Sophie related the conversation she'd had with the policeman to her husband. "He said he was adopted when he was a baby. Said his adoptive parents never kept the truth from him, but he still wants to find his real family."

Darren laid his cutlery on the table, choosing his words carefully. "Do you know how old he is?"

Sophie missed the keenness in his voice, hungrily preparing her next forkful. "Of course not, but I'd guess at early thirties, thereabouts. Maybe my age, give or take."

The same grey-blue eyes and curly brunette hair, the strong nose. Surely not. But if his suspicions were correct, she would pay through the nose for her long-lost son's details... He had to see Mary Miller again.

Having anticipated cuddling up on the sofa to discuss the arrangements she had made for the move, Sophie was disappointed when Darren said he was going out, and the ugly thought of another woman surfaced. She repressed it, blaming hormones and insecurity.

I, however, was pleased to welcome Darren into my scruffy apartment, hurriedly clearing a space for him on the sofa. "I think I may have found your son."

I moved the wooden chair from beside the table and flumped down to face him. "I have four sons, so that wouldn't be so difficult."

I suppose it had never occurred to him that I may have had more children, and I admit to bending the truth to portray myself as a woman who had ceased living at the age of fifteen, only to be reborn when I found my long-lost babies. He looked uncomfortable. "Um, the boy twin that was adopted."

I sat straight, stunned hope fluttering through me, and removed my glasses, exposing the red dents made by the heavy frames at the top of my nose. I wiped my watering eyes with the back of my hand. "I'm sorry, it's the shock."

Darren grinned, loving every powerful moment, not that I saw anything untoward in his intentions; sometimes I could be ridiculously naïve. "Calm down, love, I wouldn't want to raise any false hopes. Look, I'll find out a bit more about the man, but I will need a birth certificate to make sure I've got my facts straight."

Without hesitation I was on my feet, glasses in place, rummaging through the overfilled top drawer of the sideboard. "They're both in here somewhere." Soon I brandished a tatty, yellowed certificate. "That's Anna's, now for Andrew's... ah, here it is." By now I was sure I had misjudged Darren, that Beryl was prejudiced and Sophie had provoked the beating. Idiotic fool that I am.

Looking back, it must have been hard for Darren to not punch the air with glee, the prized blackmail possessions now his to control us like puppets. Four people: his wife, me, his father-in-law and possibly the unsuspecting Officer Taylor. We were all in his power. He almost ran from my flat, assuring me he would return soon.

Darren drove straight to Coalville Police Station and demanded to see Taylor, whose inquisitive expression on seeing him was the spit of my own. "Can I help you?"

"I need to talk to you. In private, if that's okay."

Taylor guided Darren to a small interview room and they sat, Darren smiling roguishly, a glint in his yellow eyes. "Sophie told me last night that you were adopted, that you're looking for your mother."

Alan was irked that his private life had been discussed with the man he hated with a passion. "What's that got to do with you?"

"Have you ever seen your birth certificate?"

"My parents have been open about my adoption."

Darren took a document from his pocket and unfolded it. "Is that it?" Taylor grabbed at the paper, but Darren snatched it back.

Taylor's anger bubbled; he wanted to beat the shit out of Darren Delaney, and only his professionalism stopped him. "What are you doing with that? Where did you get it from? What are you playing at, you scheming bastard?"

Darren laughed, enjoying his power. He stood, tucking the certificate into his pocket with a pat for extra effect. "I know who your mother is."

Sure that Taylor's curiosity would bring great rewards, Darren tugged the door open, but it slammed shut with the force of his body as Taylor punched him, dragging him back by the collar, pummelling him over and over, thumping out the smugness, beating out the arrogance. "Give it to me, you fucking bastard."

Darren grinned with every blow, blood trailing from his mouth and nose, and when Taylor came to his senses and backed away, Darren pulled the door wide once more. "I also know who your father is. And your twin sister. Give me some money and I might just tell you who they are." And he was gone.

Alan sat in the chair, his busy mind driving him crazy as the minutes ticked by. How would Delaney know so much about his history... unless he was involved in that history too... Sophie... Mary Miller's insistence she was her mother, that her twins had been named Anna and Andrew... His adoptive parents had changed his name from Andrew to Alan... And then, sickened, he remembered Sophie's middle name was Anna.

That was why he had been drawn to her: not lust, or love, as he had thought, but genetic sexual attraction. He had an overwhelming urge to vomit.

Chapter 10
Puppets

Sophie suspected Darren had gone to the local after his mysterious trip to Derby and was miserable that he was drinking to excess every night again. Not only did it cost a fortune, especially when she paid the bills and housekeeping with her credit cards - money better spent on things for the baby - but it made his breath reek and, quite frankly, he became a bore. Not to mention the violence.

She didn't look at him when he returned home, shrugging off his jacket and throwing it across the sofa instead of hanging it up. He didn't like her mouthy, but she couldn't hold her tongue. "White Horse again, was it?"

Darren took a crystal glass, a wedding present from his parents, from the cabinet and poured a large whisky, gulping, replenishing. "Nope, I've been to see your copper friend at the police station."

And now she noticed his swollen and bruised face, dry blood on his lips and chin. "Oh my god, Darren, what happened to you?"

He sat beside his jacket, arrogant and smirking. "Just your best buddy taking his pathetic anger out on me, that's all."

"Alan Taylor did that to you?"

"You bet he did. He's jealous because he's in love with you and you're mine."

Averting her eyes, Sophie sipped her hot chocolate; she had suspected as much from the way Alan gazed at her. "Don't be silly, of course he isn't."

"Why don't you go and ask him yourself?" Darren was loving every second. "I also had a very interesting chat Mary Miller." Sophie gasped. "Nice enough lady, a bit crazy about the edges maybe, but she seems sound."

Sophie's chest was tight, breathing hard. What was her husband doing? Why was he saying these things to her? Shaking, tears dripping, she slid the mug onto the table and poured a brandy, while he watched with amusement. "Same old Sophie, eh, can't cope without a drink. Ah, some things never change." Darren refilled his glass and sat beside his wife, arm around her shoulders. "It's okay, I'll look after you, I'll take you away from all of this. Less than three weeks until we go now. Once we're in Mallorca you can start a new life, you and my son, away from all of this."

Confused, Sophie clutched her child from the outside, protective. Was he being nice? But he visited that woman, had a fight with Alan Taylor. "I don't understand, why go and see them both?"

That sneer. Those ochre eyes, snakelike and empty. "Just searching for the truth. I have your birth certificate, the real one. Mary Miller wasn't lying."

"But I phoned Mum, she said she gave birth to me."

"Harold and Beryl adopted you. Mary's your mother."

Clutching her chest, heaving, breathless.

Darren hugged her close. "Shhh, sweetheart, shush. Beryl's a liar, I've always said as much. You're better off with me."

"But I look just like my dad?"

"Coincidence, that's all. I promised Mary I'd try and get you to see her."

Disgusted, her face twisted. "No way. Absolutely no way."

"That's fine." Darren gulped his whisky. "You don't need anyone but me."

Head swirling, no distinction of truth or lies, the dizziness was overwhelming. Had her whole life been a lie? Tired, exhausted. She shrugged from Darren's grip. "I'm going to bed."

As soon as her head hit the pillow, Sophie let the tears flow, not understanding. Not wanting to understand.

I can see how ridiculous it is now, but I had no idea how cruel Darren could be, that I was only seeing the public side of his character. Oh, how wonderful it would be to have the ability to see into the future and stop yourself from making mistakes. But I had been sucked into his web, just like poor Sophie and no doubt many more before her. The next morning, I bounced from my bed with a wonderfully unusual spring in my step, hoping to see Darren sooner rather than later.

The removal company delivered the boxes in the morning, and Sophie relished the mundane task of packing to take her mind off the despicable revelations. But still the thoughts hammered her. Mary Miller - dismissed. And again - dismissed, with hatred. Beryl was her mother and Harold was her father. Mary was just a crazy weirdo who messed with lives because she had nothing better to do in her sad little world. And then, Mary wasn't a liar, Beryl and Harold were.

She was desperate to escape, run away from the angst and doubt; Mallorca couldn't come soon enough.

Preparing another cup of tea, wrapping and boxing the excess crockery as the water heated, Sophie was oblivious that Darren had pulled another sickie and was climbing the stairs to my flat.

I cracked the door and grinned, wide and welcoming. "Come in." His face was swollen and bruised and my smile waned. "Oh my, what happened to you?"

He shook his head, cold from the frosty morning, hugging his jacket close. "It's nothing. What with the baby and everything, Soph gets angry sometimes. Just a few bruises; they'll heal.' He followed me to the living room and sat in the same spot as the previous evening.

Steadying myself on the table, I eased my bulk onto the hard chair. "Sophie can't have done that, she's a gentle soul."

Darren stared sadly at the carpet, his voice pained. "It's just her hormones. She's always been a bit feisty, gives me a few scratches here and there." And his woeful eyes met mine. "She's a bit of a drinker, you see, gets angry sometimes, but when we move I'm sure everything will be better." He was small, a shell, throat dry and crackling. "Can we change the subject?"

I gulped, struggling to accept this shocking revelation. "Of course, I understand." Now I was certain I had misjudged the man. "Did you find out anything last night, you know, about my son?"

Marvelling at how gullible - stupid - people could be, Darren smiled gently, his evil plotting reaching fever pitch. "Yes, I did. He's definitely your son, Mary. Nice guy, respectable sort, you know."

I grasped my chest, supporting myself woozily against the table. "I've waited so many years for this moment. Does he look like me? What's his name? What's he like?"

Darren laughed, waving his hands for ceasefire. "It's early days, Mary, and I've been driving all over trying to sort out your family. I think it's about time you gave me something for my trouble, don't you?"

I grimaced at my selfishness, heaving from the seat. "Of course, silly me, I didn't mean to be rude. Would you like a cup of tea? Coffee?"

"Money, Mary, or should we call it expenses. You reimburse me and I'll make sure you have your nice little family back together." He laughed, eyes sparkling.

Dismayed by the lack of family spirit, I took a tenner from the drawer beside me and passed it across, but the twinkle dulled, the chuckle now a sneer, lip curled and nostrils flared. "Large expenses, you stupid cow."

Momentarily blank, I realised this was blackmail. He had duped me. Me, a master manipulator; I'd been had. The initial hatred I had felt for him flooded back. Furious, I grasped his arm and marched him to the front door, onto the balcony. "Get out of here and don't even think about coming back, you vile bastard."

His cocky laughter echoed through the slammed door as the footsteps dissipated, taunting me, contemptuous and cruel. Of course I wanted my family back together, desperate to hold my twins once more, but I was resolute I had done the right thing. What amateur Darren didn't know was that once I was crossed, I was dangerous.

That night, I opened a book I hadn't consulted before and followed instructions, making a crude effigy of Darren from scraps of material. One day soon, when it felt right, I would get my retribution.

Darren was unperturbed, sure the importance of the information he had would sway Mary eventually, it would just take a little time. In the meantime, there were more people to work on and he parked outside the Waller household.

When Harold came home, he was astounded to find his son-in-law draped across the spare seat of his study, clutching a mug of steaming coffee. "Darren, what are you doing here?" Unnerved, he set the paperwork from his last lecture on the desk.

"Harold, Harold, dearest daddy-in-law, just sit down and relax. Chill. There's some business we need to discuss."

An easy-going soul, he had welcomed Darren into the family initially, but time and circumstances had raised his hackles and he had come to dislike Darren as much as his less-trusting wife did. He was wary, and the ominous atmosphere that he couldn't put his finger on was disturbing. He crossed his arms, head cocked. "What do you want, Darren?"

"Ah, come on, Dad, no need to be so thorny. Let's chat." Harold winced, hairs rising on his nape. "Have you spoken to your daughter recently? Oh no, of course you haven't. Silly me. Thing is, I know you and the old dragon don't like me, that you think your little darling's too good for me, but that's tough really. After all, she loves me, we're married, and you can't have her back." The sinister iciness was unsettling, but Harold refused to show vulnerability. "Have any little birds told you we're moving abroad?" Harold's jaw tensed. "Pretty soon, actually, nice villa, bit of sun. And of course she'll have my baby there. Mam and Dad will love having their first grandchild to dote on, they'll see him every day. You know, we can't wait."

Harold was tense, a body of steel under mocking tendrils of malevolence, and he forced his hands to unclench, hiding his emotions from the wicked and taunting tormenter.

"I know about your dirty little secret, daddy dear, I know that you shagged an underage girl. Had it from the horse's mouth. You are a naughty boy. I have to admit I'd never have expected you of all people to have such a raunchy past. Couldn't Beryl have babies then? Is Steve the fruit of your loins with some other little schoolgirl as well?"

Fingers of angry red crept across Harold's psyche and he itched to wipe the provocative smirk from Darren's face. Instead, he waved, dismissive. "Go away, you ignorant idiot, go and find somebody else to bully because I'm not falling for it." His restraint was tremendous, sitting, sorting through paperwork, nonchalant.

A derisive chuckle. "Oh, Harold, I won't go away until you to buy my silence. A couple of thousand should do for now. Of course, if that's not acceptable to you, I can always let Sophie know what darling daddy is really like. Or perhaps I could introduce Mary Bryce to the old dragon, let them talk about old times, compare notes on your sexual performance maybe. What do you reckon, Dad?"

Harold glared, unwavering, loathing. "I told Beryl all about it at the time, it was her idea to adopt Sophie. So forget your extortion, it's not going to work on me."

121

His goal achieved, Darren stood; he had Harold Waller in the palm of his hand. "The old dragon may know, but sweet Sophie, the apple of daddy's eye; it would ruin her. You'll never seen her again." Darren stalked out, his vindictive chuckle echoing from the magnolia walls, and Harold locked the door, leaning against it, breathing hard, panting. Faint.

He slumped onto his chair, head in hands on the desk. "I'm so sorry, Sophie, I should have told you."

Now, I tell fortunes purely for gain, there isn't a psychic bone in my body, but the cards spread on the table before me were riddled with doom and gloom. Beryl had shuffled, asking me for a general reading, but my mind had been bursting with Sophie and Darren as I had dealt the Celtic cross and if one believed in such things, the results would be remarkably appropriate of the situation I knew and Beryl didn't.

I reached the ninth card, Hopes and Fears, and turned over The Sun, which was completely out of place amongst the other cards. I relaxed; of course it was all piffle. A wonderful card suggesting happiness on all levels, but I knew the truth of the horrendous mistake Sophie was about to make. It was essential I dispose of the husband, stop my girl moving out of reach.

Nonetheless, I trotted out the banal patter that Beryl wanted to hear, soothing, reassuring.

Not for me, though. I needed to see my daughter, warn her about Darren and the dangers the cards were predicting. But if I visited, she would call the police.

I even considered calling them myself in the hope they would be receptive, but dismissed the ridiculous idea in seconds. People, society, had labelled me mad for years; why would things be any different now?

I had to come up with something, but what?

When Darren returned home at just gone three, Sophie was buzzing with excitement. "Hey, Soph, calm down. What's going on?"

She was gushing nonsense, sentences tripping into each other in her quest to relate everything at the same time, and she followed him to the kitchen. He opened a cupboard and found it empty. "Where are the glasses?"

"I've packed them, we're down to two of everything." She passed him a tumbler from the side. "Have you heard a single word I've said?"

Darren raised an eyebrow. "If you want the truth, then no, you're talking a load of mumbo-jumbo." He took the blended whisky he had bought from the carrier bag and poured a large measure.

Sophie breathed deeply to calm herself, arms and fingers outstretched. "We've sold the cottage."

In one glorious moment his dreams came to fruition, his long-term plan suddenly, unexpectedly - wonderfully - now short-term. He beamed, eyes twinkling, speechless.

"The estate agent called asking if I could show a couple around at short notice. I told them we were packing - the boxes came this morning - and the place was a mess, but they said these people had seen the cottage from the outside a few times and were really keen. So I said yes. Anyway, this Ian and Laura, they loved it. They're from down south, and bloody rich, said this will be their second home. They run a business, not sure what, but they can buy the place outright, no mortgage, nothing. A surveyor's coming out as soon as possible. Isn't it fantastic?"

Darren took the other glass from the side and poured a smaller whisky. "Drink this, Soph, I think you need to calm down."

Sophie sipped, enjoying the warmth, the cheap kick. "Don't you see? It means we won't have to stay with your parents too long, we can buy a place of our own."

Darren drained his drink and replenished it, raising the glass to clink against Sophie's. "Here's to us. The future."

Chapter 11
Countdown

Darren didn't return for his fraudulent money, which was good, seeing as I had none, and two weeks hurtled by with no contact between any of us. If Darren had been telling the truth about their November emigration, there was only a week before he and Sophie were due to fly off to their new life.

Sophie's organisational skills had proven priceless: the removal company was booked and storage for their furniture until they found a place to buy, flights arranged and suitcases packed, bar the essentials. She had scrubbed the cottage from top to bottom - paintwork, scuffs on walls, kitchen, bathroom - and it was clean as a show home. Their life was in limbo, surviving on takeaways from wrappers and bar meals at the White Horse.

Darren had continued his self-employed joinery to earn as much money as possible before the move, working on a new build designated to be a care home for children with cerebral palsy. Hodgekinson, Neville and Barton, although disgruntled by Sophie's absence, had no choice but to pay out her notice as long as her willing doctor supplied medical certificates. She hadn't divulged that she was leaving the country, and the black cloud over her resignation was of no concern.

I was clueless that Darren had also tried to blackmail PC Taylor and Harry, not that it would have shocked me. Eternally honest, Harry had related the events to Beryl, who, as she had done thirty-one years before when told of his affair with a teenaged girl and the resulting pregnancy, coped by blocking it out, pretending it had never happened. Obviously there had been arguments and tears, but underneath her anger, Beryl understood why he had needed to reopen the wound: for Sophie's sake.

I had met endless brick walls trying to figure out how to stop Sophie from leaving, dismissing hundreds of ideas after rational thought, and I was at a loss. The miserable frost had set in and showed no signs of abating, and the murky skies had dumbed the high spirits of summer. I had taken to keeping my winter coat on inside as I couldn't afford to heat the flat and had given up hoping that Darren would grow a heart and pass me details of my son without the payment I couldn't afford. I often wondered whether I would have succumbed to his blackmail had he showed his face, but I couldn't raise two pounds, let alone two thousand.

Then Harry and Beryl turned up on my doorstep.

Harry could have been anyone at first, but I soon recognised the familiar - older - eyes. Beryl must have been heartbroken that her personal mystic was the Lolita who had ensnared her husband, but she kept her dignity, polite yet distant. Few words were needed before we understood our common goal: Sophie's welfare. "As far as I know she's due to move in a week or so. Darren said he'd been in contact with you, Mary, is that true?"

My face twisted with distaste at the mention of his name. "Yes, he's been here. He says he knows who my - our - son is, tried to blackmail me."

Harry was astounded. "You mean he knows about Andrew as well?"

It was like he had unblocked a dam and years of anguish flipped to anger. "Why did you only take Sophie? They should have stayed together."

A tear trickled from Beryl's eye and I felt an uncommon pity for her. "That was down to me." Quiet, barely there. "I already had Steve and I desperately wanted a daughter, but after two ectopic pregnancies damaged both fallopian tubes, the only solution was to adopt." Her shoulders squared and she caught my eye. "Don't ever kid yourself that I condone your tawdry affair with my husband, but at least our daughter was his flesh and blood. I couldn't, however, have coped with two babies, I was very anxious at the time."

"You would have, had they been yours." I quipped maliciously, and Harry silenced me with a glare. I wasn't to know that her use of anxious was a euphemism for the severe depression she had suffered following the failed pregnancies. Regardless, I was jealous: her life could have been mine.

Beryl's decorum was intact, and she continued, "We can't change the past, but in the near future our daughter - I accept we are all her parents - is moving to another country with a man we know to be scheming and violent bully. Our joint quest is to work out how to stop her?"

I would never have been capable of such poise and my sudden respect for Beryl, the other woman, surprised me. A trickle of understanding emerged for why Harry hadn't ended his marriage for the pretty airhead I used to be. I felt like a dandelion beside an orchid, sitting next to her, and my voice was gravel as I said, "We're doing this for our unborn grandchild too."

Harry had always weighed the situation up before wasting words, and he thought for a while. "The thing is, as a grown woman it's her choice if she wants to move away, but I'm especially concerned about the violence and her refusal to acknowledge it. It's only a few months since she was... oh, gosh, Mary, you won't have known she was in intensive care."

"I do, Harry," Beryl winced at my use of the affectionate nickname, "I went to see her. Darren tried to tell me that *she* was the violent one."

"Rubbish." Harry cleared his throat, calming himself. "I think the best thing we can do is go and see her at home. If we voice our concerns together, she may at least consider our reasons for being unsettled with her emigration."

So off we went, united in our concern for Sophie's future. Harry politely opened the car door open for his wife and me, his ex-mistress, and we traipsed along the driveway to Sophie's cottage. But nobody appeared to be in and we glanced at each other, awkward. On the point of giving up, we heard giggling, footsteps approaching.

Sophie was shocked when she came through the gate, Darren's worried face a picture. "Mum, Dad." She shot me a filthy glare. "What's going on?"

Shaking his head, Darren let himself in and closed the door. Beryl broke the ice. "Sophie, we need to talk to you."

Her flushed face and easy smile left me in no doubt she had been drinking, and Beryl's judgemental raised eyebrow showed she had thought the same, but with less understanding. Sophie beckoned her parents into the house. "Not you though, I want nothing to do with you."

I shied away, embarrassed, but Beryl charitably took my arm. "Mary is part of the discussion we need to have with you." I was so grateful; damn the bloody woman for being so nice.

Sophie reluctantly moved aside.

We dodged around neatly labelled boxes to the kitchen, where Sophie filled the kettle. "Shit."

Beryl's indignant expression was priceless. "Sophie!"

Our daughter chuckled, pulling a bottle of wine from the fridge and clicking the kettle off. "I've packed all but two glasses and Darren has one upstairs for his whisky. We'll have to neck this instead."

"You shouldn't be drinking with a baby on the way." Harry put his arm around Beryl's shoulders to calm her, but her tone was curt as she nodded to the ceiling. "Can he hear us?"

Sophie swigged from the bottle and stared wryly at her adoptive mother.

Harry sighed. "Look, love, I know you're an adult, but please reconsider your move abroad, or at least slow it down a pace. We're worried about you."

"For god's sake, here we go again." She breezed to the hallway and we followed like sheep, shuffling awkwardly. "I know you don't like Darren, but he's my husband whether you like it or not, and when I said my vows, I meant them for life. So, if that's all you have to say, I'll say goodnight now." She waited impatiently by the open door, but we weren't about to be beaten.

"Sophie, close the door, let's go and sit somewhere." The fact the furniture was buried under

129

boxes hadn't gone unnoticed and Harry flushed. "Or just stand." He took a deep breath, sad eyes imploring forgiveness, while Sophie crossed her arms defiantly. "I know this will be hard for you to accept, but what Mary told you is true: she is your birth mother. We adopted you."

"Darren has already told me the story, which, I might add, should have come from you many years ago."

He took her hands, but she shrugged away. "I *am* your natural father, but…"

Swigging. Beryl wincing. "I told you already, Darren told me everything. So I know she's the little slag who got herself knocked up when she was fourteen, and I know you are a paedophile and mother dear is a blatant liar. So, as I said, goodnight."

"Sophie, it's not as cut and dried as…"

"I don't want to hear your bloody excuses. I said goodnight." The shrillness was biting. "Now get out." A freezing wind gusted from outside, matching the icy atmosphere.

Tears welled in Harry's eyes and it was clear his heart was breaking. "Sophie, please listen."

"Out."

Footsteps on the stairs, and Darren swaggered over triumphantly, glass in hand. "Well, come on, you lot, you heard the lady: she wants you out of here." Arrogant and grinning, he sipped his drink as we filed out of the house, the door slamming behind us. Nobody noticed me take his keys from the side.

We had no idea of Sophie's forwarding address, whether we would see or hear from her again. Whether

130

our grandchild would ever know us. We had tried, shown our unity, been truthful, but Darren had her captivated and we'd lost her.

The drive back to Derby was in silence.

Cradling hot mugs of tea amid the chaos of my flat, our minds were in turmoil, the atmosphere miserable and our daughter inaccessible. I was amazed by Beryl's fortitude; I had expected her to fall to pieces, a sobbing wreck. "What do we do?"

"We give him the money he asked Mary for, pay him off."

Hope touched me, but Beryl was adamant. "There's no way we are succumbing to his bribery, Harold. One of us will get through to her somehow. Maybe the three of us turning up at the same time was overwhelming for her, especially in her current condition. Perhaps if one of us - it's probably best if it's not you, Mary, please don't take offence - were to see her alone, try and at least get the address of where she'll be staying. Harold, she dotes on you, I think you're the one who needs to do this."

The doorbell rang and we glanced at each other, but PC Taylor wasn't the face we had hoped for. "Mrs Miller, I... um... I need to talk to you."

I was irritated, mindful of Sophie's threats of harassment. "I suppose you'd better come through." A restraining order was the last thing I needed and Sophie's intolerance irked me. After all, she was about to leave the country. "Harry and Beryl, her parents, will explain why I was there."

Alan removed his cap and moved a pile of magazines from the cluttered sofa, sitting. "I think you've got the wrong end of the stick. I'm here for personal reasons, it's not an official matter." He glanced apologetically at my visitors. "Actually, this is a bit of a private matter."

Fed up with his blithering, I was dismissive. "There's nothing you can say to me that can't be said in front of my friends."

Taylor awkwardly scanned the room and Beryl diplomatically suggested they leave, but I adamantly declined. He stuttered lightly as he said, "Obviously you know Sophie Delaney." He now had Harry and Beryl's attention. "Well, I had a visit from her husband a couple of weeks ago and it was pretty unpleasant. He didn't say in so many words, but I believe he wanted money from me for the details of my birth mother. I've added two and two and think I may be the male twin you gave birth to on thirtieth of August, nineteen-eighty."

A collective gasp, three gaping mouths.

Uncomfortable, Alan glanced between the three of us. Beryl was the first to speak again, the least affected by the announcement. "What makes you think that?"

But I could see now: the eyes, my blue-grey, the brunette curls and slightly turned-in toes. Could it be true? "It's only what Darren Delaney implied, but I do have this." He unfolded piece of paper from his pocket and passed it to me. My heart stopped and I struggled to catch my breath. "It's a copy of my birth certificate, my parents gave it to me when I left home."

I was hot, yet shivering, scanning his delightful face - the one that mirrored mine - though my bottle-bottoms. I yearned to hold him, the baby they had stolen against my will. I had never even had a chance to say goodbye. I felt sick with emotion. "I have a copy of my adoption certificate if you want to see that."

I caught Harry's eye and he was equally winded, skin pale and breathing stilled. He took the document from Alan and read, eventually nodding to me.

Alan, of course, knew nothing of the recent events and was on tenterhooks, tempted to run away and forget he had found the courage to approach me. "Should I go?" Slowly, I stood, arms out and heart full to bursting. "Oh my god. Oh my god." Tears swimming down his face as he embraced me tightly, never wanting to let go.

Harold sat with his head in his hands - I'm sure he was crying - but Beryl stood and greeted Alan kindly. The situation was devastatingly painful for her, but an outsider would never know. "I guess I'm your stepmother."

Alan surveyed her blankly.

"Harold, are you going to speak or shall I?" Harry shook his head, pointing to her, and Alan looked on, bewildered. Scared. She took his hand. "It's nothing to worry about, dear. Harold here is your natural father."

Alan propped himself against my table, stunned. Ecstatic, yet overwhelmed. The past couple of weeks had been tough, drinking himself to a stupor most nights to block out the nonstop confusion. He had reasoned, rationed, but the direst consideration was that just two weeks ago, before this can of worms had opened, he would gratefully have bedded the woman who was in fact his twin sister.

The next hour past in a flurry of explanation, concluding with the news he already knew of Sophie's plan to relocate. When I told him of devious Darren's blackmail attempt, he admitted he had also been approached, responding, he said shamefully, with violence. Having loosely come to terms with finding his birth parents, he agreed to try and help stop Sophie before she made such a terrible mistake. "She doesn't know any of this."

I raised an eyebrow. "Darren may have told her."

"No, she would have called me, I'm sure of that. I'm going over there now. Perhaps we could meet up for a meal later - my treat - and catch up with the last thirty-one years."

Happier than perhaps he had ever been, Alan approached the cottage with a spring in his step, and was surprised to find Sophie was also cheerful; he wasn't sure he had seen her smile before. "Hi, Officer Taylor, come on in. It's a bit of a mess, but we're moving soon."

"You seem very happy today." He could see the resemblance now. She took after her father and he his mother, but little things, mannerisms, their walk. Turned-in toes.

She switched the kettle on and rinsed the two unpacked mugs. "My husband said it was you who gave him the black eyes, is that true?" Embarrassed, he fidgeted with his hands, but she rolled her eyes, smiling. "Thing is, he's a bit jealous. I think because you're a good-looking guy he saw you as a threat. I'm just pleased he's at the pub, it might be a bit awkward if he were here."

He wanted to blurt out the truth, to hold her, hug her, but, "When are you moving?"

She chuckled, happy and carefree. "Four days now. We leave here in three, stay at an airport hotel in

Manchester, then fly out in the morning. I'm so excited, Officer Taylor."

"Please call me Alan, I'm not here on official duty."

Her smile waned. "Oh, why are you here then?" Maybe Darren's suspicions had been right.

"Sophie," he was struggling to find words that wouldn't scare her, "your pregnancy, your baby..."

She patted her tummy lovingly, a proud grin. "I'm fourteen weeks now, nearly half way."

"What about your maternity care, surely you need antenatal things, scans, stuff like that?" Aware he sounded like a father, he winced.

"That's no problem. Darren's parents have arranged insurance to cover everything, they've been wonderful, and the Spanish hospitals are supposed to be amazing. This baby's going to have the best."

"Sophie, don't go." He was desperate.

Her face fell, irritated, fed up of people interfering with her life. "He was bloody right, wasn't he? You do have feelings for me."

"At least give me a forwarding address."

"What, and risk getting battered again because..." She turned away, busying herself with the drinks to avoid his concerned face. She had never admitted what was happening behind closed doors and realised she had said too much. "I can't keep in touch. You're a copper who helped with some vandalism to Darren's car, and everything is sorted now. End of story."

"Sophie, it's true that I have feelings for you, but not in the way you think." It was all or nothing. "I'm your brother, your twin, and Darren was the one who told me."

Floating, unaware. Tormented and faint. Why did everyone keep challenging her family unit? She heard screaming, but was deaf, blind and mute.

How she got to bed, covers tugged up to her chin and a balloon of brandy in her hand, she had no idea. She had a vague recollection of a policeman being in the house, but couldn't remember why. All that mattered was that in four days she would be away from this place, away from the darkness, the scheming, the hurting.

I should have known that Darren, like a bad smell, wouldn't go away. He pushed past me and slammed the door, arrogant and condescending. "Give me a couple of thousand and I'll give you our forwarding address, it's as easy as that."

I have to admit it was tempting, having been told Sophie's dramatic response to Alan's pleas. "I haven't got any money."

He towered over me, too close, threatening, and scowled. "You're back in touch with Huggable-Harold and he's got shedloads of money. Get him to fucking pay up, you stupid cow. Just remember, Sophie's my property, and so is that baby, so if you don't show me the readies pretty fucking quick, you'll never see them again."

I was scared, intimidated, and I slunk to the phone, sifting through used envelopes and scraps of paper for Beryl's number. I dialled, while Darren spat, "I've got special plans for Sophie, she's going to have a big shock once she's had my son."

I glared into his malevolent yellow eyes. "Harry, it's Mary."

Harry stopped by the next morning on his way to work and handed me two thousand pounds, having withdrawn it without consulting Beryl; he knew she would be horrified. "Don't give it to him until you get an address."

Once he had gone, I sat at the table and counted the money. It felt so good, the crisp, powdery texture, the smell; I'd never seen so much cash in my life. I stared at the phone, Darren's mobile number scribbled on a coupon beside it, then at the banknotes.

Dinner that night would be beans on toast, my messy flat was freezing and I wore second hand rags because my finances were so bad. If Harold Waller had done the decent thing and stuck by me all those years ago, it would be me, not Beryl, living the privileged life. Instead, I was poor. Harry owed me.

I caressed the money for a while, wondering if I could justify keeping it and use my manipulative skills on Darren instead. It was wrong, but so tempting, thinking of all the things I could do with two thousand readies. I made up my mind: it was worth more in my pocket than in Darren's.

Stashing the wad at the back of my sideboard drawer, I took the effigy I had made of Darren weeks before, short tufts of brown wool stitched into the head and ochre eyes marked with a felt pen, and attached the house keys I had lifted from their hall to the doll with an elastic band.

Chapter 12
And Gone

The storage company had arrived early to take the furniture and boxes to their depot, ready to transport abroad when the Delaneys found a house to buy in Mallorca, and Sophie had taken their cars to the garage that would be selling them. Darren had finished working now, but instead of helping with the chaotic arrangements, he had gone to see his parents in a borrowed van, their own lives in disarray, to discuss plans. Sophie was too busy to be annoyed, focusing on everything running smoothly, and excited about the hotel later, the flight tomorrow.

She had blocked the intervention by her parents from her mind; it was easier that way.

Maureen poured a coffee each from a flask while the removals company emptied the house, and they sat on the low garden wall. "I've been giving her alcohol, Mam, I've done my research. If I tell the doctors she's got a secret drink problem, then they're likely to give the baby withdrawal drugs when he's born."

She nodded, smiling. "Are you sure it's a boy?"

Darren laughed, cocky. "Come on, Mam, it's my baby, of course it's a boy."

"And you're quite sure the alcohol won't damage the child?"

"Not in the quantities she's been having. Just enough to register she's a drinker, but not enough to cause problems." He tapped his nose. "I'm being careful. It's my son, remember."

138

Alan knew he was abusing his position in the police force, but worrying about repercussions could come later. He had spent the morning calling removals companies in the area and finally, trusting of his status, Archie's reluctantly admitted they were moving the Delaney's belongings to Mallorca. They refused to say any more without seeing identification; Alan was in the car within seconds.

Archie's Master Removals tenanted a grubby building with graffiti walls and wind-blown rubbish littering the parking area, and Alan questioned their professionalism. He asked the receptionist for Tony Archival and introduced himself to the gruff man, showing his ID.

Archival waved his hand. "I can see your uniform. Why the interest?"

"I'm not at liberty to say, I'm afraid, but we do need a forwarding address."

He scanned the handwritten booking form, coffee stained and curled at the edges. "Puerto de Pollença." He showed Alan the address.

"Plot one-two-three, number two, Calle El Nogel."

"It's pronounced kiy-ye, it means street. Is that it?"

Alan nodded at Archival's abruptness, resolute that if he were ever fortunate enough to move abroad, Archie's Master Removals would absolutely not be the company he would choose to deliver his chattels.

Maybe I should have been happy for my daughter, pleased that her future appeared so positive, but I had a gut feeling that Darren was up to no good and intended to pre-empt him in some - any - way. He didn't love

Sophie the way she thought he did, I just wished she could see that.

I may have acted differently had I known Alan had procured an address, but I was giddy with panic. There was no way I was parting with Harry's money, so messing with the supernatural was the only option left to me. I had bought a book about Voodoo from the charity shop the previous Christmas, following the instructions to make an effigy of Darren a few weeks before, and now I blew the dust away and flicked to the index, searching. *Spell for Revenge* seemed appropriate and read carefully, studiously.

Confident I understood the procedure, I rummaged through my sewing box for some pink material, from which I cut a small square, threading it onto a pink-ended pin, and I took a tube of superglue from the kitchen drawer. I put them beside the effigy I had made of Darren.

The ambience needed to be mysterious, magical, so I lit a few tea-lights and scattered them around the room, moving piles of junk to make space, and switched the light off. Perfect; the flickering flames were spiritual, enchanting.

Now, I set the effigy before me and focused singularly on my vengeful wishes, reciting the words from the book. I took the pin - pink: the colour of death, according to the book - and plunged it through the doll's chest, grinding from side to side, concentrating, willing evil on the man I hated with a passion.

Engrossed in the ritual, I didn't notice the paper that had fallen from a stack of junk onto a burning candle, and by the time the smell alerted me, my sideboard was a ball of fire. Had I read the final sentence, I would have known the spell could backfire if used maliciously.

Fearful, I had only one thought: Harry's - my - money was in the drawer of the burning cupboard. I had to get it, and despite burns to my face, arms and chest, I retrieved the charred notes and zipped them into my duffle coat. About to succumb to the heady smoke, I managed to call the emergency services. Eyes drooping, the acrid smoke hurting my lungs, I crawled from the spreading blaze, but my energy was gone. Sleepy, peaceful. This was it, my life was ending. Now I would finally see if the spirit really did remain.

The fire engine and ambulance arrived within seconds of each other. A brave fireman carried my limp body from the inferno and the paramedics treated me on the balcony, and while the firefighters hosed the flames, soaking the flat and my treasured possessions, I was blue-lighted to hospital.

Meanwhile, Harry had been anxiously awaiting my call to tell him if his investment in Darren's blackmail had gained Sophie's contact details. Time running out, he had driven to my tower block, arriving at the same time as Alan, who had heard of my predicament on the grapevine. "Mary's flat is on fire." Harold ran up the stairs behind his son, adrenaline pumped and desperate.

Reaching the balcony was an anti-climax. The turquoise door was propped wide open, water spilling over the step, and two firemen guided the hose. "Where is the lady who lives here?"

"Went to hospital about twenty minutes ago. We've nearly finished here ourselves, just dampening everything down now."

Alan was riddled with confusion. He wouldn't have chosen oddball me to be his birth mother, but I had given him life and he owed me everything. He felt no love, yet there was compassion and protectiveness. He grabbed Harry's arm, leading him back to the concrete stairs. "Come on, let's get to the hospital." And at the firemen. "Is it the Royal Derby?"

He shrugged. "I guess so, mate."

Annoyed that no money had been forthcoming from Sophie's family, Darren put the suitcases into the taxi and climbed into the front. In the back, Sophie emotionally watched her beloved house disappear as they rounded the corner. A new chapter. A new life, away from the gut-wrenching drama her parents, Alan Taylor and the awful Mary Miller had bestowed on her.

After leaving the keys with the estate agent, they headed for the Radisson Blu Hotel in Manchester, a silent journey spent watching scenery through the windows, the dull grey sky turning charcoal then black.

The room was comfortable, beige walls and carpet, pristine white bedcovers and oak-veneered furniture. Darren dumped the cases and opened the mini bar, a kid in a sweet shop. He lined the double-measure bottles on the bedside cabinet and poured the first, downing it, then the second. Third.

"Go easy, Darren, we've got an early start tomorrow." Eager for a shower, Sophie was unpacking her cosmetics in the en-suite.

Lounging against the pillow, flicking through television channels with the remote. "Stop nagging, I'll be fine. Shall we go find the bar? We can have a couple of drinks, then have something to eat in the restaurant when Mam and Dad get here."

"What time are they arriving?"

"Didn't say, Mam said she'd call me." Darren found South Park and chuckled.

Sophie closed the door and turned the shower on, undressing, unaware that her mobile was ringing. Darren reached across the bed and, seeing an unknown number, answered. "Hello."

"Is Sophie there?" Darren bristled on hearing his father-in-law.

"Are you aware Sophie deleted your number from her phone? That means she doesn't want any contact with you."

"I don't care. I need to speak to her?"

"Tough, because you can't."

Through gritted teeth. "Can you pass a message to her?" No response. "There's been a fire in Mary Miller's flat and she's been injured. She's in the Royal Derby."

"So why are you telling me?"

The cold arrogance was exasperating. "I'm not, I'm telling Sophie. Mary's her birth mother and she needs to know."

Darren had no intention of passing the message on. "If you wanted me to be your go-between, you should have given me the money I asked for."

Astounded, Harold growled, "I did."

"Don't fucking lie, old man."

"I gave it to…" And now Harold realised what had happened. He shivered, broken.

"Face it, Harold, you've lost her." Darren switched Sophie's phone off and buried it deep in his hand luggage.

I was woozy from morphine but awake and reasonably coherent. My burns had been cleaned, smeared with a thick layer of antibiotic cream and covered with Telfa dressings, and an intravenous drip replaced the body fluids I had lost. Ibuprofen helped with the pain. My condition wasn't serious and I would be in hospital for two nights, maximum.

Alan sat by the bed, trying to coax what had happened from me, but I ignored his questions, my insides twisted with guilt.

Having left the ward to phone Sophie, Harold, reddened by the chilly air outside, marched to the bed. "What did you do with the money I gave you?"

I shifted, feigning pain while working on a feasible explanation. "I gave it to Darren, but he said he'd need another two grand before giving me any details."

"You're lying. I've just spoken to him and he told me he hasn't had the money."

"Then he's lying, not me." Further conversation was pointless and Harry reluctantly accepted he was two thousand pounds poorer and still had no address for his daughter.

Alan was confused. "What's going on?"

I was eager to tell my story first, keen for the lies to become facts in my head. "Harry gave me two thousand pounds for Darren in return for Sophie's address in Mallorca, but he just laughed and said he wanted more."

144

Angry that his birth parents had buckled to blackmail, Alan thrust a scrap of paper at Harry. "You idiots, why on earth get involved in his evil games. I already got the details from the removals firm."

Chapter 13
Countdown

I had nowhere to live until my flat was stripped and redecorated, so was grateful when Harry and Beryl offered to put me up in the meantime. The council had no urgency to make my place inhabitable as long as I had somewhere else to stay, and a month on, the situation was grating poor Beryl. Not a bright woman, Harry had been attracted to her homeliness: she was an excellent cook, kept a clean and tidy house and was well-presented, dignified. However, underneath my eccentricity was an intelligent and inquisitive mind and the regular debates and discussions Harry and I shared pleased him. But she was never threatened; I was obese, my clothes scruffy, aged before my time with wiry, grey hair. She still felt, however, as if she were on the side-lines, unwanted, unneeded, a spectator to our playful mind games and conversations.

To oust Beryl further into the coldness of being a spectator to the family, Alan had become a regular visitor. She had been dismayed when Harry, unaware of her distress, had suggested we all spend Christmas together, but was too polite to say.

At first, having Sophie's address was comforting, but as time passed, the weather cold and naked trees waving in the strong winds, we realised it didn't make the slightest difference; we were still estranged. Harry and Beryl had hoped their Christmas card to her might provoke a response, but realised their expectations had been futile after the postman came on Christmas Eve.

Harry had marched restlessly around the house for the best part of the day when Beryl finally had enough.

"Harold, for heaven's sake will you just sit down, you're driving me batty." Always intrigued by true drama, I listened through the door.

Beryl had rarely raised her voice in their forty-year marriage, and Harry slipped onto a chair in the kitchen, stunned. "I'm sorry, darling."

She breathed deeply, soothing, calming, and lowered her voice, leaving me struggling to hear. "The past few months have been a nightmare and I'm not sure I can cope any more."

"I know it's been hard, darling, but Sophie..."

Shouting again. "That's just it: Sophie this, Sophie that, it's all about Sophie. Our life together doesn't get a look in. Has it ever occurred to you how selfish she's being? If she had any sense she would have left that man the first time he hit her, but no, she cries on our shoulders then toddles back to him to get battered again. When I point it out to her, she strops off to another country. She's a selfish, spoiled brat, Harold, and it's your mollycoddling that's made her that way."

I was astounded, protective of the man I loved and our daughter. "Don't talk about my Sophie that way."

Beryl spun around, furious. "You're just as bad, Mary Miller. First you steal my husband and spit him out when he's given you what you want, and now you're in my house, claiming the daughter I raised and loved. You never give us any money towards your food and board and you don't lift a finger to make the council hurry up with your flat. You're sponging off Harold's good nature and taking advantage of my placidity."

She ripped off her apron and slammed it on the side, storming from the room, leaving Harry dumbfounded. "I've never seen her like that."

I sympathetically touched his shoulder, but jumped back; the bolt of electric that had passed through me was a shock. Had he felt it too? I knew I still loved him, always would, but all I had wanted from him was revenge for the years I had lost. But now I realised I wanted him, not revenge. I wanted what Beryl had.

I caressed his shoulder, savouring the delicious warmth that flooded my body. I was going to make sure he became mine again.

The first month in Mallorca had been wonderful, an extended, exotic holiday. Sophie and Darren spent luxurious days drifting the quaint streets, relaxing at sidewalk cafés with coffee and bars with cold beer, sampling delicious selections of tapas. The comparative warmth of the winter was perfect for lazy strolls by the marina, marvelling at the splendid scenery, palm trees with a backdrop of mountains. Each moment was new and precious.

They had made their temporary home in the underbuild of Maureen and Bob's villa comfortable, while looking for a place of their own. After paying off credit cards and loans, even with Darren's hidden savings from the sale of his house and a hefty gift from Maureen and Bob, they could only afford a small place, but at least they would be mortgage free. Unsurprisingly, they differed on the property style and location. Sophie wanted to avoid tourist areas, find a peaceful village inland, learn the language and live the

Spanish life, but Darren and his parents overruled her, insisting they buy close to Maureen and Bob. For the baby's sake, they said.

They moved into their apartment two weeks before Christmas, Archie's Master Removals bringing their belongings from England, and Sophie relished setting up their new home. Darren found a job to start in January, which would give them a comfortable income. Everything was perfect, and as far as Sophie was concerned, she had arrived in paradise.

Days before Christmas, Sophie slipped on her shoes and called out to Darren, who was painting the baby's bedroom. "Back soon."

He poked his head around the door. "Where are you going?"

"I thought I'd pop down to the early market and get some food in for Christmas. Maybe look at the clothes too, mine are getting a bit snug over my bump."

Darren came through, dripping pale blue emulsion on the tiles. "We don't need to get food, we're going to Mam and Dad's for Christmas."

Sophie's shoulders fell. "Do we have to?"

"Yes, it's all arranged and Mam can't wait, she's really excited. Go and get some new clothes, though, you look ridiculous squeezing your fat body into those jeans."

The cruel words slapped Sophie on both cheeks. She had been eating healthily, was still trim, but her growing abdomen was out of her control. Forcing back tears, she snatched her bag and left.

Minutes later, the intercom buzzed and, swearing, Darren set the paintbrush down, pressing the button. "Hello."

"It's Mam, baby." He let her in and she took the lift to the third floor, kissing him on the cheek as she passed. "I thought you weren't giving our address to anyone back in England?"

She sat at the breakfast bar, while Darren collected a can of lager from the fridge, pouring a large white wine for her. "I didn't."

Maureen rummaged through her bag and produced an envelope bearing a British stamp, handing it over. "Well, someone has, because this was in our letterbox this morning."

Darren's brow furrowed. "For Sophie? But I didn't tell her your address before we moved." He tore the envelope and flicked open a Christmas card, a handwritten letter falling on the side. "It's from her bloody parents, interfering bastards. How did they get your address?" Sticking the card and unread note back in the envelope, he handed it back. "Take it home and bin it, Mam, we can't have them ruining our plans now."

Christmas Day was a raucous and drunken affair with plenty of laughter and the biggest turkey Sophie had ever seen. Die-hard party people, Maureen and Bob had invited their best friends, Peggy and Bry, who had flown over the day before. Sherry was served at ten in the morning, the first drink of many, and they played games at the table for small change: poker, blackjack, cribbage, cheat. The sky was dark by the time they finished, and drinks were then taken to the fresh and cool patio, where wine and spirits dripped and spilled as they staggered about drunkenly.

Sophie hadn't intended to drink, but Bob, Bry and Darren had thrust glass after glass in her hand and her resolve was gone after the third sherry. She wasn't keen on Peggy and Bry, their brashness grating, and although her in-laws were welcoming and generous, she was aware they only tolerated her for the sake of their pride and joy, or 'baby', as Maureen disturbingly called Darren too often.

Her husband's comment about her weight had struck her deeply, affecting her appetite and self-esteem. He liked his women slim - skinny - and the resort was swarming with pretty, deep-tanned ex-pats with glorious hair and abundant confidence. Her pregnancy hormones didn't help with the insecurity.

They returned to their apartment at three in the morning and Darren collapsed fully-clothed on the bed, snoring and grunting within seconds. Sophie lay with her back to him, lonely tears soaking the pillow. She missed her parents - or the parents she thought they were - and brother. Why had they told her so many lies? Her whole life had been a lie. She looked at her husband, open-mouthed and dribbling, and was grateful that she at least had him.

Meanwhile, Christmas in Littleover was placid and respectable, but although she was a marvellous host, Beryl was reserved. On reflection I suppose her outburst the previous day was troubling her, not usually one to show her emotions. Or maybe she had sensed that our relationship had altered its course; she was my enemy now.

Always poor, I normally celebrated with a small chicken, so the delightful meal Beryl prepared - and she really was a marvellous cook - was a treat. But I didn't indulge, which left Beryl nonplussed. Used to me piling mouthful after mouthful into my fat face - a packet of biscuits rather than one, a family-sized bar of chocolate instead of a piece - she worried I may be ailing. However, I had decided that 'mountainous Mary' was a thing of the past. I knew what I was doing.

The loveliest part of the day was when our sons, half-brothers, met for the first time. Steve, the image of his mother in a man's body, and Alan, the spit of me, gelled instantly, sharing their father's gentle sense of humour. But Sophie's absence affected every member of our peculiar family, and we all quietly hoped she would call. She didn't.

Christmas week was also nondescript and I couldn't wait for a bit of fun and rowdiness to see the New Year in, but apparently the docile couple usually went to bed before the big celebrations at midnight, and this year was to be no different. I wasn't having that, no way. After years of loneliness, feeling bitter and hateful when Big Ben struck twelve, I had company and intended to enjoy it - such a shame the man I loved still had a wife - so I insisted we crack open the Champagne at midnight to welcome the New Year with optimism. Beryl agreed begrudgingly, yet Harry had a sparkle in his eye.

Early evening was unremarkable, watching crap telly and sharing a bottle of merlot, and I was eager to spice things up. I suggested another bottle and Harry wasted no time in collecting some cabernet sauvignon from the cabinet, leaving Beryl astounded. "Harold, we've had enough to drink. Have you forgotten there's still a bottle of Champagne to come? We don't want to get silly."

She was too boring for words and I rolled my eyes before winking at Harry. "Come on, Beryl, let your hair down for once."

She was uncomfortable, an outsider in her own home. "You're a bad influence, Mary." Said jokily for Harry's benefit, I felt the cloaked hatred she bore for me. She had reason though, because I planned to steal her husband. The weight was already dropping off me and I had new outfit, courtesy of Darren's misplaced blackmail money. I had also coloured my hair and discovered the delights of make-up. Beryl slipped from the room and padded up the stairs.

Harry and I sipped wine and discussed environmental issues, an educational and enlightening debate for us both. He was innocent of my plans to replace Beryl and manipulating him was a breeze, his trust in human nature so great. I subtly shuffled closer, squeezing my exposed cleavage, tittering at his jokes. "It's ten to twelve, Harry, you'd better get the bubbly ready. Shall we watch the countdown on the telly?"

"Goodness, doesn't time fly." He clicked on the set and headed for the kitchen, and I darted to the cabinet, pouring a good measure of single malt into two crystal glasses. I was back on the sofa when he returned. "I see," smiling, he had spotted the drinks, "trying to get me drunk, are you?" He set the Champagne on the table and took three flutes from the cabinet… and finally noticed his wife's absence. "Has Beryl gone to the loo?"

I grinned. "She was tired, said she'd leave us to it."

I passed him a whisky, taking the other in my hand. "To us." We clinked glasses. "And to our daughter." I sipped, but Harry was reticent. "Come on, get it down you, we'll be opening the plonk in five minutes."

The excitement on the screen was mounting, flashing between Big Ben and thousands of revellers whooping and laughing with anticipation, back to the studio and the enthusiastic presenters. His nose and cheeks pink, Harry finished the whisky and removed the foil from the bottle when the countdown began, easing the cork into his hand.

Screaming and cheers from the telly; 2013 had begun. Bubbles popped and crackled from our full glasses, and I leaned close to Harry. "New Year kiss?"

As planned, the alcohol had relaxed his inhibitions and briefly his lips met mine for the first time in thirty-two years. We gazed into each other's eyes, intense, dangerous, kissing passionately, touching, moaning.

Under my spell now, the man was mine.

Chapter 14
The Affair

Darren found Sophie's pregnant body repulsive and despite having needs, the idea of having sex with her appalled him. Her personality had also suffered, sitting around like a beached whale, plodding miserably around the house, hormones raging, whinging constantly about tiredness and heartburn, or piles and backache.

He was earning a decent wage and his philosophy was work hard and party harder, but she wouldn't leave the house unless necessary. He was sick of the never-ending pregnancy. "Come on Soph, we never go out any more. It's Friday night, I've been working all week and I just want a few drinks."

"I'm too tired. You try carrying another human around all day every day and see how you like it."

"Fuck this, Sophie, I'll go out on my own then."

She waved her hand, dismissive. "Fine, go. Maybe I'll get some peace and quiet."

Fists clenched, wishing he could punch the sarcastic bitch, he stormed out, slamming the door. Sophie was past caring about his tantrums, the only thing that mattered now was the baby.

BarStudz was crowded with familiar faces, mostly drunk having finished work for the week, and Darren sat beside Jonathon at the bar. Darren sank three pints within ten minutes and ordered a vodka orange, salivating at the generous measure.

Then *she* walked in, flowing black hair and a gorgeous tan, come-to-bed eyes and pouting lips. She sat beside him and he smiled. "Drink?"

She eyed him, head to toe. "Sure, dry white wine." She wasn't playing hard to get, and neither was he. Within an hour they were pumping each other hungrily in a nearby alley.

Sophie was sleeping peacefully when he returned to the apartment, the grotesque mound under the covers reminding him why he had strayed.

The day had come for me to move out of Harry and Beryl's house, my own flat now redecorated and ready for habitation. Harry and I hadn't mentioned the New Year kiss, but every time we made eye contact there were a million words unsaid. Beryl must have noticed, but at fifty-nine was too old to consider her marriage failing; it was better not to know.

The weight was dropping from me, especially since joining a gym early in January, and I had replaced my severe glasses with contact lenses, colouring my grey hair a pleasing sandy blonde. The transformation had taken most of the money I had stolen from Harry, but it was worth it for his puppy-dog affection.

I imagined Beryl's sigh of relief as Harry drove me to my flat, purchasing cleaning materials on the way, eager to scrub every trace of Mary Miller from the hovel I had inhabited for too long. I stepped over spewed rubbish and climbed the depressing concrete steps to my newly-painted turquoise door. The council had dumped the charred remains of my furniture, leaving the flat empty, an acrid tinge to the air, and I despaired. I had become accustomed to the luxurious life now and was desperate for a way to return; if only Beryl would disappear. I dropped the borrowed suitcase and removed a bottle of wine, before checking the flat to see the canvas I had to work on: the bedroom was intact, as were the kitchen and bathroom.

Harry brought the last of my belongings from the car and surveyed the barren living room with disdain. "Oh my, you've not even a place to sit."

"I'll be fine, at least I've got my home back. I'll cope. Somehow."

The sympathy I had been angling for was heartfelt. "At least let me buy you some bits, a sofa maybe. Whatever you need to make this," he sorrowfully scanned the room, "easier."

"That's really sweet of you, Harry, but I couldn't do that. I'll tell you what would make this more bearable," I picked up the wine, brandishing it, "you could share this with me. I bought it yesterday to celebrate coming home, but it'll be much more fun with some company."

Harry was torn. We always had such an interesting time together, after all, I had so much more to say - so many thought provoking opinions - than his irritable and strait-laced wife. "I can't, Mary, I'm driving."

I waved dismissively as I headed for the kitchen for two glasses. "One or two won't hurt."

Three glasses later, Harry noticed the time. "It's been wonderful fun, but I'm going to have to get home."

My heart sank. "I wish you could stay. It's going to be so quiet without you and Beryl around for company. I used to get so lonely before the fire."

His brow furrowed, guilty. "I'll tell you what, I'll come back later and take you to the Furniture Superstore, get some things in here to cheer the place up."

"You're such a good hearted man, but really, I'm sure Beryl would go crazy if she found out."

Taking my hand, smoother than it had been for years now I was using moisturiser, he gazed at me intently. "I insist. I'll be back as soon as possible."

Beryl heard the front door, the jingle as Harold hung his keys up, and poured thick soup into waiting bowls. Buttered bread was already on the table, cutlery neatly beside placemats, and Beryl brought lunch through. "You were a long time."

"Yes."

She waited for him to elaborate, but he took a mouthful, avoiding her gaze. "It's nice to be just the two of us again." Another mouthful, no words. "I'm going to make your favourite tonight: boeuf-en-croute with mashed potatoes and gravy."

"Mmm," he waved, swallowing, "you haven't prepared it yet, have you?"

"No, but…"

"Good. I won't be back for dinner; I'm taking Mary out to get some furniture."

Beryl slammed her spoon on the table. "Harold."

He shrugged. "Be charitable, Beryl, the poor woman lost everything in that fire…"

"And I'm losing everything to that woman. Just remember that it's you and I who are married, not you and Mary. For crying out loud, you had an affair with that woman, she bore your children. It took me years of pain to come to terms with that. I've had to put up with her dishing you doting looks for the past two months, and now I just want her out of our lives."

"I'm sorry, but we can't leave her destitute. I know I was wrong to stray, but it was over thirty years ago, and you were horribly depressed at the time."

"I don't believe you've passed the blame to me." With a filthy glare, she stormed upstairs, her untouched soup cooling on the table.

I could tell from Harry's sheepishness that an argument had taken place and this pleased me deeply. I made choosing furniture fun to help him forget the dispute with Beryl and my enthusiasm was catching, he was laughing in no time. He assembled a couple of cupboards, promising to return the next day for the others, and I promised him a meal in return. He was under my spell, and I was ready.

He was stunned to find Beryl's car gone, the house empty, when he arrived in Littleover late evening. He searched for a note, an explanation, but when she hadn't returned by midnight, he called Steve; he hadn't a clue either. Fretting, Harold went to bed, resolving to find her tomorrow.

The doorbell rang repeatedly at four in the morning and he jumped out of bed, worried. "Mr Waller?" He nodded at the two officers. "Can we come in, please?"

Harold moved aside and showed them to the living room, where they sat. "It's about your wife, Beryl Eveline Waller."

Trepidation. "Yes."

"I'm afraid there's been an accident," he paused, hating his job, "a lady we believe to be your wife has sustained serious injuries in a fall."

Tense, bile in his throat, a sensation of utter emptiness. The officer was still talking; he needed to focus.

"… a mugging gone wrong, we believe."

"I don't understand."

"I'm afraid she was killed instantly on impact."

Angry. What were they blithering about? "Killed? Who?"

The officers glanced at each other. "Mr Waller, your wife fell from the balcony of a block of flats. We think there may have been a struggle as there were numerous defence bruises on her arms and hands, that she fell or was pushed over the railing during the conflict."

Harold gasped and stood abruptly, pushing the policemen from the house. "Please go."

Darren drove into the driveway of his parents' villa; he'd had lunch with them the past week, intolerant to Sophie's nagging. Maureen sang cheerfully with the radio as she prepared ham rolls, and when he entered the kitchen, she passed him a beer from the fridge. "Go and sit down, baby, I'll bring your lunch through in a mo."

Darren sat next to his father and they eagerly watched the satellite football, helping themselves to food when Maureen brought it through. When they had finished, Maureen remembered the letter that had arrived that morning. "This came addressed to your wife."

Recognising Harold's handwriting, Darren rolled his eyes, throwing the note aside and returning his attention to the game. "It's from her dad again, probably just sentimental rubbish."

"Aren't you going to read it?" He shook his head and, curious, Maureen tore it open. Gasping, she clicked the television off. "Beryl Waller is dead."

Darren laughed. "The old dragon? Can't be, she's invincible."

Maureen read aloud: "I'm terribly sorry to have to tell you that your mother has died."

Bob was intrigued. "Does he say how?"

She scanned the note. "Seems there was some violent altercation and she fell from a fourth floor balcony."

Missing the game, Darren turned the telly on. "That'll be the birth mother I told you about, Mary something or other; she lives on the fourth floor. No loss to society I can assure you, just a benefit scrounging good for nothing."

"Thank god for that. We don't want your wife flying back to England for a funeral with our baby due in less than three months." Maureen frowned. "I'm assuming she won't go. Will she, baby?"

Darren downed his beer thirstily. "She hated the woman, she'll be pleased if anything. You never know, she might actually raise a smile for once."

However, when Darren told Sophie the news - without mentioning the letter to avoid an argument - she dismissed it easily. She caressed her stretched belly, relishing the baby kicking. "She meant nothing to me."

Harry remained housebound for a week after Beryl's death, unable to face the world, wishing he could step back in time to their final lunch, do things differently.

Eventually, he came to see me, staggering dizzily when he reached the balcony where Beryl had taken her last breath. Feigning shock when he told me that the woman I had *heard about on the grapevine* had in fact been Beryl, I helped him to sit, wrapping a blanket around his knees against the bitter cold of my unheated flat, and made him a strong mug of tea.

We talked for a while, coming to the conclusion that Beryl must have come to visit me on the fated night and been attacked before she could reach me. He wasn't suspicious in the least, especially as my crocodile tears ran copiously while he held my hand in comfort.

After several hours of reminiscing, I offered him a meal and he declined, explaining his appetite had disappeared on hearing the tragic news. He left, but I knew he'd return; Harry would need a friend. And the more he shared his grief with me, the more he would rely on my company.

I had won the game; it was only a matter of time before I could leave my freezing flat for the luxurious semi I had spent the most comfortable two months of my life in. And this time I would be the lady of the house.

Poor Beryl.

The only people to attend the funeral were Harry, me - she would turn in her coffin - Steve, Alan and a couple of close friends. I was actually distressed by how few people cared about the woman.

Everyone was disgusted that Sophie hadn't shown, a subject much discussed at the private wake held in the home Beryl had once run with utmost efficiency but now gathered dust. Harry reasoned that Sophie was in the final trimester of her pregnancy, but even he had to admit that the absence of a wreath or card was cruel.

The few guests gradually tailed off, leaving me, Harry and Steve to clean up. "How are you feeling, Dad?"

He sighed, deflated. "I don't know. It never occurred to me when I married your mum that I'd face my dotage alone. We thought we had forever. Part of me has died with her, but I have to move on, however hard. But I don't know how."

"Why don't you move in with me?"

"No, you're a grown man, you need your privacy. And, come to it, so do I. Anyway, this place holds years of memories of your mother, I'm not ready to let that go."

I brought a tray of empty glasses through. "Of course you're not, but you're not doing so well on keeping the place clean."

"Really, Mary, that's the pot calling the kettle black, don't you think?"

I chuckled at his cheek. "Why don't I move in again, take care of the housework. Of you. I won't want payment, just board and food. At least you'd have some company."

Harry slipped a plate onto the drainer. "You know, I think that's a wonderful idea."

Darren had never met anybody as impulsive and wild as Vicki, she intrigued him and he was smitten. Their sex sessions had become more frequent and he had even spent the night with her. She had hinted at commitment a few times, eventually suggesting she move in with him and give up the flat she could barely afford on her low wage. He had no choice but to admit the truth.

"Married? And it didn't occur to you to tell me before?"

Darren stomped to the fridge in Vicki's pocket-sized kitchen and grabbed the vodka bottle and some orange juice, pouring a generous measure each. "Babes, it's awkward. We're not married in the conventional sense any more, that stopped months ago, but she's expecting my baby and…"

"A fucking baby." Incredulous. "A wife and a bloody baby in one fell swoop. Darren Delaney, you are so, so history." Vicki stood, pointing at the door. "Piss off back to wifey."

"Look, my son's due in two months and I'm leaving her once she's had him. I don't love her any more, in fact maybe I never did. I've certainly never felt the way I feel about you before. You're spontaneous and fun, you live life to the full, no rules and regulations. Sophie's not…"

"Sophie is it? Fucking bitch."

"Vicki, she's too boring for me, she hates going out, she's let herself go, she's just…" He shook his head. "She's just not you."

Vicki marched back and forth, digesting his sincerity. He was such a laugh, especially after a few beers, and was handsome, hardworking, great in bed. But he was married with a son on the way. He wrapped his arms around her, warm, comfortable, loving, protective. Reciprocating his kiss, they shuffled back to the bedroom.

Sophie slept alone in the marital bed now. Every night after dinner, Darren would shower, overdoing the aftershave, and head to BarStudz, reeking of perfume when - if - he returned. He was obviously having an affair, but she no longer cared; her love had begun to die the day he had hit her knowing she was pregnant. She had excused him throwing her down the stairs when he hadn't known about the baby, but the second beating... His verbal abuse continued, but the words floated over her head now, not listening, not believing.

The marriage was over, but divorce was hard to consider too, and at the moment she needed the money he brought in. Once the child was born, she could find work - waitressing, shop work, cooking - and with no mortgage, she would only need enough for food and bills.

It was the boredom and loneliness that troubled her, and she excused the *vino Espanol tinto* that Darren bought for her as a necessity; the baby kicked and punched for England, so was clearly healthy.

She often thought of her family and their lies, yet time had made her view the difficult situation from their perspective. Ready to forgive, she called her father at the university after Darren had left for work, only to find Harold had retired, as had his secretary. Unable to remember her parents' or brother's numbers, Sophie searched for her address book, oblivious that Darren had disposed of it before moving, and having failed to transfer them to her Spanish mobile, she could only remember their addresses. She wrote to them, praying they would respond.

Chapter 15
A Welcome Holiday

The sky was blue and cloudless, sun tickling the new daffodils and tulips, and I marvelled in my luck on this happy mid-April day. I had settled into Harry's home easily, and although I still slept in the spare room, we were becoming closer by the day. Messy Mary was long gone, the house so clean it bordered on sterile, and I relished being a wonderful and inventive chef. Mirrors now reflected a person I had once only dreamed of: fitter, slimmer, with neat hair and smart clothes. Having access to Harry's healthy pension helped on all counts. Our routine was comfortable: Harry would read his broadsheet newspaper from cover to cover in the living room, while I pottered in the kitchen, preparing the evening meal in advance.

This morning was no different until the postman rang the bell. I dusted my hands off and answered, curious, and he passed a package addressed to The Wallers, postmarked *España*, which I excitedly took through to Harry. He threw the newspaper aside, tearing at the brown paper and a bunch of photographs fell onto his lap. He unfolded a letter. "It's from Sophie."

"What does she say?"

Harry scanned the note. "Well, the photos are of the Puerto de Pollença area, and of the apartment she and Darren have purchased. She sounds a bit lonely though, says Darren's out all the time and not wholeheartedly supporting the pregnancy." He glanced up, shifting his reading glasses to the end of his nose to focus on me. "I don't think that comes as a surprise really, does it?" I shook my head, and he pushed his

166

glasses back. "She's invited us over. Oh, you'll like this, Mary, she's calling you mum. She must have come to terms with the situation."

Obviously, I was thrilled by both her acceptance and the prospect of a sunny holiday. "Tell me we'll go; it'll do us the world of good to get away."

He laughed. "Of course we're going, no question about it. In fact, I'll get down to the travel agent without further delay."

Later, Harry and I scoured the photographs, the dramatic scenery with a stunning backdrop of mountains, her apartment, and the few pictures of Sophie carrying our grandchild. "We should let her know we're coming over, has she put a phone number in the letter?"

Harry glanced at the note. "No, and I doubt a letter would get there in time."

"We've no choice but to turn up unannounced, then."

"I'll tell you what, I'll drop a card in the post in the hope it'll get there before we do. If it doesn't, it'll be a nice surprise anyway." He pulled a postcard from the bureau and scribbled a short message, finding the address in his book. Neither of us noticed it was different to the one at the top of the letter.

The postcard was delivered to Maureen and Bob's villa the day before we were due to arrive and Maureen passed it to her son. He swore under his breath.

"Don't worry, son, they've sent the card here, so they'll probably turn up here. We'll just tell them you've moved away and we have no idea where to." Bob's idea made sense and they decided Darren would have lunch elsewhere the following day. "After all, we don't want them ruining our plans at the eleventh hour."

"No," Maureen sipped her wine, "we've made it this far; there's only three weeks before we have our baby."

Harry and I stepped from the taxi into the balmy spring sunshine, the azure sky complimenting the plentiful bougainvillea that adorned the delightful gardens. We glanced around. "I can't see an apartment block."

Harry asked through the window, "Are you sure this is the right address?"

The driver shrugged, dismissive. *"Inglés? No, señor, arrepentido. No olvide sus maletas."* Harry sighed at his incomprehension, opening the boot for the suitcases, and the cab drove off as soon as the lid slammed.

Harold took the slip of paper containing what he thought was Sophie's address from his bag and checked the street name, the number on the gate. "It's Calle El Nogal, and it's plot two, number one-two-three. Let's see what we find."

The gate was locked - a deterrent to the illegal immigrants that plagued the ex-pat communities - so I pressed a doorbell button that Harry hadn't noticed, and Maureen hastened out within seconds to let us in. She noticed me and did a double take. "Who's this? Where's Beryl?"

Harry paled. "But..."

Maureen rolled her eyes, tight-lipped, and guided us into her pleasant villa, indicating the sofas and offering us drinks. Bob was in the garden, sweeping red sand from the patio.

"Is Sophie not here? It's such a long time since we saw her. I expect she's nearly fit to burst that baby out any day soon."

Maureen's sorrowful performance was worthy of an Oscar. "We got your card yesterday so there wasn't enough time to let you know before your flight as we don't have your telephone number. Darren and I fell out shortly after we came across and they moved away as soon as they could. We have no idea if they're even still in Mallorca as we've not heard from him. It's been such a terrible time."

Harry grasped Maureen's arm, comforting. "I'm so sorry to hear that. How terrible for you."

She may have reeled him in, but I didn't buy her lies for a minute. I had met women like her time and again, my block of flats had been full of them: women protecting their vandalising sons or thieving husbands from the law. "Maureen knows exactly where our daughter is, she just doesn't intend to tell you."

Not a person to be crossed, Maureen shot me a withering glare. "I don't know who you are, love, or what you're doing here, but you can keep your bloody nose out of our business. Neither my Darren nor his wife are any of your concern."

And I wasn't a person to threaten; years of living in poverty had given me a spine of steel. "Sophie is my daughter and her whereabouts is very much my concern. Give me their address."

Maureen took a moment to digest my words. "You mean it was Beryl who died, not the birth mother?"

Harry was stunned, but I was enjoying the spat. "Oh, is that what you told her?" I took Harry's hand. "That'll explain why she didn't come to Beryl's funeral.

I told you she wasn't the vindictive type." My cold, blue-grey eyes settled on Maureen. "She just wasn't given the facts. This woman has intercepted every attempt you've made at contacting Sophie. She's been lied to, Harry."

Harry stood, fierce. "Is this true?"

Maureen's sneering, victorious chuckle taunted him. "You can ask her if you find her, can't you. But you won't, Mallorca's a big haystack for one little needle, and she's got no NIE number, my baby made sure of that, so you won't be able to find her in the official records. As far as the Spanish government is concerned, little Sophie Delaney doesn't exist." She loved the effect her words were having, Harold pale and drawn. "She's just an illegal immigrant."

Towing our suitcases, Harry and I struggled through the heat to a shopping area the taxi had passed and sat in the shade outside a café. Harry was distraught. "She's right, you know, we're never going to find her. I mean, if we knew she lived in Puerto de Pollença, we'd stand a chance, but if she's moved to a different area, we've no hope."

I sipped my strong coffee. "That's not like you; you're the optimist in this relationship." I surveyed the scenery, the mountains, the glittering buildings with terracotta tiled roofs. "She does live here, remember the photos had Puerto de Pollença written on the back. All we have to do is find the apartment block from the pictures." I noticed his pained expression. "You did bring the photos?"

He shook his head, focusing on the tapas the waitress had brought over. I dipped bread into the

170

steaming *carne mechada*, savouring its flavour. "No problem, my memory is good; I can see the details in my head as if they were laid on the table before us. We've got a week to find her, remember. Come on, have something to eat, then we'll check into a hotel so we're not towing the bags around with us."

We had searched desperately for three days, to no avail. Usually upbeat, Harry had a despondency that I had never seen before and my patience was wearing thin. Having reached the outskirts of yet another urbanisation, we stopped for a drink, tired. The café was tiny, set in a valley underneath towering mountains that was abundant with colourful flora. I had always found languages easy to pick up and said to the bronzed waitress, *"Holà, señora, por favor. Uno café con leche, y uno café san leche."*

"It's alright, love, you don't have to struggle, I'm English."

Embarrassed, I chuckled with her; she had stunning slate eyes and jet flowing hair, and I would have sworn she was a native. "I thought I was doing so well, too. We want something light to eat, maybe some Russian salad with tuna, something like that."

"Sure, I'll be right back."

As she entered the café, I had an idea and I called her back. "I'm sorry to be a pain, but we're looking for our daughter who came out to live here five months ago and we stupidly forgot to bring her address. Age gets to you like that. She lives in an apartment block, quite tall, painted a peachy colour."

"You could be talking about a million places around here, hun. Have you got anything more than that?"

I brought the photo to the forefront of my mind and noted the scenery. "We're searching this urbanisation because of the backdrop," I pointed to the mountains, "the balcony overlooks a similar scene. Also, there was a heart-shaped pool, with a tots' paddling pool beside it."

"Sounds like my apartments, the Montaña Vista, that's got the only heart-shaped pool I know of in the area. I might know her, come to think of it. What does she look like?"

"She was dyed blonde last time we saw her. She's pretty, dark-brown eyes, about five foot five…"

"And she'll be heavily pregnant by now." Harry's pessimism had gone, his eyes glinting.

Vicki's shoulders sagged as she realised they were describing her lover's wife, but then she considered that miserable Sophie may go back to England with her parents, leaving the coast clear for her and Darren. "Is her name Sophie Delaney?" She waited for the excitable clamouring to die down and smiled. "Look, you relax and have your food; my shift ends soon - they close the café for siesta - so I'll walk you there after and show you where she lives."

I jumped up and hugged her, grateful. "Thank you, I can't tell you how wonderful this is."

Scheming Vicki knew what she wanted. "Just one thing: Sophie's not been happy and I know she's having problems with her husband. Maybe you should suggest she returns to the UK with you."

172

Sophie ignored the intercom, but the persistence of the caller was irritating. She dropped her book and answered the machine. The shock of hearing her father's voice made her tremble, heart speeding, and she pressed the door-release button, waiting at the top of the stairs, hugging him, not wanting to let go. He held her face, gazing into her deep brown eyes, at her tanned, healthy glow and glistening, sun-bleached hair that she no longer dyed.

Expecting Beryl, she saw me and gasped; Darren had told her I was dead. "What the hell are you doing here?"

The door to the opposite apartment cracked open and Sophie dragged us inside to avoid being the subject of gossip. I began to explain, but Sophie raised her hand to show her disinterest in anything I had to say. Harry took over. "I understand you were told Mary had died. Sweetheart, it was your mother who died in a fall." Sophie staggered, falling onto a stool at the breakfast bar. "We buried her six weeks ago. I thought you'd not come because of that silly rift you'd both had, but now I can see it wasn't your fault."

Tears coursed down her cheeks, dripping onto the hand that clasped her heart, and Harry cuddled her gently as she shook with grief. Eventually her sobbing calmed. "How did she fall?"

"It doesn't matter right now. It was quick, she felt no pain and there was nothing anybody could have done."

"I can't believe you thought I'd ignored the funeral. You don't know me at all, do you?"

Having been angry himself when Beryl had died, he understood and stayed calm. "I thought it wasn't like you, we all did, and I wish there had been another way of finding you. The address we had was for Darren's parents and they've been throwing the letters I've written to you away."

Too much. Darren's - his family's - cruelty slapped her. No words. Why would they do that? She unscrewed Darren's brandy, gulping from the bottle. "I know I shouldn't, but right now I need this. Beer's in the fridge if you want some."

We sat in silence, sipping our drinks. Eventually Sophie remembered that I was there, but her aggression had gone. "You never told me why she's here."

Harry sighed. "After you left, Beryl and I, your twin brother, Alan, and Steve got to know each other. We were all concerned for you."

"Alan Taylor?" A vague recollection of the handsome policeman who had made ludicrous claims she had forced herself not to hear.

"Yes."

"So he was telling the truth when he came to see me. I screamed at him to get out."

"Alan's a lovely man, Sophie, a credit to his adoptive parents, and he understands you were in a difficult position."

"I can understand the birth mother and adoptive parents wanting to be friendly, but don't you think going on holiday together is a bit odd?"

Harry took my hand. "Mary moved into the house as a companion after Beryl died to look after me and the housework. Over the past few months we've become closer and I believe I've fallen in love with her again." I was stunned by the words I wanted to hear.

Sophie's stomach lurched. "Again?"

174

"Yes, again. In fact, I wonder if I ever stopped loving her."

"This is a lot to take in." She took the brandy to a doorway. "I'm going to take a nap, it's hot enough being pregnant without the heat too. We'll talk more later."

Sophie had been asleep a while and Harry dozed on the sofa. Bored, I started preparing the evening meal, finding my way around the attractive kitchen, enjoying the unfamiliar ingredients and spices. Chopping onions, peppers, mushrooms, tomatoes and chicken, adding paprika, cream and pine nuts, I begrudgingly made enough for Darren too.

He came in just before five and did a double- take when he saw me. "What the fuck?" Hands on hips, I cocked my head. "What are you doing here? You're supposed to be dead." He slammed a bottle of whisky on the side and took a glass from the draining board, filling it to the brim. "Or was that a ruse to get Sophie to talk to you. Where's Beryl?"

"It was Beryl who died. I don't know why you thought it was me." I stirred the creamy sauce and turned the heat on underneath a pan of rice.

"What the fuck. She's an old dragon, you're a crazy bitch, it doesn't matter which one of you it was." He slugged his drink and poured a second. "How did you find the apartment?"

"We're not daft, Darren."

Bristling, he took the glass to the sofa opposite Harry, who had woken now. "How did you find us?"

Harry crossed his arms. "As Mary said, we're not daft. She's kindly cooking your dinner, by the way."

Despite the tempting aroma, Darren sneered. "I wouldn't eat any shit that filthy cow prepared. You two had better find yourselves a hotel, you're not welcome in my house."

"That won't be necessary, our daughter has invited us to stay in *her* home." She hadn't, but I was feeling antagonistic. "We're here for the next four nights whether you like it or not."

Yawning, Sophie came from the bedroom and was instantly on edge. She placed the empty brandy bottle on the side and crossed her arms. Darren marched over, fuming. "So you've been contacting them behind my back, have you? I told you not to have anything to do with them."

Her mother was dead and she had missed the funeral - her last chance to say goodbye - because he had withheld letters addressed to her, plus he was screwing some tart most nights of the week; she'd had enough. "You see your bloody parents every single day of the week, yet I rarely see mine…"

"She's your parent now, is she? Quick enough to replace the old dragon wasn't she, bloody money-grabber."

About to shout a response, the baby kicked and she caressed her belly instead, and she realised he wasn't worth the stress. She sat beside her father. "I'll tell you what, Darren, go do what you do best: have a shower, soak yourself in aftershave and go shag your girlfriend. I can't be bothered with this any more, the baby's all that matters now."

"Of course it is. So important you had near on half a bottle of brandy earlier. You're a pisshead and you know it."

Guilty, she focused on the tiled floor, while Harry clasped her hand. "You'd need a stiff drink if you found out your mother had died - a small detail you decided wasn't worth letting her know - and quite apart from anything, Sophie barely touched alcohol before she met you."

"She's a pisshead and you know it," he stormed into the bathroom, slamming the door, "and she's making my son a pisshead too."

The charged atmosphere softened with Darren's departure and Harry hugged Sophie. "Are you okay, sweetheart?" She nodded without a smile. "Is he always like that?"

She shrugged. "Sometimes. Sometimes he doesn't bother to speak to me. Depends on what he's had to drink, really."

Harry caught her eye. "Why don't you just leave him?"

Sophie's finger brushed her lips and she pointed to the bathroom door, tapping her ear. Harry nodded, mouthing 'later'.

Meanwhile, I dished rice onto three plates and called them to the breakfast bar. "Enough for now, we've a few days to talk. In private. Let's eat."

Darren had taken an age to get ready, finally leaving, his scorn and viciousness following him, and we sagged with relief. Sophie brought a carton of red wine from the kitchen and poured three glasses, handing them across the coffee table before sitting opposite me and Harry. "Mary, I've been doing some thinking the past few hours and I realise I've treated you badly." She swallowed. "I apologise. I accept now that you gave

177

birth to me, although I can't deny it's hard. But if you're making Dad happy, and if Mum got to know you and accepted you as Dad tells me, then I need to accept you too."

"Thank you, that means a lot to me."

"I am leaving him; I've had enough now. I swore I would never get a divorce, but he treats me badly and I don't want the baby to grow up with that sort of influence."

Relieved, Harry said, "I'm so pleased you've finally seen him for what he is. Are you coming back to England? I'm retired now, we could help out with the baby, that sort of thing."

But Sophie shook her head. "I can't. All the proceeds from Iris Cottage have gone into this place, I'd be going back with nothing until the apartment sold, and even then Darren might not agree to selling it. No, I'll get a job and work enough to pay the bills."

"But you'll have no support here."

"I'll get by, Dad, I always do." She chuckled, indicating her bump. "I can't fly this late in pregnancy anyway"

"Please come back with us, we'll look after you, the baby."

"Thanks for the offer, and I know you to want the best for me, but I'm staying. Much as I dislike my husband, my child still needs a father. It wouldn't be fair on Darren or the baby to move back."

The next morning, we came from the bedroom to find Sophie in the kitchen and our jaws dropped when we saw the state of her. Two swollen eyes, black and blue, bruises littering her arms and wrists, a sore, reddened cheek and scratches on her neck. "Dad, I can't do this any more. Please take me home."

Harry tried airline after airline to find one that would agree to agree to fly Sophie in her late stage of pregnancy, but they were all tied by their rules and regulations. One lenient company suggested she fly with a gynaecologist and midwife, but the extortionate costs would have to be met privately.

Meanwhile, Sophie and I visited a couple of estate agents to assess the approximate value of the apartment should Darren agree to selling it.

When we returned, Harry slipped his glasses to the end of his nose and smiled. "I can't find anyone who will fly you, but I've been told you should report Darren to the police. They have a zero-tolerance to domestic violence here, and with injuries like yours they'll deport him straight away. You can have the baby here, we can stay on a bit longer and..." He realised Sophie had opened the bottle of whisky Darren had brought the night before and poured a glassful. Harry and I grimaced, concerned. She waddled to the sofa and sat. "I'd rather just go and stay at a hotel or something until the baby's born, then fly back. At least that way he won't know where I am so he can't hurt me again."

I was irritated. "Can't you see what he's doing is wrong? He deserves to be punished, otherwise he'll keep doing it."

Harry patted my knee. "If she's willing to move away to safety, then that's what matters. I agree he shouldn't get away with his atrocious behaviour, but it's her decision to make." He opened the free paper. "I'll find us somewhere to stay, you go and help Sophie to pack."

Mindful of the time, Sophie filled her suitcases with equipment for the baby and as many clothes as she could squeeze in, hoping Darren would do a full day at work. It was nearing four when I dialled for a large taxi and we took our luggage outside. Harold had found a villa in the nearby village of El Vilar and paid four weeks in advance, and we arrived in good spirits. The agent met us on the roadside with the key. The villa was stunning, a warm shrimp-pink, the gardens neatly tended and a small pool for the warmer days, and inside was luxurious: three breezy bedrooms decorated in cool white, an en-suite in the largest, which Sophie had due to her condition. The kitchen was fitted with traditional glossy, cream cabinets, separated from the living room by a breakfast bar. A staircase outside the back door led to a roof terrace with an amazing view. We were delighted, and Sophie relaxed for the first time in months.

It didn't take us long to settle in, and after showering, we strolled to the village to find a comfortable restaurant.

Darren was pleased to find the apartment empty when he arrived home from work, assuming his wife had taken her parents for dinner. He poured a whisky and sat on the balcony for a while, before sprucing up for another evening in BarStudz. He and Vicki had a few drinks and headed to her tiny flat for sex. To avoid Sophie and her dreadful relations, he finally went home at two in the morning and discovered the place still empty. Furious, he threw crockery, punched furniture, kicked the walls.

Spent, Darren called his parents, sure they would be awake due to Peggy and Bry's second visit of the year. He explained Sophie's absence, but his mother chuckled. "Don't worry, baby, her maternity care is under my insurance company, remember, so we'll be able to trace her through the hospital."

"What if she's flown back to the UK?"

Her relaxed laughter calmed him once more. "She can't go anywhere, her passport's in our safe. I'll call the hospital in the morning and have note put on her records to contact us when she goes into labour. Everything will be fine."

After Harry had contacted the travel agents to cancel our return flights, we relaxed by the pool in the idyllic gardens, Sophie shaded by a parasol. As the sun hovered by the horizon and the breeze rose, I prepared a light meal while Sophie chatted to her father outside. Then Sophie felt a tightening and suspected her labour may have started. Harry fetched me and I felt her belly. "Is it uncomfortable?"

Sophie shook her head. "No, just sort of, well, painless muscle spasms."

"I'm sure it's just Braxton Hicks contractions, nothing to worry about. We'll just keep an eye on things. Anyway, dinner's almost ready, so shall we have a bite to eat, then we can prepare your hospital bag."

Now that Sophie had gone, Darren brought Vicki to see his parents in the evening, much to their surprise.

Maureen had wanted her baby back in her clutches and was irritated that another woman had sprung up so quickly. Bob, however, slapped his back proudly. "Pretty one there, son."

Darren winked. "I know, she's a stunner. She swears like a trooper, and you should hear her belch; she could win gold in the Olympics." They laughed and Vicki, reserved at first, realised she had found a home from home.

Bob lit the barbecue, while Bry handed out drinks, ensuring everyone knew to refill their glasses when needed. Vicki finished her beer and took another from the fridge. "Do you want any help in here?"

Peggy was chopping vegetables for the salad, Maureen placing beefburgers, sausages, kebabs and chicken pieces on a platter. She pointed to a tray, laden with sauces and dips. "Just take that outside, then make yourself comfortable and relax."

The evening was fun-filled, with flowing alcohol and delightful food, watching the red sunset from the patio. Once the sky had faded to navy, reminiscent of Van Gogh's Starry Night, they retreated to the comparative warmth of the balcony, lighting bug-repellent candles and opening more fine wine. Peggy gasped as a firework display commenced in the distance and Bob laughed at her delight. "We get those several times a week here. The Spanish have fireworks to celebrate the opening of a bag."

The phone rang inside and Maureen answered. "What do you want, Harold." Waiting. "Yes, we have her passport here in our safe, and no, you can't pick it up tomorrow. Do you think we're stupid enough to give it back and have you take her back to England so we can't see our grandson?" She slammed the phone down with disgust and returned to the party to relate the call in detail.

Vicki, inhibitions stolen by alcohol, was annoyed. Why were they so desperate to keep his dumb wife in Spain? Things would be so much easier for her relationship with Darren if she went home, and she said this to Darren when they had a moment alone. "It's not her we want, it's my son. If she goes back I might never see him again."

She wanted to say 'so what'. At twenty-one, she led a blissful life of sun, sea, alcohol and partying; the last thing she needed was to be tied down with somebody else's brat. Sophie leaving with the kid would be for the best, which Darren would realise in time, and anyway, she could have his child one day. Perhaps if she found their safe, found the keys?

Fishing for clues over the next hour, she gleaned that the safe was set in concrete into the floor beneath Maureen and Bob's built-in wardrobe and hidden by a wooden panel. Asking where they kept the key would be too obvious, so she needed to spend time with Maureen, get friendly and work on it from there. "So, Peggy, Bry, how long are you here for?" She couldn't put her plan into action while they were visiting.

"We're flying home the day after tomorrow, more's the pity." Peggy had tried to persuade Bry to sell up and move to Mallorca with their friends, but he wasn't keen. So Vicki would have two weeks before the baby was due to get Maureen alone, plenty of time. Suggesting a girlie trip to the market on her day off, Vicki relaxed.

Harry paced the room, his mood throwing a dampener on the contentment that Sophie and I had experienced since moving away from the Montaña Vista Apartments. Maureen's refusal to hand back Sophie's passport was downright corrupt and caused us two large problems: she would need to present it to the hospital when she went in to labour, and she couldn't fly home without it. He considered the British Embassy, or *la policia*, but Maureen had said Sophie was an illegal immigrant and he didn't want to create further problems.

Harry needed help, and to avoid involving - stressing - Sophie, he phoned Alan, who promised to find out as much as he could and call back.

After a bustling morning at the market, Vicki and Maureen returned to the villa and grabbed a drink each, unpacking bags and showing off their purchases. Vicki hadn't yet discovered where the key to the safe was kept and suspected she would have to search the obvious places - sideboard, bedside drawers, under the mattress, top of the doorframe - if the opportunity arose.

Maureen took the food she had bought to the kitchen to load the cupboards and fridge, while Vicki silently opened the bureau, digging through the stationary. No keys. She needed to find an excuse to go into their bedroom. "Maur, could I use your room to try on my new dress? I want to wear it tonight for Daz."

"Of course you can, love, you know where it is."

Punching the air, Vicki took the dress to their room and closed the door, and she hunted through the bedside drawers, clothes drawers, wardrobe. Nothing. "How's it going in there, Vick?"

"Fine, it's a bit tight though, I'll show you in a second." A key under a plant pot; she shoved it in a pocket and hastily undressed, slipping into the lacy red dress.

She opened the door and twirled, Maureen now back at the table. "That's beautiful, not too tight at all. My baby's going to love that."

"Pretty, isn't it. I'll wear it with black courts and my black shawl."

Maureen was warming to Vicki, she was sweet and fitted in well with the family, and at least she wasn't as stuck up as Sophie. "Are you going for a meal or something?"

Vicki nodded. "Yeah, he doesn't know yet, it's a surprise. My treat." She returned to the bedroom and redressed, before uncovering the safe and trying the key. It fitted, and there were the passports. She found Sophie's and wrapped it in the dress, shoving it in the carrier bag, relieved.

Bob had finished in the garden when Vicki opened the door again and she paled when Maureen said, "Show Bob the dress, Vick. She bought at the market this morning, it's lovely."

Reddening. "Sorry, I haven't got time, I just saw your bedside clock; I'm meeting a friend in five minutes." She grabbed her bags and darted to the door. "We'll have to do this again soon, it was fun. See you later." And she was gone.

Staring at each other, suspicious, Bob voiced their thoughts. "But we haven't got a clock in the there." They rushed to the bedroom.

Eager to hide the passport where Darren wouldn't find it, Vicki realised she had no idea where Sophie and her parents were staying and no phone numbers. Why hadn't she thought of that before? She would have to discreetly put some feelers out to her friends.

Showered and smart, Darren was unusually on time, but angry after Maureen's call; he detested people messing with his life. Vicki was a picture in the red dress his mother had described, her raven hair shiny and so tall in her court shoes. But she had been poking in his parents' safe and he wanted answers. He shoved her inside.

Vicki giggled. "Hey, naughty boy, you want some before we go out?" Seductive, a temptress.

His fist crashed into her cheek and she cowered, stunned. "Where's Sophie's passport?"

Hands out, defensive. "I don't know what you're talking about."

Another punch and she collapsed against the wall, face throbbing. "Don't fucking play games with me, bitch. Mam told me you took it from their bedroom this afternoon. I don't know why and I don't fucking care, I just want it back."

Seeing Darren for what he really was - a brutal and nasty, violent bastard - she grabbed the phone. "One more move on me and I call the police. Get out."

Laughing, he headed for the door. "You'll keep, bitch."

The door slammed, shaking the apartment, and tears sprung to Vicki's sore eyes. Now she knew why Sophie had let him go so easily. And she was pleased the passport was in her possession. Minutes before, she

had hated Sophie, been threatened by her, but now she
would do anything to help her.

Chapter 16
The Baby Arrives

Sophie had been having twinges for days, but this was different, it hurt like crazy. Worried she was being dramatic, she told me and Harry she needed a nap and went to her bedroom. For an hour, she timed the tightenings - seven minutes - but by the time I called her for lunch two hours later, they were coming every three minutes.

She sat at the table and the smell of Bolognese sauce made her gag, stomach heaving. Worried for her stressed father, she took me to the kitchen let me know. "Every three minutes?" Sophie nodded glumly. "And they're painful?" An intense contraction gripped her and she crouched, emitting an animal moan. "I remember that cry of pain, you're not far off. We need to get you to hospital now."

I guided her to the living room where her natural instincts took over, kneeling by the sofa, leaning on a cushion. I gently rubbed her back, feeling another contraction brewing. "What hospital are you booked into, Sophie?"

She roared as the pain ripped through her, concentrating on her body and nothing else. Harry was hiding in the kitchen area, scared of the process he had never seen before. "Harry, if we don't get her to hospital now we're going to be delivering this baby ourselves. Do something."

Flustered, he darted to the neighbour, hammering on the door, and the elderly Spanish lady finally answered. "My daughter's having a baby. We need an ambulance."

"*Bebé? Ambulancia?*"

"*Oui*, no, *si, si! Bebé, si!* Urgento!"

Almunda chuckled at his panic, slowly dialling one-one-two. "*Usted significa urgente, señor. Uno momento.*"

Once the call had finished, Almunda, enjoying the entertainment, followed Harry back to the villa, finding Sophie with her dress hitched up over naked buttocks. Harry turned his head, embarrassed. "The lady next door has just called an ambulance. At least, I hope that's what she was doing."

Sophie roared, blood-curdling, agonised, and I rubbed her back, but she shoved me away roughly. "FUCK OFF! DON'T FUCKING DO THAT!"

Now I was worried. "She's in transition, birth's imminent. I hope you told them it was an emergency."

"I did, I said it was urgento."

"*Urgente!*" Almunda corrected. I hadn't noticed her before. She went to the kitchen and filled the kettle, clicking it on. "*Usted quiere la agua caliente, y una toalla para el bebé.*" Throwing her hands in the air and muttering at Harry's blank look, she hobbled to the bathroom to find the towels herself.

Sirens wailed in the distance, but I doubted they would arrive in time. My instincts were right. "I need to push. I feel like pushing." Breathless, fearful.

My shoulders fell, beaten. "You do what your body's telling you to, Sophie." Squeezing her eyes, mouth tense, cheeks puffed, Sophie complied with nature, and reluctantly accepting I was about to deliver my grandchild, I placed my hand where I really didn't want to, feeling wet, fluffy hair as the head crowned. Sophie puffed, exhausted, before pushing again. Little wrinkly eyes appeared and I felt a rush of love and pride. Excited now. "One more, Sophie, one more and the head will be out. You're doing brilliantly. Come on, darling."

Paramedics burst through the door just as the baby plopped into my waiting hands with a gush of amniotic fluids, rushing over to replace me, and the emotions, the shock, hit me. I began to cry and Harry did too, cradling me in his arms, relishing the kittenish mew from our healthy grandchild. A paramedic helped Sophie to her feet and guided her to the ambulance, while the other spoke to me and Harry. *"El bebé es sano, pero tenemos que llevarlos al hospital para un chequeo."*

"I think they're going to hospital," I said.

Almunda grabbed my arm. *"Eso era un nacimiento rápido, es él su segundo bebé?"*

A blank stare, then, "Rapid? Baby?"

Muttering, she shook her head and tugged Harry's shirt, pushing him towards the ambulance. I grabbed Sophie's bag and followed.

As the ambulance drove away, Almunda found the keys and locked up, sighing. *"Idiotas inglés!"*

Four pints down and about to start on vodka, Darren answered his mobile, and Harold bluntly explained what had happened and where they had been taken. Darren raced around the corner to the Montaña Vista Apartments and jumped into his van, wheel-spinning to his parents' house, shaking the locked gate as he repeatedly pressed the bell. Seeing his son's urgency, Bob called Maureen as he grabbed the keys. "What's going on?" Running to the gate.

"She's had the baby, they're at the Inca Hospital. Come on."

Fumbling to unlock the gate, Maureen secured the villa and, feet in slippers, they clambered into the van and sped away. On arrival, the calm receptionist wrote the ward number on a scrap of paper and they rushed through the corridors.

Sophie was tired but beaming. Darren ignored her, leaning over his child, marvelling at the button nose and tiny fingers, a tenderness in his yellow-brown eyes. "My son. Welcome to the world, James."

"Actually, it's Jamie. We have a daughter."

Bob, Maureen, Darren, bewildered. Aghast. "Are you sure?"

She laughed. "Of course I'm sure."

Darren stood tall, unsmiling. "Why isn't the baby in special care?"

"Why would she be?"

"Because you've been drinking throughout the pregnancy. It should be in special care."

Again Sophie laughed. "She's been checked over and she's healthy, strong and bouncing."

Darren's mood was thunderous. The devious bitch was supposed to present him with a son. His first child should be a boy, that was his birthright. He hated Sophie. "I'll want to see it when you get home, so where are you staying?"

I was appalled. "That's none of your business, Darren Delaney." I turned to his parents. "We want her passport, and if you won't give it to us we'll contact the authorities."

Maureen stared at her slippers, uncommonly sheepish. "We don't have it. We think it was stolen by a girl we know."

Darren elaborated. "Her name's Vicki Halliday, and I'm working on getting it back."

Harry recognised the name from when she had helped them to find Sophie's apartment. "Don't bother, I know her. I'll get it back myself."

"You know her?" Darren was incredulous. "How?" We glared at him, lips pursed and challenging, and he stormed out. "Come on, Mam, Dad, we're going."

Awaked by the commotion, Jamie mewed heartily and I passed her to Sophie. "We'll leave you two in peace and come back tomorrow, first thing." As we strode away, waving, I whispered to Harry, "We've got to get to Vicki before Darren does, I'll bet you he's heading straight there. Let's get a taxi to the café and hope to god she's working tonight."

We were relieved to find Vicki alone, swollen and bruised under heavy make-up. "My goodness, what happened to your face?"

She spat her reply. "Darren Delaney."

A few moments passed as the truth of their relationship dawned on us. "He doesn't waste time, does he?" I asked after the passport.

"It's hidden safely at home, but I don't finish here until seven. I'll want something in return for my trouble."

Glancing at his watch, Harry sighed. "Will a hundred Euros do?"

192

"Make it two hundred and it's a deal." Harry nodded. "Give me 'til eight and I'll have it ready. Meet me outside the apartments."

Bob heard the door and poured a glass of wine for Maureen, noting her new snazzy jacket, zipped up to the neck. "Have you been treating yourself?"

She grabbed the wine and sank it. "Do you like it? I got it from that English boutique, the one next to Woody's. I was a bit cold."

Surprised, Bob glanced at the clear sky and sunshine through the window. "I hope you're not going down with a bug or something, it's baking in here."

"I'll be fine when I've had a shower. By the way," she dropped Sophie's passport on the table, "I popped into the Café Paraíso to see Vicki and got this back."

"What? Just like that? Did she say why she'd taken it? Why did she have it at work anyway? Doesn't seem very responsible."

Maureen chuckled. "That's a lot of questions. No, I didn't give her the chance to say anything, I told her it was criminal offence to steal a passport and I'd contact the police if she didn't give it back. It was easy, I don't know what we were worried about. Now, I'm going to get cleaned up. We'll pop round to Darren's after, let him know it's safe and sound."

Harry withdrew five hundred Euros from the ATM, figuring we would need plenty of cash for taxis to and from the hospital, and we stopped at a restaurant for some refreshments and tapas. At five to eight, we walked to the apartment block and sat on the low wall outside. Five minutes became ten, twenty, fifty. At nine we asked another tenant, who luckily not only spoke English, but knew which apartment Vicki rented. She let us in and directed us to the first floor, where we knocked on the door. It fell open. Hesitating, I called, "Vicki?"

No reply. Pushing our way inside, the scene and smell had us reeling, stomachs churning, bile rising. Vicki lay on the tiles, rich red glistening on her, around her, wide eyes sightless and opaque, mouth twisted, gaping. A carving knife, blade blackened with drying blood, was nearby. Trembling, heart speeding, I gasped. "Darren got here first."

Darren answered the intercom and waited in the corridor as his parents took the lift to the third floor. The door opened and, shocked by his reddened eyes and tearstained cheeks, Maureen rushed over, grasping his hand. "Baby, what's wrong?"

"It's Vicki. She's dead."

"You're joking." Maureen guided her son to the sofa. "Bob, fix us some drinks. What happened?"

"I went round after her shift, I was going to get the passport back, but when I went in she was there on the floor. There was blood all over the place."

"Jesus, what did you do?" Bob placed three whiskies on the table and sat, intrigued.

"I panicked, I was so scared. I could see she was dead, her eyes were wide open and sort of different, sort of misty. I knew she was dead. I didn't know what to do. I would have phoned the police, but they would think I did it so I just ran. I came back here and had a drink. Mam, it was awful."

She patted his hand, gentle, reassuring, and Bob passed his whisky over. "Drink this, son, you look like you need it."

Darren knocked the drink back, wincing, and Bob refilled the glass. "They'll think it was me who killed her, but I didn't, honest. But I've been seeing her a couple of months and we've argued and everyone at BarStudz knows we fell out. And what about the passport? I can't just go back to her flat and look for it now, can I?"

Maureen caught his eye. "Darren, let's get two things clear. First, you have an alibi, you were here with us the whole time, and second, I have the passport."

Choking a mouthful of whisky back into the glass, he stared at his mother. "What? How?" She told him of her visit to the café and Darren snorted, disbelieving. "I know Vicki and she is," he faltered, "was stubborn as a mule, she'd never have given it back without a fight."

"Well, she did and that's that. You know perfectly well that nobody says no to me."

Harry and I had been taken to the police station for questioning, through a translator, and were both suffering from shock. Within minutes of meeting Detective Inspector Garcia, who was heading the investigation, he had assessed that we were innocent of any wrongdoing, but had difficulty understanding the complex situation. Eventually, my patience ran out. "The bottom line is that we think Darren Delaney killed her."

The accusation translated, Garcia paced for a while, despising the British who were too lazy to learn his language. Sighing. "*¿Donde vive el?*"

"Do you have his address?"

Harry wrote Darren's and his parents' addresses on a scrap of paper.

An urgent knocking on the door stopped the conversation and Darren glanced nervously at his mother. His father hastened to the door and moved aside for DI Garcia and three uniformed officers. "I told you they'd think it was me."

Lips tense and shoulders back, Maureen grabbed her handbag from the table. "You have nothing to worry about, baby, we're coming with you."

"*Señor* Darren Delaney?" Darren nodded, shoulders sagging. "*Creemos que es posible que tenga alguna información acerca de una mujer que fue encontrado muerto en su apartamento, por favor nos acompañara a la estación.*"

Not understanding a word, but confident of the gist, Darren allowed the officers to lead him away and Maureen, indignant, pushed Bob to follow, locking the apartment behind them.

Maureen and Bob hadn't been allowed in the interrogation room, which angered her, as she told anybody who would listen. They had constructed a watertight story before the police had arrived, and Darren now insisted he and his parents had gone to his flat after leaving the hospital, where they'd had dinner and a few drinks, chatting about the new baby. He explained that although he and Vicki had argued, he had wished her no harm.

Harry and I had told them about the passport and he denied any knowledge of a theft, telling them it was, as far as he knew, in the safe at his parents' villa, where it had been since the day they moved over. DI Garcia was suspicious as passports were needed for any official matter - banking and buying property, for example - but Darren explained their bank account and the apartment were solely in his name, so Sophie hadn't needed her passport.

His parents were interviewed individually and related the same story, and Garcia instinctively knew they were lying, but none would budge on the details.

Maureen and Bob eventually fell asleep, while Darren consistently pleaded innocence, regardless of Garcia's many attempts to catch him out. But at three in the morning, exhausted and confused, he admitted finding Vicki dead, running, panicking. The needling accusations increased and Darren cried with frustration, tiredness, but he wouldn't admit to something he hadn't done. At five, Garcia left him in a cell, feeling he would achieve nothing more in persisting further. He also needed sleep.

But tests showed that the DNA of the skin cells scraped from the victim's nails was from a female. Vicki's attacker was a woman.

After a caution for not having informed the police when he had found the body, Darren was free to go.

Chapter 17
Revelations

Both needing a comforting cuddle, Harry and I had shared a bed, but worry had kept us awake. As chirruping birds welcomed the new day, I prepared tea and climbed back under the covers. "What are we going to say to Sophie?"

Harry sighed, tired and cranky. "I don't know. I think the best thing is to get her and the baby away from this damned place as soon as we can. Now we've seen what Darren's capable of, I fear for their safety. And ours, for that matter."

"What about the passport?"

"There must be something we can do. I mean, people lose their passports all the time so there must be a way to replace it. Maybe the embassy can help. I don't know, I can't think clearly at the moment."

Having dropped Darren at his apartment, Maureen went to bed, but Bob needed a drink or two to settle after the dreadful ordeal. After an hour he crept to the en-suite to read his book, take his mind off things, and was about to unzip his trousers when he noticed the sleeve of Maureen's new coat hanging from the linen basket. Reasoning she had dropped it along with her clothes by accident, he dragged it out and chucked it by the door.

But it fell open to reveal a vast patch of drying blood on the lining and his heart stopped, initially concerned his wife had hurt herself, then common sense took over. He emptied the basket, dragging out the clothes she had worn the previous day. Blood soaked. A carnage. Unable to move, unable to think, he realised with dread how much being a hands-on grandmother meant to Maureen.

Sitting on the toilet seat, the offensive clothing glaring at him, displaying her desperation, he shuddered, disconsolate. Did he report her and send her to prison? Did he say nothing and live a horrendous lie? Despite everything, if she was prepared to murder for a passport, what else was she capable of? No wonder she had insisted they relate the same story to the police: she was protecting herself, not Darren.

Minutes ticked by as Bob recounted the recent months. He had been compliant with Maureen and Darren encouraging Sophie to drink alcohol throughout the pregnancy, reassuring him they wouldn't give enough to cause foetal alcohol syndrome in the child, just enough to declare Sophie an unfit mother and claim the baby for themselves. It had seemed harmless. But that had backfired when the baby arrived fit and healthy, and without Darren's presence at the birth, the issue of alcohol had not been raised.

Maureen was a woman possessed. He recalled her statement the previous evening: *nobody says no to me.*

Much as Bob relished the idea of raising their grandchild while Darren worked, maybe Sophie taking Jamie back to England was the best solution.

He had no choice but to take the passport back. He would insist on an address and reasonable visitation rights, perhaps an agreement drawn up by a solicitor, before handing it over, but Harold was a decent man and he was certain he would be fair.

Bob replaced the clothes in the laundry basket and crept into the bedroom, checking Maureen was asleep. He took the key from under the flowerpot and tiptoed to the wardrobe, removing the passport from the safe and tucking it into his pocket.

The sweet whimpering woke Sophie and she beamed at her new daughter, tenderly retrieving her from the crib for a cuddle. Breastfeeding hadn't come naturally the day before, but now the baby latched on without hesitation.

Bob, unshaven and wearing yesterday's clothes strode in and sat beside the bed. Sophie pulled the sheet higher for modesty. "What are you doing here?"

"When are you getting out of here?"

Sophie shrugged. "Jamie's doing well and I'm fine, so I'm hoping it'll be today."

"I need your address. I'll give you your passport back, but I want to arrange formal visitation rights first."

"How do I know you'll give it back when I give you the address? Who knows what games you lot are planning?"

He sighed. "I want to help you leave. The others don't know I'm here, and I'm fed up with the silliness. Look, let me know when you're ready to go and I'll drive you home, give you the passport when we get there. Darren and Maureen won't know a thing about it until after you've left the country."

Sophie considered for a while, unsure. "How do I know you're not lying?"

"You don't, I can't prove that. I'm just asking you to trust me."

She had never seen her brash father-in-law so humble, so anxious. Was she being naïve? Stupid? She nodded.

He exhaled, relieved. Arms out, smiling. "Can I hold her?" Sophie passed the baby and he grinned adoringly at the alert blue eyes, cherub lips and mop of chestnut hair. "She's beautiful."

"I know. I wondered when one of you would notice her."

Maureen was still asleep when Bob arrived back at the villa, and he was relieved, although he knew she would go mad when she discovered the passport missing. The short time with his granddaughter had been enough to fall in love and he would miss her when Sophie returned to England, but it was best for both to get as far away from this mess as possible.

He poured a stiff drink and relaxed on the sofa, closing his eyes. In moments, he was asleep, his conscience clear; he had done the right thing.

DI Garcia took the file on Victoria Halliday's murder to his superior and briefed him, detailing the little forensic evidence they had. He believed that Victoria had inadvertently disturbed an intruder on her return from work, and the chaos in her bedroom supported his conclusion: drawers had been thrown, the contents strewn, clothes ripped from the wardrobe, and her unzipped handbag contained no cash. Ransacked in a search for something, most credibly money. He suggested the burglar had panicked and stabbed her in a tussle. Case cut and dried.

Guerra sifted through the paperwork. "*Supongo que es factible. Si se obtiene una coincidencia de ADN, tenemos nuestro hombre.*"

"*Mujer, señor.*" Why had he corrected him? A female thief was unusual, would warrant further investigation. But he wanted the case closed; resources were already strained with the drunken and violent British, and they weren't worth it.

Guerra eyed Garcia, digesting the uncommon information, pondering if his officer's time was better spent on other work. Finally, Guerra decided. "*Archivo.*" Garcia grinned with relief.

He wasted no time closing the case, which came as no surprise to his colleagues; he shamelessly hated foreigners. But Benita López was furious. An intruder couldn't have entered without either having a key or being invited in as the door lock hadn't been damaged, so Victoria must have known her killer. Garcia waved, dismissive. "*Extranjeros estúpidos*"

López slammed her pen on the desk and stormed out, not prepared to leave Vicki's death unsolved, and returned minutes later with the news that Guerra had changed his mind, that she was now the investigating officer in charge.

López took the file and left, intent on finding out as much about Victoria, her life - her death - as possible.

Refreshed, Bob woke to the delicious aroma of bacon and trotted to the kitchen to find Maureen and Darren. "You were sleeping like a baby, how come you weren't in bed?"

"Ah, this and that."

"We were just discussing how to get the baby away from Sophie, bring her here where she belongs." Bob grabbed a roll and took a bite to avoid replying, and Darren continued, "I think we should tell the hospital about Sophie drinking during the pregnancy. It must have affected the baby somehow, has to have, otherwise they wouldn't say in all the books that you shouldn't have alcohol in pregnancy. It's common sense."

Maureen took a butty, nibbling at the crust. "You'd think so, wouldn't you? I suppose that's our best option really. Other than snatch the baby, or kidnap her with her mother, what other choice do we have?" She and Darren laughed, Bob taking another gigantic bite to avoid being part of the conversation. The phone rang and Bob dropped his lunch, hoping it would be Sophie, an end to the ridiculous plotting.

It was. Moments later, he returned to the kitchen, took a final bite and grabbed his car keys. "Just going out for a while." He pecked Maureen on the cheek. "I'll be a couple of hours at most."

Maureen tugged him back. "Where are you going?"

He had already prepared a lie. "Paul needs help moving some furniture. Back soon."

He rushed away, jumping into his car and screeching away, leaving Maureen fuming, the yellow eyes that Darren had inherited fierce. "He's lying. Paul went to the UK yesterday for his daughter's wedding. I'm going to find out what's going on." Snatching the phone, she found the last number to call and dialled.

"Hello."

It was Sophie's voice and Maureen slammed the phone down, already on her way out and dragging Darren with her. "We're going to the hospital."

Bob arrived sooner than Sophie had expected and took her suitcase, leading her swiftly through the maze of corridors to the car park. Having strapped Jamie into the back, Sophie climbed into the passenger seat. "Have you got the passport?"

Bob pulled the book from his pocket to show her. "Where are we going?"

"Head towards Puerto de Pollença, I'll direct you from there."

He pulled onto the main road, passing Darren's van, and without checking the traffic, Darren swung a U-turn, falling into place three cars behind. "Sophie's in his car, Mam, what's he playing at?"

"I don't know, but I'm bloody well going to find out."

Alerted by the dangerous manoeuvre, Sophie watched the van in the wing mirror, heart racing and crestfallen as she realised Bob had lied to her. Without a clue where to direct her driver, she had no intention of taking him to her current address in El Vilar.

The owner of Café Parisio told López that Vicki had been a regular at BarStudz, so after questioning him about his deceased employee in pigeon English, she headed to the bar. The clientele, most drunk or well on their way, talked freely and López left with a plethora of gossip in her notepad.

Vicki's affair with a married man was no secret, making his wife the number one suspect, but a couple of calls showed she'd had a baby the previous day, so popping out to murder the mistress was unlikely. She would get a DNA sample all the same.

Vicki had been promiscuous with no respect for the sanctity of marriage, and the spouse of a former partner was also possible. But there had been many; it was a can of worms.

Intending to scrape Mrs Delaney's cheek for a sample to rule her out, López headed for their Montaña Vista apartment; maybe Darren would know the names of Vicki's previous lovers.

Harry and I had visited Sophie and Jamie early in the morning and she had told us of Bob's visit, that he would bring her home and return her passport. She had asked Harry to find a solicitor to draw up a visitation agreement, and subsequently help us to register Jamie's birth, apply for a British passport and instigate the divorce. Carlos Mendosa was confident and spoke fluent English, so Harry made an appointment for the next day.

Bob was becoming twitchy as they entered Puerto de Pollença. "I thought you'd moved away from here. Are you sure you haven't missed a turning?"

Sophie chuckled. "I haven't missed anything, Bob."

But when she told him to stop outside the Montaña Vista Apartments, Bob's anger rose. "No way are you in the same block as Darren. Just remember I still have your passport, so I don't want any funny business."

Noticing Darren had parked a short distance behind, Sophie unbuckled the baby seat, while Bob retrieved her suitcase from the boot. He followed her inside and they took the lift to the fourth floor, Darren running up the staircase two at a time. Sophie pulled the keys from her bag outside the flat she had inhabited for several months and Bob lost his temper. "What the hell do you think you're playing at, Sophie, we had an agreement."

She took the baby inside. "Yes, Bob, we had an agreement. So why have Darren and your wife been following us?" Sophie glared at him, defiant, just as her husband reached the floor.

"Darren." Bob was furious. "What are you doing here?"

"I could ask you the same thing." Darren grabbed his father's shirt and dragged him into the apartment. "Why have you collected Sophie without..." A tap on the door interrupted him and he shouted, "Come in, Mam, you don't have to knock."

"Darren Delaney?"

He was astounded to see López. "Oh, for fuck's sake, not you lot again. You already know it wasn't me, so what do you want now?"

López waited while Sophie set the baby seat on the floor and caught her eye. "Sophie Delaney?"

"Yes."

"This needs you also. Come." Nobody moved. "Who are you?"

Arms crossed, Maureen strode through the door, nervous when she saw the uniformed officer. "I'm, er, Darren's mam."

López waved her over. "Come. You sit. You all sit." They followed orders, while the policewoman took some testing kits from her belt-bag. She indicated for Sophie to open her mouth, brandishing a swab, and scraped the inside of her cheek, placing the bud in the tube and scribbling her name on the label.

"What's this for?" Giddy, Maureen's heart raced.

"Vicki Halliday was, er, kill by woman, so, er, I need DNA sample, please." She waved the second kit at Maureen. "Your mouth, please."

Maureen stood up, disgusted. "No, you bloody well don't. We've already told you we were all here last night, we have alibis, so you can stuff your bloody cotton bud up your jacksy."

"You have the alibi, you have not to worry. Please."

Maureen stomped to the door. "You want my DNA, you bloody get a warrant."

A flurry of action and López had slammed handcuffs on her wrists, leaving Maureen stunned. "What the hell are you doing?" Bob's head was bowed, while Darren and Sophie looked on, incredulous.

"You don't give sample here, you give in station."

"Okay, okay, I'll give you the bloody sample, just get these bloody things off me."

A thousand thoughts ran through Bob's mind. The police must have found DNA at the scene and his wife's was going to match it. But he would tell them his wife visited Vicki frequently to explain the hairs, or whatever they had found. It would be okay. He forced himself calm, and when López left, he was no longer concerned, suspecting he was paranoid because he knew of her guilt. When he returned home, he would burn the incriminating clothes she had been wearing.

Darren, however, didn't know what he knew. "What was all that about, Mam?"

She hesitated. "Nothing, baby, it just feels like Big Brother, having my personal details on a criminal database. It's ludicrous. Now, where were we? Robert

Delaney, you lied to me. Had you forgotten that Paul's gone to his daughter's wedding?" Bob's head fell again, angry at his useless memory. "Obviously you had. So you went to pick Sophie up behind our backs. I think it's about time you told me just what you're up to."

Now Sophie realised Bob hadn't lied to her, she needed to save his neck. Thinking quickly, she said, "He can tell you later. Jamie's going to wake for a feed soon and I want to get back home. Bob, you can drive me. You two," she glared at Maureen and Darren, "had better stay here, or I'll direct Bob to the police station and tell them you stole my passport."

"Bob, you're staying right here, and so is she."

"You can't keep me here, Maureen, have you lost your marbles or something? You're crazy."

Pointing at Jamie, asleep but squirming. "That, young lady, is my grandchild, my Darren's daughter. You are not taking her anywhere."

Bob rarely challenged Maureen, but he was fed up with the games. They had come to Mallorca for an easy life, not this jiggery-pokery. "Come on, Sophie, I'll take you home. Don't try to follow us, because if you do, I'll tell the police about the blood-stained clothing in the linen basket. I know what you did, Maureen, and I think it's about time you admitted you need some help."

Bob, Sophie and Jamie left and the flat was silent. Reading between the lines, Darren hoped he had misunderstood his father's threat.

Five minutes. Ten. Fifteen. Finally, "You killed Vicki?"

Lips taut and defensive. "I did it for you, baby, so you could keep your baby here."

208

Darren shook his head. "No, don't try and offload your guilt onto me, Mam." Pouring himself a brandy, one for his mother, bringing them and the bottle to the table. "What on earth possessed you?"

"It was an accident, baby, just an accident."

"No." Angry now. Confused and scared. "I saw her body, remember, and that bloodbath was no accident. She was hacked to pieces. I want the truth, or you'll never see my child again."

Maureen's neat little world was falling apart and she licked her lips, beaten. "I went to her apartment to get the passport back and she wouldn't give it to me, said she was going to give it back to Sophie, that she deserved it. She said you gave her the black eye, kept taunting me, over and over, and I snapped. We all have a breaking point."

He sneered, disgusted. "But murder, Mam. This was murder."

"It wasn't like that for me, I just wanted her to shut up, stop saying those awful things about you. I don't know how it happened. I remember seeing the knife and the next thing she was on the floor, blood everywhere. It happened so quickly. I don't know."

Darren refilled his glass and tormented minutes passed in slow motion. Eventually, common sense prevailed. "They'll have found your fingerprints on the knife, the door latch. They'll put you away for this."

Ochre eyes reflecting his. "Not if we stick to the alibi. We can say I was always visiting her. That'll explain the fingerprints."

"Not on the knife."

His mother had never cried in front of him and it broke his heart. He sat beside her, hugging her close as her guilt flooded in heaving sobs.

Harry and I were relieved when Bob drove up, worried they had taken so long. I took the car seat and unstrapped Jamie for a cuddle. "I'll take her for a bath to give you three some space to talk."

Bob sat on the armchair, Sophie and her father on the sofa, and Harold patted some paperwork on the table. "I've been in touch with a solicitor, Carlos Mendosa, and he's happy draw up an access agreement that will suit us all. I'm seeing him tomorrow at eleven, perhaps you and Darren, if he's interested, would like to come."

"We'll be there, at least I certainly will, and I'm sure Darren will want to put his views across."

"Before we make any arrangements though, we need to be clear of your plans, Sophie. Are you coming back with us?"

This was the first Sophie had heard of the arrangement and she had to ensure she made the right decision for her child's welfare. "So much has happened in the past few weeks and," she caught Bob's eye, "after what just happened in the flat, I think your family may be in some trouble." Harold raised an eyebrow, quizzical, but Bob shook his head, and Sophie headed to the kitchen. "I need five minutes to clear my mind, so I'll fix some drinks."

Considering matters carefully while she prepared a tray with glasses, a bottle of red wine and some snacks, she returned to the silent room. Bob poured the drinks, passing them around.

"Right, here goes. The thing is, it would be difficult being a single parent here, trying to work, trying to get by. Plus, I'd be completely alone and a social life would be impossible. Not that it matters, Jamie's wellbeing is central in all of this."

"You'd go stir crazy without a chance to be an adult, your social life is important."

Sophie ignored her father's input. "But my money is tied up here, so how could I find a place to live in England?"

"With us until you sort yourself out, of course."

Unchecked tears brimmed. "Dad, please don't take offence, because I've quite come to like Mary since you two have been out here, especially after she delivered Jamie. But with everything that's been going on, I haven't had a chance to digest Mum's death, I haven't grieved, and with you and Mary cohabiting in a house I associate with Mum, I'm not sure I could cope."

Harry nodded sadly.

"I think I want to try and make a go of things out here, but have a passport arranged for Jamie, just in case everything goes wrong. I'm sure I'll find a job and a childminder, and I only need to work enough to pay for food and bills because there's no mortgage to worry about."

Disappointed, but accepting. "Then we need to agree on what access Darren should have, give Carlos something solid to work on tomorrow. Right, Bob?"

"That sounds good to me, and Maureen and Darren will be delighted you're not taking Jamie back to England. Are you still planning to divorce Darren, or…?"

"I know this must be hard for you, but Darren has been violent throughout our marriage and I can't deal with that now Jamie's here."

Bob stood, appalled. "Now, listen here…"

"Calm down, Bob, she's telling the truth; I know, I've picked up the pieces. Darren drinks a lot and loses control when he's had too much."

Sophie continued, nervous of Bob's reaction. "I do want a divorce."

"What if Maureen and I pay for marriage counselling?" He knew his wife would never agree to it, but he had to try.

"No."

Maureen was a stranger to walking, but today she needed fresh air, time to think the sordid situation through. She had begged Darren to come for dinner, but he was busy sinking the brandy. Bob's car wasn't outside when she arrived home, which pleased her, grateful for the quiet. A baking day, maybe, but first she had to get rid of the clothes. Shredding them with scissors, she bagged the rags and dumped them in the communal dustbin at the end of the road.

By the time Bob returned, the smell of fresh savouries filled the house, and she placed a tray of steaming bread and scones on the table. They ate without words.

Suddenly, sirens, slamming car doors, shouting, baying. Faces at the patio door, officers breaking down the front door, guns waving. Maureen was handcuffed and led away.

As if he had been watching a film, Bob returned to his food. Washed the dishes. Tidied the kitchen.

Once the kitchen was spotless, he fixed a large whisky and dialled his son. "Daz, would you mind staying here tonight?"

Chapter 18
Legal Arrangements

The sun was hot, spring heralding summer, and the gardens of El Vilar flourished in the gentle breeze, but Harry was inside, pacing the room. "They should have been here twenty minutes ago. We'll have to leave without them or we won't get there in time."

Sophie hadn't mentioned the previous day's fracas to me or Harry, repudiating gossip. "I don't think they're coming, let's just go. We can get a taxi." I came from the bedroom with the baby. "Are you sure you don't mind watching my little angel?"

I grinned, enjoying the cuddle. "Of course not, you'll be able to think clearly if you don't have to worry about her. Besides," I gazed into Jamie's alert, crystal blue eyes, "we're going to have fun, aren't we, sweetheart?"

Harold ensured that the agreement Carlos Mendosa arranged was fair: Sophie would have custody, but Darren could have her overnight on Saturdays. "So what now, Carlos?"

"My secretary will type this and Mr and Mrs Delaney will both sign."

Harold was pleased with his choice of solicitor, a kind and honest man in a million. "How long will it take? You see, we've travelled a fair distance to get to Palma…"

"Is not a problem. You go, have some, er, some meal, have coffee. You return in one hour and Teodora have ready for you. *Si*. You go."

Darren had arrived drunk and staggering the night before, but had sobered immediately on hearing the news. They had slept off the alcohol and, after phoning to find out Maureen's whereabouts, visited the police station.

López explained that Maureen had confessed to killing Vicki, and they had charged her with manslaughter as the attack wasn't premeditated. A hearing in court was due the next day.

Deflated, they were heading home when Bob noticed the time. "Shit, it's two o'clock. With everything that's happening I'd forgotten we were due to see a solicitor with Sophie this morning."

"A solicitor? What for?"

"After I took her back yesterday we discussed arranging a formal agreement for your visitation rights to Jamie."

"Nice of you to consult me."

"She's staying in El Vilar, we'll go and see them now."

Sarcastic. "Are you sure you should be taking me? I mean, God forbid I find out her address."

Bob issued a withering glare. "I don't think you'll be causing any further problems with all of this shit that's going on, will you."

I took the baby to the bedroom to give the others some peace to discuss the paperwork. Harold explained what Carlos had told him and presented the document, showing Darren and Sophie where to sign.

Darren almost spat his beer out. "You want me to have it at the weekend. You can stuff that up your bloody arse, Sophie." Harold couldn't understand the problem and said as much. "She only wants me to have it at the weekend because she knows I like to have a drink on Saturday nights. I work all bloody week, which is more than she does, and I deserve to unwind at the weekend, not look after some little brat."

"How dare you." Sophie was livid. "You can't even say 'she' rather than 'it'. You knew things would change when we had a family and you've got responsibilities now. Your daughter should come before drinking, Darren Delaney."

"Get off your bloody high horse, you self-righteous cow. I'm not taking it for the weekend and that's that." Darren drained the beer bottle, slamming it on the table, and stormed to the garden for a cigarette.

Ashamed, Bob said, "I'm sorry, but if I'd been at the meeting I would have told you that men always go out on Saturday nights where we come from. Can we not change it to, say, Tuesday or Wednesday? Maureen and…" Remembering her arrest, that Harold and Sophie were unaware and he didn't want them to know. "Maureen and I will look after Jamie while Daz is at work, we'd be happy to."

Sophie snorted. "Jesus Christ, talk about Darren being a pampered, spoilt, irresponsible jerk. Isn't the whole point of access that he sees Jamie, not shove her onto someone else to look after. Sod this, sod it all. Do what you want, I'm past caring." She stomped to the bedroom to join me and the baby, slamming the door.

An agreement made, Harold neatly changed the wording on the document to allow Darren to have Jamie on Wednesdays for the night, and they signed, initialling the corrections. Bob took Darren home, and

Harold found us in Sophie's room, lounging on the double bed with the baby sleeping peacefully between us.

"Have they gone?"

He nodded. "Finally. Shall we go for a meal to celebrate the end of a rotten situation?"

We strolled languidly to a nearby Chinese restaurant and sat by a shaded table, and while waiting for the food to arrive, Harry said, "Now everything is agreed, may I suggest that," he caught my eye, "we stay in the villa until the rental period runs out, get Sophie and Jamie safely back in the apartment, and then we can go back to our lives in Derby."

"Extra holiday? That's fine with me." I winked at my daughter.

She wasn't so enthusiastic, her mind elsewhere. "Sounds good."

Concerned, Harry took her hand. "What's the but?"

Sophie shook her head, leaning aside while the waiter placed drinks on the table. "I'm just a bit scared, that's all. I'm kind of diving into the unknown."

Harry smiled at me. "Mary and I have been talking, we'd like to buy you a car. Will that independence make you a little less anxious?"

Sophie was flabbergasted. "You can't do that."

"Let's call it a gift to welcome my granddaughter into the world."

Mentally calculating, frowning. "I'm not sure, what with running costs, and…"

"We've thought about that too. Look, I have a good pension and apart from visiting you a couple of times a year, we don't have much else to spend it on, so we're happy to pay for the associated costs."

Sophie jumped up, hugging her father. "Thank you, so much." She saw me watching, grinning, and hesitated before including me in the cuddle. Amazed, I was ecstatic that her protective walls had started to fall.

Blissful weeks passed, enjoying, relaxing, getting to know the beautiful new member of our family, and sadly the time came to leave the villa. Darren had reluctantly moved into the underbuild of his parents' villa, so we took Sophie and Jamie home to the Montaña Vista Apartments in the runabout Harry had bought for them. Harry and I spent our final night there, and we whooped and gasped at a colourful storm that raged for over an hour.

Sophie took us to Palma the next morning, despondent, sorry to see us go, waiting until our plane took off and waving tearfully. I had been a huge support since Jamie's birth, helping her adapt to motherhood and babysitting when she desperately needed to sleep. And Harry's jolly and gentle presence had comforted her when she needed to be vulnerable.

Now she was truly alone.

Entering the silent and still apartment, she put Jamie's car seat on the floor and poured a glass of wine. She would rest today, start searching for work tomorrow.

Chapter 19
Going It Alone

We arrived in Littleover early afternoon and I put the kettle on, yearning for a mug of hot tea. Harry and I believed Sophie was in a better frame of mind than when we had first seen her, and our own relationship had come on leaps and bounds.

Sorting through the stack of mail, the phone rang and Harry answered. "Hi, Dad, I just wanted to make sure you got back okay."

I caught his eye and mouthed, 'Is that Sophie?' He nodded. "Can I speak to her?" He passed me the receiver. "I was thinking about you on the way home and, well, with you on your own with a baby, you'll need to someone to offload your day onto; perhaps you could call us every day. If the cost of the telephone cards is a problem, we can…"

Sophie chuckled. "If it makes you feel better, I'll call every evening to tell you what's going on, update you on Jamie's progress."

I couldn't put my finger on what, but something didn't feel right and I was eager to keep the lines of communication open. Let's just say, Harry - even Sophie - may have been taken in, but I didn't trust Bob in the slightest.

Sophie and Jamie had settled into a comfortable routine in the past few weeks, meeting the locals and making friends, familiarising with the area, spending sunny days relaxing by the communal pool. Evenings were a mix of scouring the free papers for a job and watching mindless TV. It was a bland way of life, but she was pleased to be done with the drama, and Darren hadn't caused problems when he had picked Jamie up and dropped her home.

Until this Wednesday. Midday came and went without him showing, without even a phone call. By eight o'clock, Sophie was thoroughly fed up with Darren's lack of responsibility. She bathed the baby and tucked her into her cot, a gentle kiss goodnight, and watched until her eyes closed. Pouring a glass of wine, she sat by the breakfast bar and opened the paper, but a knock on the door disturbed her.

She clicked the chain her father had fitted in place and opened up to see Darren, letting him in, temper fraying. "You're too late, I've just put her to bed. The arrangement…"

"Oh, shut up, woman, I didn't come here to listen to your bloody nagging." His breath stank of alcohol and Sophie calmed herself to avoid provoking him. He grabbed her wine from the side and slumped onto the sofa, lounging back, feet on the table.

What had she ever seen in him? He was revolting. "If you're not here for Jamie, then what do you want?"

"Get a drink. I want to talk to you." Bristling, she filled another glass and sat opposite him. "You're a bitch, Sophie, you've ruined our lives."

"Thank you. Is that all you wanted to say?"

Darren sat upright, gulping his drink. "My mother, my wonderful Mam, was sentenced to eight years in prison today. She's gone down, leaving me and my dad to cope for ourselves, and it's all your fault."

"What? Why's she in jail?"

"Dad's in pieces." He drained the wine and swayed drunkenly as he reached into his bag, retrieving

220

a bottle of whisky, filling the glass to the brim. "If it hadn't been for you, Mam would be at home having a nice drink to round off the day, but oh no, she's locked away in some dingy cell while you live happily in my bloody apartment."

"We've got to stay somewhere," she pointed to the bedroom, "there's a baby in there, or have you forgotten. Anyway, my money made up over eighty percent of the purchase price, so it's more mine than yours."

"In your dreams, stupid." He took some paperwork from the holdall, throwing it on the table. "This place is in my name, see. My name. No mention of you, is there?"

"Maybe so, but it was bought mainly with the proceeds from Iris Cottage."

"Haven't you worked out yet that you can't buy anything over here? And you're supposed to be bright. Get this into your stupid head: you can't buy anything here without an NIE number, that's why your car had to go in Dad's name. Nothing, nada, zilch. This flat belongs entirely to me, and if I want you to leave I'm completely within my rights to ask you to go. And that's what I want."

Sophie's thought of Carlos Mendosa. "No. Any solicitor would be able to prove that the money was transferred from my account in England."

Darren cackled, pompous, triumphant, replacing the documents and whisky in the bag. "Doesn't make any difference over here, you pathetic cow. You've always looked down on me like I'm stupid, just because you're a solicitor and I do manual work, but who's the stupid one now, eh? You can sleep on the sofa tonight, but I want you out of here tomorrow." Collecting his glass and the bag, he swaggered to the bedroom.

Swollen-eyed and tearstained, Bob opened the gate for Sophie, showing her into the villa, and fixed a drink each. "So why are you here?"

She explained, but Bob shrugged, dismissive. "He's just had a few drinks because he's upset. He'll have forgotten all about it by morning."

"At this very moment he is asleep on my bed, with my baby, leaving me to sleep on the sofa. It's not on."

"Look, I've got enough on my plate without having to constantly intervene in yours and Darren's petty arguments." Sophie hadn't heard Bob shout before. "Just go home, have a drink, sleep it off, and everything will be fine when you wake up."

Tears brimming and humiliated, she hastened back to the apartment block. The tone of Darren's voice had been malicious, yellow eyes shining hatred, and regardless of Bob's indifference, she was worried. Cautious of being alone with Darren, she climbed the stairs to the second floor and knocked on her friend's door. Kerry led her to the kitchenette. "What's happened, hun?"

Through tears, Sophie related the story.

"What a bastard. Look, if need be you can stop here for a couple of nights, but what with four kids and all, plus their dad's coming home this weekend, you'd have to be gone by Friday."

Grateful, Sophie took her telephone card from her handbag. "Can I call my Dad from here? I daren't do it at home in case Darren hears me."

"Of course you can. I hate to say this, but if your husband does carry out his threat, you haven't got a leg to stand on over here. If the flat's registered in his name it doesn't matter where the money came from, it's still his. You should have got an NIE number as soon as you moved here. And residency, have you got that?"

"I don't even know what it is." Sophie's insides were twisting, an aching, physical pain.

"Girl, you've got problems. Go phone your dad, I'll get you a beer."

Harold was horrified. "Phone Carlos first thing tomorrow, tell him the situation and that you need Jamie's passport urgently, then get yourselves back to England. We'll find a good solicitor here who will work alongside Carlos to get your money back. Okay?"

Deflated, she knew he was right.

Darren was snoring noisily when she returned to the apartment, reminding her how grateful she was not to have to put up with the hideous racket every night, and she crept into the bedroom for a pillow and blanket. A carton of wine sent her to sleep.

She awoke the next morning to find Darren clattering about in the kitchen. She initially hoped that Bob had been right, that her husband would have forgotten his tirade, but Darren swaggered through, whisky in hand, demanding she pack her bags. Enough. "I am not going anywhere. You can't get rid of me if I refuse to leave." He raised his fist, threatening, but she remained firm. "Stop being so dumb and go back to your parents' house. We can sort this place out through solicitors." He punched her and she fell back, scrambling up immediately, standing up to him. But the next crack knocked her head against the wall and she slithered down in agony, defeated.

Chuckling and dominant, Darren stood over her. "Your brat's crying, hadn't you better go feed it?"

While Sophie attended to the cut on her face, Darren nipped to the shop on the ground floor for a newspaper, and she kicked herself when she realised she could have put the chain on the door, locked him out. Instead, he relaxed on the sofa while she packed her and Jamie's essentials, unwanted tears spilling. With a heavy heart, she dragged the suitcases outside the front door and went to the bedroom to fetch Jamie. "What do you think you're doing?"

Swollen-faced and broken, Sophie didn't reply. He rushed through and grabbed the child, but she held on tightly. "I said you have to leave, you're not taking her with you." The first time he had acknowledged Jamie's gender.

Sophie dodged past and placed Jamie in the car seat, lifting it onto the pram frame, clipping it in place. Darren unclipped the baby from the harness and ran back to the sofa, clutching her close.

Maternal instinct burgeoned and she growled, "Put her back."

"Fuck off, you stupid cow, me and my dad are going to look after it. Just get your bloody ugly face out of my apartment."

Sophie launched at him, scratching, biting, and he dropped Jamie on the sofa, fighting Sophie to the floor, kicking, over and over, face, head, chest. Finally, she stopped resisting and Darren lay back on the sofa, watching for movement. She was stilled.

He took the screaming baby to the cot in the bedroom. "Shut up, you stupid brat, or I'll give you some and all."

Keen to see how her friend was, Kerry trotted to the fourth floor, through the fire door to the corridor, and noted two suitcases outside Sophie's flat. Sensing trouble, she hurried closer and saw feet, a bruised and bleeding body. Checking for a pulse, breathing, she was relieved when Sophie stirred. "Can you hear me, hun?"

Sophie groaned, grimacing, trying to speak, and eventually Kerry understood: "Jamie."

"We need to get you to hospital."

Sophie opened her puffy eyes, summoning her last ounce of strength, and slurred, "No. No hospital. He's got Jamie."

"She's with her dad, he'll look after her, she'll be fine. But we need to get an ambulance for you, darling." Tapping one-one-two into her mobile.

Wincing, throbbing, Sophie struggled to sit, clutching her pounding head. But blood gushed from her mouth instead of words and she slumped to the floor. Floating amidst waves of pain, she heard disconnected voices, noises, ebbing between black and consciousness. The paramedics soon arrived, assessing her injuries, strapping her to a stretcher once a neck brace had been fitted. Fitful, Sophie tried to form words with her distended tongue. "My baby. Not safe. Baby."

Kerry explained to the clueless medics: "*Ella tiene un bebé y está preocupado porque el padre es violento. Ella ganó 't dejar sin el bebé.*" One paramedic called for the police on her radio, while the other asked if the violent father had beaten her patient so badly. Kerry nodded. "I think so."

The police arrived as Sophie was carried towards the ambulance and, unable to get sense from her, they questioned Kerry, who detailed what she knew about Darren's savage history and the previous night's visit from Sophie. They headed to the fourth floor and knocked, receiving no response, but the sound of a wailing infant from inside was enough to justify kicking the door open. They found Darren splayed on the sofa, snoring, empty glass in hand, the contents spilled on his T-shirt. Barely waking, Darren was led to the police car.

He faced deportment, and his father faced a life in Mallorca alone.

Chapter 20
Hospital

On hearing the heartbreaking news, Harry immediately arranged flights to the island we had recently left, and our journey was sombre. We arrived at the hospital past midnight to a scene he had already witnessed at the Royal Derby. She had been beaten mercilessly, her broken body melting our hearts. This time it me, not Beryl, holding her other hand, and unlike her I shed no tears; years of hardship had toughened me. Harry and I spent the night beside her.

The English-speaking doctor explained in the morning that she would recover well in time, and Harry asked, "When will she be able to fly?"

A pleasant man in his thirties, Juan Murillo was both handsome and clever. "Two, three day maybe."

On cue, Sophie opening her bulging and bruised eyes, squinting, confused. "Where am I? Where's Jamie?"

I patted her hand. "Jamie's fine, love." We had been informed that her neighbour, Kerry, was kindly watching the child.

Juan stooped over her, shining a torch into her eyes. "You have nasty attack, Sophie. Your husband, *la policia*, they have. You soon go to England with *momia y papá*." He laughed sweetly, hugging his chest. "With your *bambino preciosa*."

Her face was too swollen to smile, too sore, but she wanted to. And she wished she wasn't in hospital, in a surgical gown, because the stunning man before her had just made her heart double flip. Watching Sophie, I knew.

Sophie's injuries weren't as severe as those she had incurred in England, but she was in hospital for longer, and she wasn't complaining; Doctor Murillo was a pleasure with his wide smile and joyful outlook. Sometimes she wondered if he spent longer with her than with his other patients, but berated herself for being silly.

Her injuries started to heal over the next three days, the swelling reducing and the bruising an array of colours until settling green-yellow. Miraculously, she had no broken bones, but the repeated kicks to the head were a cause of concern and Juan refused to release her until brain function tests were complete - officially, at least; he also wanted a forwarding address.

Nurse Carmela Ramos - one of Doctor Murillo's many admirers - enjoyed spending time with Sophie, chatting, laughing, discussing and debating. Having finished her shift, she perched on the edge of the bed. "How are you today?"

Although Carmela spoke good English, Sophie had been trying to grasp Spanish, much to the amusement of the staff. "*Hola*, I'm good, *gracias*. Um, *cómo usted es?*"

Carmela giggled, correcting her. "*Cómo está usted*. You are crazy lady. You have seen the doctor this morning?"

She checked her watch. "Not yet. Doctor Murillo must be busy, he's usually done his rounds by now."

Carmela shook her head. "Doctor Murillo not work today. *Día vacación*, how you say, er, holiday."

Sophie's face fell, exposing her crush, and Carmela, who had long accepted Juan's disinterest in her, said kindly, "He like you, Sophie. He like you a lot."

Sophie reddened. "Don't be silly."

"He does, he look at you with *amor*."

Carmela jumped up as a consultant and his junior strolled in. The doctor silently scanned Sophie's notes and raised his eyebrow, confused. Dropping them on the bed, he regarded her for a while, then shined a torch into her eyes, moved her head side to side, back and forth, and gently palpated the bruising. "*Panza?*" He gestured his abdomen and she tugged up her nightdress, exposing a mottle of bruising, which he examined. "*Usted, enfermera.*" Carmela nodded. "*¿Por qué todavía está este paciente aqui? Ella no necesita estar.*"

Carmela blushed. "*Doctor Murillo dicho ella no estaba lista para salir todavía.*"

"*Él mantiene su adentro porque ella es bonita. Ella puede ir.*"

He stomped from the room, leaving Sophie perturbed. "What's going on, why was he angry?"

Carmela grinned. "He is angry at Doctor Murillo. He say you better, you can go. He say Doctor Murillo only keep you here because you pretty."

"Mon Dieu... oh, no, that's French, what is it in Spanish?"

"*Mi Dios.* Your parents come take you home, yes?"

Sophie was already dressing, packing her bag. "Yes, they should be here soon."

Carmela looked at the door and whispered, "I take your address, we write when you go to *Inglaterra*. And I give to Doctor Murillo."

Harry and I had consulted Carlos about the impending divorce, how to comply with The Hague Conventions on removing Jamie from Spain, and the seemingly fraudulent behaviour of Darren buying the apartment solely in his own name. Carlos was confident he could resolve matters fairly, that Sophie wouldn't be out of pocket, and he informed us that Jamie's passport had arrived.

Arriving at the hospital to find Sophie had been discharged, we eagerly informed her of the arrangements as we said our goodbyes to the nursing staff and caught a taxi back to the hotel. Harry arranged flights for the following day and we decided to go for a celebratory meal. Embarrassed by the bruises on her face, Sophie layered the make-up thickly, but she had a spring in her step at the prospect of going home.

We knocked on her door as she was fastening Jamie into her pushchair, and were about to leave when the phone trilled. Sophie answered, heart speeding when she heard Juan's voice. "Doctor Murillo, is everything okay?"

"I call hospital, see you okay. Carmela say you gone and tell me hotel." She barely dared to breathe. "She say you go to England soon."

"Yes, we go tomorrow."

"*Mañana*, no. I want to see you. I meet you today, please."

So Carmela had been right. Stunned. "I'm going for a meal with my dad and Mary, you can come too if you like." What was this madness?

"*Gracias, usted son hermoso.* You wait five minutes, yes?"

230

She put the receiver down and I crossed my arms, tutting. "Am I right in thinking you've just asked that gorgeous doctor to join us?" Coy, she smiled, butterflies fluttering in her tummy.

Harry and I walked ahead with the buggy to avoid cramping Sophie's style, and Juan tooted as he drove past, waving, beaming a manic grin. He parked and bounded to Sophie, wrapping his arms around her. I watched gleefully, but Harry was cautious. "I don't think this is a good idea."

I winked at him, wheeling the pushchair with one hand, taking his with the other. "It'll do wonders for her self-esteem."

Trapped in a spiral of depression without his murderous wife and violent son, Bob was staggered when he answered the gate-bell. "Darren, you're out." Opening the gate, he hugged him briefly before remembering his manliness and withdrawing to shake hands. Inside, he brought out the whisky.

"The solicitor said they were going to deport you. How did you get out?"

"She wouldn't press charges, said she was going back to England so there was no point. They let me off with a caution and told me to stay away from her."

"That's fan-bloody-tastic, son, you must be so relieved. What are you going to do now?"

"I'm going to get pissed with you, then reclaim my apartment and live a life of luxury in the sun without any women nagging me and little brats howling all the time. Sophie made a big mistake when she didn't have a boy, I'd still be with her if she'd given me a son."

Bob understood, remembering the relief when Maureen had produced their healthy son all those years ago. "You're not going to see the child again?"

Darren downed his drink. "No, she's welcome to it. I'll play the field until I find someone who can give me a son. Let her fuck off back to the UK, I don't care if I never see her or that brat ever again."

Laughing, they finished their drinks and Bob brought the bottle to the table. Tonight, they were going to get hammered.

Juan led us away from the tourist area to a quaint and cosy *bodega* we would never have found ourselves. Frequented by the locals, eating and drinking, laughing and dancing, the place was full of life. One wall was stacked high with barrels of *vino* - different grapes and strengths - and he filled a couple of empty plastic containers left for this purpose to take home. He ordered a selection of *tapas* that we wouldn't have tried without his insistence, and the food was delicious. It was a lovely night with excellent conversation, and great food and wine in an electric atmosphere. And seeing the besotted lovebirds - adoring, sweet - I thought it so romantic.

Even Harry's initial reserve about the doctor relaxed as the evening progressed, he was obviously a genuine, kind and generous man. But Harry was Harry: blundering, what you see is what you get. "So, you two are clearly smitten with each other, what's going to happen after you fly back to England tomorrow?" I doubt he meant to break the magic, but he had succeeded all the same.

Sheepish, Sophie realised she was behaving like a silly, lovesick teenager. Of course they had no future; he had a good job at the hospital and she had no intention of leaving England again. It was a daft and hopeless scenario, a pipe dream.

But Juan stunned them all: he stood, eyes everywhere focusing as he shouted, *"¿Hay alguien aquí habla bien Inglés? Necesito un traductor."*

An elderly man, gnarled and stooped, stood slowly, resting on his walking stick. *"Sí, me enseñado Inglés en la universidad."*

Exuberant, Juan joined him and they had an intimate discussion over a glass of wine, and we glanced at each other, bewildered. Juan soon helped the man over, dragging a chair across for him. *"¿Puede usted recordar lo que le dije?"*

"Si, señor." He turned to Sophie. "He said he has never felt for anybody the way he feels for you. He says it is quick and early days, but he will move to England for you."

Sophie blushed so deeply it showed through her heavy foundation and I had tears brimming. Harry was simply boggle-eyed.

Juan and Sophie strolled behind us on the way back, arm in arm, lovesick. Harry and I took the baby to our room, leaving them in privacy.

Having shared their first kiss - brief and gentle due to her bruising - Sophie watched him drive away. She collected Jamie, deflecting my million questions to ensure her happy tears flowed only once she was alone.

Chapter 21
Return from Paradise

We boarded the Airbus, grateful to leave the harrowing Mallorca chapter behind. With Jamie asleep on her lap, Sophie was pleased to be going home. The previous evening had been amazing, but she was under no illusion that Juan would join her in England; he was passionate and overenthusiastic about everything, but would have forgotten her within a week. However, thanks to his loveliness, her confidence had soared and the memories would last a lifetime.

As the plane taxied to the runway, Sophie had no idea that Juan watched forlornly through the departure window, hand resting on the pocket that contained the ring he had bought that morning to remind her of his intentions over the coming months. Nightmare traffic had made him miss her by minutes.

Harry wasted no time in helping me move my belongings to his bedroom so our daughter could have her childhood room. We replaced the equipment that had been left in Mallorca, a new cot at the foot of her bed, and would later create a pretty nursery in the boxroom for when Jamie was older.

Sophie had an excellent reputation as a solicitor and was confidant of finding a part-time position once things settled. We adored having her and Jamie around, watching the latter change and grow by the day.

Two weeks passed. We were having breakfast, and Harry answered a knock on the door, returning with a package, postmarked Spain, addressed to Sophie. "I hope it's not bad news." With trepidation, she ripped the brown paper, struggling to get through the excessive tape, and finally retrieved a letter and a bubble wrapped box from within. Unfolding the letter, she beamed. "It's from Juan." The box contained a stunning diamond ring that reflecting the light into a thousand glistening colours. She stared, stunned.

I had never seen diamonds so large. "I thought you said he wouldn't be in touch. No man buys a ring that expensive without being hopelessly in love."

Sophie read the letter, written in his appealing pigeon English, telling her how he had missed her at the airport, how he thought of nothing but her. Asking her to help him find a job so he could join her in England, support her financially. It seemed too wondrous to believe.

I was still enthralled by the ring. "Is it an engagement or friendship ring?"

"I don't know."

"Try it on. If it fits your ring finger, then there's your answer." It was a perfect fit.

Meanwhile, unromantic and straightforward - all the worse for me - Harry sifted through the post. "Here's another one from Spain." Opening it, his face furrowed as he read. "Sophie, this is from Carlos. I'm afraid he's sending some bad news."

Admiring her ring, disinterested. "Let me guess, Darren has contested the divorce and doesn't intend to give me any..."

"Sophie," stern, she felt five years old again, "Carlos says that as the apartment is solely in Darren's name, you legally haven't a leg to stand on."

She moved to the window, staring sightlessly. "But I can prove the money came from my account."

"I know, sweetheart, but Carlos says he's tried everything and can't find a loophole in the law."

"I've worked all my adult life to earn that money, just to be told I've lost everything? No. I won't accept that nothing can be done, there must be justice somehow. How can I buy a house over here for me and Jamie if I don't get the money back? This is ridiculous."

Harry's heart ached for her. "What if I call Bob and appeal to his sense of fairness?"

She grabbed some wine from the fridge and poured a large glass, and Harry and I exchanged a glance. "Well, I haven't got his number, have you?" She didn't wait for an answer, snatching the bottle and drink. "Forget it, Dad. Watch Jamie will you, I need to lie down?"

I nodded and she left. "I don't think calling Bob is a good idea, I don't trust him. The Delaneys are a bad lot, I knew that from the moment I met them."

Harry waved my comment away. "I'll try Carlos, reaffirm that this is fraud. I need to speak to him about their divorce anyway."

I was horrified. "She can't go ahead with that now. If something happens to him - and his liver's probably pickled with the amount he drinks - then at least she'll inherit the apartment if she's still married to him."

He debated my reasoning. "Yes, I see what you mean."

He picked up the phone and I left, heading for Sophie's room. "Can I come in?" She didn't reply but I could hear her crying, so I entered anyway. She was on the bed, an open bottle of brandy and the ring on the bedside cabinet. "Come on, love, there'll be a solution, there always is." I wasn't so sure.

"He didn't treat me well, and he hurt me on so many occasions, but I didn't hate him, I always knew it was the drink talking, and that's why I stayed with him for so long. I gave him the child he wanted, I went along with his plans, I was a good wife to him. So why does he hate me so much?"

I sat and hugged her as the tears spilled. "The simple answer is he wanted a son and you gave him a daughter. He's not the man you think he is, it wasn't the drink speaking, it was his nasty self. Remember he was willing to throw you out of that apartment even though you mostly paid for it, he was willing to take your baby despite having no interest in her. And he beat you so badly you were in hospital for three days. Again. You owe that man and his family nothing."

"Just keep reminding me how horrid he was to me and Jamie, Mum, don't let me forget, because that way I can hate him enough to fight this to the end."

Did she just call me mum? A strength I never knew I had appeared from nowhere; somehow, some way, I would get the justice my child deserved, even if it meant playing as dirty as Darren. Later, when Harry was playing golf and Sophie was sleeping the alcohol off, I would call her twin. He was a policeman, after all, he would know what to do.

Nurse Carmela gratefully left the hospital, eager to go home and rest her aching feet, but Doctor Murillo shouted after her, dodging through staff and patients reach her. "Carmela." She blushed, surprised he knew her name. "*¿Usted quiere venir para un café conmigo?*"

She nodded, cheeks reddening, and walked towards the nearest café. Coffee with dishy Doctor

Murillo; never in her wildest dreams had she expected that to happen. His crush on Sophie must have petered out now she was in England. Whatever, Carmela wasn't complaining.

They sat by a small and shaded table on the terrace and she devoured his strong features and foppish dark hair that reflected in the sun. He had the most beautiful eyes she had ever seen on a man, long black lashes framing the clearest of blue. And his mouth - full red lips, slightly crooked teeth that added to his appeal - how she wished she could kiss him.

While she had been daydreaming he had ordered two coffees and the waitress brought them over. "Carmela," the Spanish lilt was creamy and deep and her cheeks burned, "you were close to Sophie Delaney, weren't you?"

Ten tons of shame dropped on her. Nodding, crestfallen.

"Do you have her phone number?" She shook her head, scared to talk in case she cried. "Damn. I sent her a ring the day she flew home, four weeks ago, but I've not heard anything. What do you think I should do?"

Forget her, screamed her head, ask me instead. I would never ignore you. The man of my dreams and she casts him aside like a piece of trash. "I don't know, are you sure she got it?"

"I sent it recorded delivery and her father signed for it."

"Did you give her your phone number and address?" *I wish I had your phone number and address.*

He sighed. "Both, and the hospital address. And my mobile and email."

Regardless of her unrequited crush, Carmela had a soft spot for Sophie and a true friend should want the best for her friend. "You have three choices: keep waiting and hope something arrives soon; accept she's moved on with her life; or go and see her in person."

Juan grasped her arm, triggering a tingle from head to toe. "*Las gracias, Carmela, usted es un amigo verdadero.*"

A true friend, she thought, *he has no idea how much of a true friend.* She finished her coffee and said sourly, "*De nada.*"

Although Juan had enjoyed watching subtitled British films and television, visiting had never appealed to him, but he would do anything to be with Sophie. He'd had many girlfriends who had been pretty, or smart, or witty, but never all three. Sophie had an ethereal, haunting quality; delicate, yet strong. And she had a wicked sense of humour.

He landed at Heathrow Airport and flagged a taxi, terrified of Sophie's reaction when he turned up unannounced on her doorstep. This was crazy; he should ask the driver to take him back to the airport, consider the money he had lost on the ring a learning curve and get on with the life he knew.

But the car parked outside a house. He paid and, inhaling deeply, rang the doorbell.

I did a double take when I saw Juan and ushered him in, leading him to the kitchen. "Can I get you a drink, you must be thirsty?"

"Er, may I speak with Sophie?"

I filled the kettle. "She's taken Jamie shopping, you'll have to make do with me for now."

He sat at the table, while I prepared tea for me, coffee for him. "I think you know why I come."

"Well, no, actually."

"I send ring, she no answer."

They had seemed so happy on the final night in Mallorca, I'd assumed she had replied. Darren's spite had hit her hard, but she could at least have sent a thank you. I was seeing a side to Sophie I hadn't realised existed.

Sophie was flustered when she saw Juan on her return. She wasn't wearing the ring and his rejected heart sank, asking her why, but she returned it, still boxed, running upstairs to hide. He was about to leave but I persuaded him not to give up, explaining about her apartment and Darren's nastiness. I offered to babysit so Juan could take Sophie out, but she refused, barricading herself in her bedroom.

Angered by her rudeness, I left Juan with a fresh coffee and rapped on Sophie's door, letting myself in. "What do you think you're doing? He's come all this way for an answer to his proposal and you behave like an ill-mannered child. Most women would give their eye teeth for that sweet man, what the hell is wrong with you?"

"I don't want to be rude, but I have to be. If I'm nice, he'll think everything's going to go ahead, and it can't."

"Why on earth not?" Incredulous, appalled.

"Firstly, he's Catholic and I'm not religious; second, look how disastrous my move abroad was, if he moves here he'll miss his homeland, his family and friends; third, Darren and this ridiculous money lark is doing my head in; fourth, I have a baby, how's that going to look to a Catholic family? God, Mary, I could go on and on about why it won't work."

Unknown to us, Juan had followed me and was listening from the landing, needing to hear the answers himself. I said, "Do you love him?"

"I barely even know him."

Shouting. "Do you love him?"

Sophie glared hatred at me and stormed from the room, stunned to find him outside. "Juan, I didn't know you were there."

"I know."

Fidgeting, embarrassed. "How much did you hear?"

Juan stared at her, confused. He thought women liked romance. He had been a fool. Slowly, he traipsed down stairs, took his bag and left, slamming the door. Sophie burst into tears, pushing me out of her room, locking the door.

Outside, Harold was parking when Juan stormed from the house with a face like thunder. He opened the car door and greeted him, but Juan kept walking.

Harold trotted after him and clutched his arm. "What's going on? Why are you in England? Why the bad mood?"

Juan related the humiliation he had just experienced in stilted English and gasped when Harold laughed. "Get in the car, Juan, let's go for a drink. Sophie's a complex character, but I know her better than anybody."

Over drinks and a meal, both men enjoyed the comprehensive and informative discussion greatly.

Harry booked Juan into a hotel for one night and arranged to pick him up at lunchtime the next day. I was on the sofa feeding Jamie when Harry arrived home. "Where's Sophie?"

"Drunk again, hence me having the baby. So much drama has happened here today, you want to thank your lucky stars you avoided it."

Harry poured a glass of sherry each and sat in his armchair. "I didn't, I've just been out with Juan and he told me all about it."

I lifted Jamie to my shoulder, patting her back. "I don't understand what Sophie's playing at. He's a lovely man and she's throwing him out with the rubbish."

"She's been behaving oddly since that letter from Carlos, and she's not been a day without a drink either."

"Tell me about it, I'm more like a mother to this little one than a grandmother."

"If she can't even look after Jamie properly, then we've got to put this right, because things will only get worse."

Sophie burst into the room, raging. "Have you forgotten I've lost everything I ever worked for, my house, my husband? I've had a bloody rough time, but now all I am is a lush and a bad mother? How fucking dare you judge me."

Harry remained calm. "That's not what I said, but we are worried for you. We don't like what's happening any more than you do." Eyes not leaving her father, Sophie defiantly snatched some brandy and swigged from the bottle. Harry winced, weary. "Put the bottle down, it won't do you any good."

Wide-eyed and glaring, challenging, Sophie gulped again. "No. I can't handle this any more, any of it."

He sighed. "You're an adult, Soph, you have to. I don't understand why you won't have Juan by your side through this battle. With all the rubbish you've got going on, at least he can bring some happiness into your life, surely."

Vehement. "Juan bloody this, Juan bloody that. I can't bloody let him into my life with what's going on, I don't even trust myself at the moment, let alone another man."

In her selfishness, my daughter wasn't bothered about how her cock-up affected me or Harry, and the man I had loved for more than thirty years was also exhausted, emotionally drained. It seemed I was the strongest member of the family right now and I had to make this crap go away. "Sophie," I waited until she gave me her full attention, "what if this situation were resolved and you had your money back, or if it had never happened, would you be pushing Juan away then?"

Her anger crumpled. "No," she whispered, sagging onto the sofa, "no, I wouldn't, Mum." Harry's stunned eyes met mine. "It feels like everything I touch turns to filth and I'm scared that if I get together with him our relationship would be doomed too. Every time I try to stand up and cope, something new kicks me down."

I hugged her, protective, maternal, warm. "I know. You've reached rock bottom and the only way from there is up. Trust me, things will be better soon." My venom went unnoticed.

Sophie soon relaxed, falling asleep on the sofa, and Harry tiptoed up to bed, leaving me - again - with the granddaughter I was more like a mother to.

I received an unexpected letter the next morning and my mind whirled with how best to deal with the news. I found Harry weeding his begonias in the garden. "The housing association has found out my flat is empty. I'll lose it if no one is living there."

He dropped the trowel. "But I thought you were happy here? I've proposed, we work well as a couple, we share a bed. Why would you leave?"

I chuckled. "No, silly, I don't want leave, but perhaps we could sublet to our daughter. She'd be forced to take responsibility for Jamie if she had a place of her own, and she'd have freedom and privacy. I know it's not the nicest of areas, but it's a start, a chance for her to pick herself up and move on."

He sifted roots from the soil, debating the pros and cons, the realisation he would miss his daughter and grandchild if they left now. "I'll have to think about it, give me time. And don't mention anything to Sophie yet."

Chapter 22
Alone Again

I signed a new tenancy for my flat, convinced Harry would come to my way of thinking - which he did - and while Steve and Alan decorated in subtle neutrals, I found suitable second-hand furniture, linen and kitchen equipment. After a fortnight, the place looked better than it ever had during my many years there, and we collected a bottle of Champagne for when we told Sophie that evening.

I prepared a sumptuous meal, the kitchen table set beautifully - candlelit and homely - and the boys arrived at seven. Sophie was ecstatic to see her brothers, chastising them for not visiting enough. Jamie was now sleeping through the night, so we put her to bed after her last feed and the rest of the evening was ours.

We hadn't seen Sophie drink alcohol since the altercation two weeks before, so weren't worried about handing out aperitifs and wine, and after the first course - baked tuna pâté served with French bread and salad - we told her the wonderful news.

Her reaction wasn't the one we had anticipated.

What we didn't know then was that Sophie had been nipping to the corner shops when nobody was home, bringing booze secretly into the house, drinking discreetly when she was sure nobody would know. In her mind, she didn't have a problem - that was Darren's department - it simply blocked out the unhappiness and gave her a best friend, helped her to sleep.

So, fuelled with the hidden brandy she had been sipping most of the day, she screamed, "You're kicking me out? I can't believe this."

"No, sweetheart, it's not like that at all. We love you being here, but thought this would help you get yourself back on track, you and Jamie."

She poured more wine and I noted the tremble in her hand, believing it to be caused by shock, as she downed it in one and poured another. "You're as bad as Darren. Why is everybody so desperate to get rid of me?"

Steve and Alan, me and Harry, stunned. Deflated after all the hard work we had put into creating a lovely home. And this time our boys noticed Harry's tiredness as well as me. "You can't compare me to Darren, I do nothing but care for…"

"I can compare you to him. He threw me out, you're throwing me out. Simple." She grabbed the Champagne from the side, fussing with the foil, her coordination awry.

"Darren is a violent bully, yet I've never hit anyone in my life." Harry's temper was beginning to fray and Steve went outside for a cigarette, non-smoker Alan joining him for the peace and quiet.

"No, you never hit Mum, you never hit us, but it didn't take you bloody long to move the next woman in as soon as she died, did it?"

Reeling, he took a deep breath and walked from the room. The front door closed and his car started up, drove away.

I panicked. I switched the cooker off, dinner ruined, the evening ruined. My carefully devised plans ruined. Keeping check on my temper, I took the bottle and Sophie's hand. "Let's get you to bed. Have a good drink tonight, sleep it off, and we'll talk about things tomorrow. We shouldn't have sprung things on you like

246

that." I took her upstairs, tucking her in, handing her the Champagne. And noticed the half-drunk brandy on the floor beside the bed; I had thought the bottle when Juan had been here had been a one-off, but now I wasn't so sure.

Steve was pouring a drink in the living room when I came back down and he fixed one for Alan and me. "What now?"

"She'll be fine." I bristled with frustration.

"But what about…"

My plotting was hush-hush and I silenced him with a glare, annoyed. "Not here." Nodding my head for him to join me in the hall. "That will be fine too. Everything's booked, it'll go ahead as planned. Not another word on the matter."

I took Sophie to a small café in Derby centre for lunch the next day, emotions no longer running high. Harry was minding Jamie so we could speak without distraction, and I had worked half the night honing my manipulation skills. Sophie remembered her behaviour the previous night and was quiet, fiddling with her fingers and staring at the table. When I gripped her hand reassuringly, everything tumbled out in a flurry. "I'm so sorry, I was shocked. I hate that I was so unpleasant, that I ruined the evening, that my brothers won't ever want to talk to me again." She stared at me, imploring. "I've been so confused, Mum dying, Darren going, having Jamie. Everything has been getting on top of me and I know I have to sort things out, but I'm not sure I'm strong enough to go it alone yet."

I stroked her hand softly. "You're stronger than you think, Sophie, I know you have it in you. We'll still help with Jamie, there's no question about that, but being in the house you grew up in isn't going to help you in the long run. Look, we've furnished and decorated and it's ready to move into, except Jamie's equipment, and the boys will bring that across for you. Just come and see it, it's beautiful. I can stay a while to help you settle in, give you space to look for a job, or sort out benefits…"

"No, I'm not accepting handouts. I'll get a job."

"Then that's what we'll do, and I'll make sure Steve and Alan check on you all the time, get their backsides into gear now they're uncles."

It had been weeks since I had heard Sophie laugh, and she tucked into the salad with gusto. I relaxed gratefully, proud of myself, the all-knowing matriarch. The cuckoo in the nest.

Later, the household quiet but for sleepy breathing, I tiptoed silently down the stairs to the bureau and retrieved the letter I had intercepted from the postman, reading, formulating my reply. At last I put pen to paper:

'Dear Carlos, thank you for your letter. I'm surprised you haven't received my copy of the divorce agreement as I sent it three weeks ago. Please provide me with a new form, which I will deal with on receipt. Many thanks for your patience, Sophie Delaney.'

I sealed the lies into an envelope and hid it at the back of the bureau, ready for posting the next morning.

The five of us moved Sophie and Jamie's belongings across Derby to my old home at the weekend. Although the area was undesirable, it was a mini palace inside, especially now the housing association had laid a new carpet. They had also fitted kitchen cabinets and I had bought white goods from a charity shop. Harry had given his spare television, and Steve had found an economy DVD player online.

Now her initial worries were forgotten, Sophie was excited. She had applied for several jobs and found a list of childminders and nurseries nearby, and with strength and determination, she was confident of her new start. Life seemed good.

Once Jamie was settled in her new bedroom, Harry collected fish and chips from the takeaway on the corner and we watched Saturday night television as we ate. I couldn't remember a time when there had been so much laughter in the flat, high-spirited jokes and witticisms plentiful, and it seemed that the troublesome period was firmly behind us. Except for two things: the divorce, and the man holding it up.

The night passed in a whirl of fun and eventually the boys left, Harry not far behind. He kissed me on the cheek at the door. "How long do you think you'll stay for?"

I removed the glasses I rarely wore now, Harry's pension affording me the luxury of contact lenses, to wipe my eyes. "Until I'm sure she's settled. We'll be under each other's feet in no time anyway, she'll be begging me to go."

I stayed a week before leaving Sophie to cope on her own for a couple of days, returning on the Tuesday to see how she was doing. Her face was drawn, but she seemed happy enough. She had rearranged the kitchen to suit herself and unpacked most of the boxes, and the place was clean and tidy. We enjoyed time with Jamie, who rolled about on the floor, gurgling and chuckling, growing fast and bonny as a button. Sophie had settled well into motherhood, clearly adoring her bundle of fun.

I had told Harry I was staying a further week, but omitted the part about my trip abroad; my plans were coming to fruition. I put essentials into an overnight bag and checked my watch for the hundredth time, while Sophie settled Jamie in her cot for a nap. But today things were different and she brought the sobbing child back through. "She won't settle. I'm going to try some of that baby rice I bought, see if that fills her up."

"Aha, you've reached the solids stage. You're going to love her nappies from now on."

She prepared Jamie's first grown-up meal in the kitchen and I quietly made a call while strapping the baby into her bouncer, and when my daughter returned with the bowl of mush, I was ready to go. She looked at me, scared. "I thought you'd at least stay until evening."

"You're managing so well, you'll be fine, and I'll be back tomorrow to stay another few nights, so don't worry. Anyway, Jamie's food is getting cold. She won't eat much on her first attempt, but that will improve as she gets used to the texture. Your dad's picking me up in five minutes or so."

Petulant, she exaggeratedly shrugged her shoulders and shoved a gloopy spoonful into Jamie's mouth. "Can't see what the hurry is."

There was no point talking when she was in a mood, so I waited by the window, and after a minute or two she snatched the baby from the chair and wiped her mucky face. "I'm putting her to bed."

I was too excited about my forthcoming trip to let a sulk ruin my mood, so I shouted, "See you tomorrow," as I closed the door, eager to start the fun.

Tonight was the night.

Sophie ran to the hallway, dumfounded by my hasty disappearance, but had no choice but to be a mother, be responsible, and she returned to her crying child.

Healthier and more sprightly than I had been in years, I ran down the stairs to the waiting car and climbed onto the back seat, slamming the door. The two men in the front seats peered at me over their shoulders and I grinned. "Are you ready, lads?"

Steve was apprehensive. "As ready as I'll ever be." Alan started the engine and pulled into the light traffic.

Chapter 23
The Surprise

I had never considered that Harold would miss me. He knew Sophie needed support, but the loneliness was unbearable. While the tasteless microwave meal for one heated, he gazed mindlessly through the window at the autumn leaves dancing on the ground, remembering my homely cooking and friendly laugh. I had been gone three days, and he had only phoned once to check on us, so surely he had given us enough space? The microwave buzzed and he took the soggy cardboard lasagne to the table, resolving to visit us later, maybe with flowers and chocolates to apologise for his neediness.

The flat was quiet, an orange hue streaming through a gap in the curtains, and Sophie answered after only one knock. "Dad, what are you doing here?"

Smiling sweetly, he handed Sophie a bouquet as he entered. "I thought I'd come and see how you and Mary are getting along."

She lay the flowers on the table, glancing at the time. "But Mary left two hours ago, said you were picking her up." They stared at each other for a while, until, "She was going to spend the night with you to see how I coped on my own."

"I don't remember anything being said, but I must admit I'm getting quite forgetful. Maybe she took the bus." Smiling. "That'll be it, we must have crossed each other travelling."

"I guess so. Well, now you're here, do you want a cup of tea?"

"What a good idea. I'll call her soon, make sure she's arrived safely."

Three mugs later, the autumn sun peeping over the horizon, Harold replaced the handset in the cradle, his brow furrowed. "There's still no answer."

Sophie shared her father's concern. "She's been gone four hours now, that's plenty of time to get across town even if the buses were delayed. I'm getting worried."

He paced for a while, heart hammering, and then chuckled. "I'll tell you what's happened, sometimes she doesn't answer the phone if she's engrossed in a book, or doing embroidery. She probably hasn't even noticed I'm not there. I'll find her at home."

Darren had discovered to his delight that his deep tan and roguish looks attracted a constant stream of female holiday makers; he hadn't had as many conquests since his twenties. He would shag the tarts in dark alleys or deserted copses if they didn't have a hotel room, unwilling for them to know his address. Tonight, three attractive women vied for his attention, eager for an easy fling, and he checked his pocket for condoms while deciding which one would give him a good time rather than an unproductive goodnight kiss.

His eighth pint warming in the heat, condensation dribbling down the glass, he summarised the candidates:

> • Tanya: Natural blonde - rare these days - rough chopped bob, obviously looks after herself. Big nose, but so what. Endless legs above towering heels and a sedate shift dress, nipped in

all the right places. But it was tight; would he be able to lift the skirt over her hips without taking the entire outfit off? Maybe wait and see what wears tomorrow.

 • Annabel: Equal height to himself, at least with the elegant courts, so shagging would be easy. Dyed brunette, the ends unattractively frizzy. Massive green eyes, unusual colouring. But, wow, the skirt: Lycra, mini, stopping right at the top of her thighs. And huge tits bursting from the tiny boob-tube. She would definitely be up for a fuck.

 • Kyra: Petite and trendy in a tight Black Label Society vest top and cropped beige combats, the loose waistband displaying her hips and G-string. No, she wouldn't bang on the first night, too sassy.

He took Annabel's hand and pulled her close, sultry, staring into her soul while he whispered well-worn patter. She responded and he was satisfied he had selected the right one. He had mastered the seduction process over the months: buy a couple of shots to get her drunker than she already was and pretend she was the most perfect woman he had ever seen. Never failed.

Life in Mallorca was great.

Harry shouted my name as he entered our house in Littleover, confident of a reply, but the silence concerned him and he searched upstairs, downstairs, the garden. Should he worry Sophie, maybe unnecessarily? Surmising it would only be fair, he dialled her number.

Her voice was grave. "Then what's happened to her? Do you think we should contact the police?"

Harry sighed. "I thought of that. I didn't want to make a fuss so I called Alan, both his landline and mobile, but he's not answering either. After a few attempts at both, I called the station, but the desk sergeant said that, because of her age, sound mental health, and without any extenuating circumstances to suspect she was in danger, they wouldn't get involved until she'd been missing more than three days."

"That's ludicrous."

"Hold on, sweetheart, hear me out. They've taken her description and some basic details, and said they'll keep an eye out, but we should call all her friends and family to see if she's staying with any of them. I'm sure she's safe and sound, Mary's a feisty lady, I can't imagine a mugger or whatever would be brave enough to tackle her, so don't you worry yourself."

The gang had planned the attack in detail: discreetly stalk the victim to a suitable area, grab from behind and throw to the ground, disable - a few hefty kicks to the head and a few stabs with the knife - that should be enough. Quick and easy, with no time for reaction. Go through the pockets, take the valuables, and get the hell away before anyone sees the body. It went like a dream, perfection, taking only a few moments. Leaving the body lifeless on the ground, they raced into the darkness with their spoils.

Exhausted from a sleepless night, endlessly waiting for the woman he loved to come home, Harry tipped his uneaten lunch into the bin and drove to Derby to see

Sophie. She opened the door and her troubled expression mirrored his. "I take it you've seen the news." Harold nodded, worried his voice would crack if he tried to speak. He sat in the living room, while she silently prepared a pot of tea in the kitchen.

"Where's Jamie?" Somebody had to break the deafening silence.

"Having a nap. Have you, er," she swallowed, terrified of the answer, "have you heard from the police?"

He shook his head, sightlessly focusing on the tray, the steaming teapot. "I've called several times, but all they'll say is the woman remains unidentified as yet."

The tense quietness returned and the minutes ticked by, two, five, ten. Harold downed his tea and stood by the window. "The last news report I saw said the woman's head had been beaten severely." He crumpled, willing the unmanly tears away.

Sophie joined him, held his hand. "It's probably not her. You said yourself how strong she was. She's smart, streetwise, only an idiot would pick on her." Choking back her own tears, she gazed through the exhaust-stained glass at the rundown building across the road. "You have to be hard to live in this area, I'm already learning that one."

Heavy rapping at the front door broke their joint melancholy and they momentarily saw hope in each other's eyes. Harry followed as Sophie ran through and tugged the door wide with shaking fingers. Her shoulders sagged when she saw Alan, smiling widely and carrying a zipped suit protector by its metal hanger. "You two look like death. What's up?"

"I thought you'd have heard, I left enough messages." Harry led Alan to the living room and explained about the mugging and murder of a woman in the early hours. "We think it's Mary."

He laughed, patting their shoulders. "I know for a fact it's not Mary, I've just left her back at my house." Their shocked expressions caused Alan to laugh more and their faces twitched, unsure whether to join in. Alan passed the plastic bag to Sophie. "Go and put this on and do your make-up. And do something with your hair, it looks a right mess."

"What's going on?"

Alan tapped his nose. "I'm taking you both out. I was going to give you an hour to get ready while I took Harry's suit over, but I may as well get it from the car so he can get changed here. If that's okay, Harry." Neither moved. "Look, you've nothing to worry about. Mary stayed at my place last night, because we've arranged a surprise for you. Now," he clapped impatiently, "go and get changed."

Sophie looked stunning, a complete transformation from the weary and tear-stained woman who had greeted Alan at the door. The cream satin dress, lace-edged with a princess neckline and ankle skimming hemline, was incredible, elegant and flowing and not too young or mature, and it fitted perfectly as if made to measure. She had showered and created a shiny, elaborate up-do from the frizzy muss of unkempt curls, and her subtle make-up enhanced her strong features. Alan was bursting with pride as he surveyed his twin, and Harry hadn't seen her so beautiful since her wedding day.

The suit Alan had brought for Harold was his favourite, many, many years old, but the quality and fit were as new. They were a handsome family.

Alan checked his watch. "We've got about quarter of an hour. Does anyone want a glass of Dutch courage before we leave?"

"I'm not sure I can get Jamie ready in such a short time, she'll need a bath, a…"

His raised hand stopped her. "My sister will be here in a minute to babysit."

Aghast. "I can't leave her with a stranger. Anyway, she won't be able to cope, Jamie's…"

Talk to the hand. "Mandy is thirty years old and has three kids of her own, I can assure you she knows exactly what she's doing. Now stop panicking and get ready to have a brilliant evening."

As they approached Littleover, Harry and Sophie assumed that whatever event Alan was bringing them to would be held at the parental home, so when he parked outside a quaint church hall, they were intrigued. "Well, here we are," he said as he opened the car door for Sophie.

The trio approached the heavy oak doors, arched at the top with aging Bath Stone, and Alan knocked a coded warning to his accomplices. Waiting patiently for a few seconds, he swung the doors wide to silent darkness from within. Like lemmings, Harry and Sophie followed Alan into the void, swallowed by blackness when the doors closed. Nothing.

Suddenly, the room lit up. "Surprise!" The reality of the situation slapped Sophie on the cheeks as cousins, grandparents, friends, uncles, aunts - everyone she knew - swarmed around her with presents, gift-wrapped and tied with ribbon.

Bewildered, she gasped, "What is this?"

Arm around her shoulders, I guided her from the crowd and held her hands. "You've had a tough year and you've shown remarkable courage in the face of it all. We thought it would be fitting to arrange a surprise birthday party." Sophie opened her mouth to speak, but I silenced her, wagging my finger. "I know your birthday's not for another five days, but this was the only date the hall was free."

"I never thought something like this would happen to me. It's amazing. You must have worked so hard, my friends, my family. I can't believe it." She threw her arms around my neck, squeezing me until I struggled to breathe - a proper cuddle from a daughter to a mother - and at that moment we knew our relationship had changed forever. Holding me at arm's length, Sophie was sincere. "Thank you so much, Mum." This time I knew she hadn't said it by accident.

The caterers had prepared a wonderful cold buffet of good, old-fashioned party food, and drinks flowed amid the raucous and merry laughter and wild and happy dancing. Steve hauled the abundant presents and cards to his car for Sophie to open later.

Tired and content, Sophie sat on the side-lines to appreciate the effort her brothers and I had made, the fun balloons and streamers and tacky disco ball that reflected the flashing lights, the remains of the sumptuous buffet, the stackable chairs lining the walls filled with people she loved. She was truly happy for the first time in forever. Of course she wished Beryl were there, but knew she would be in spirit.

Juan briefly entered her mind and she shook her head to dispel him.

The hall darkened, enhancing the floodlit stage, and Steve waved his arms for the chattering to hush. After a hilariously witty speech, he invited his sister to the stage. Embarrassed, but aware she owed all the people who had travelled far and wide, she climbed the few steps to his side. "Sophie, you're the best sister and I'm so proud of who you are, what you've achieved and how you cope. But something is lacking in your life, something you had, but chose not to keep because of your understandable insecurities at the time."

She bowed her head, dreading whatever was coming next.

"Tonight, we have one more surprise for you. Please face the side of the stage and close your eyes. Don't you dare peek - I know what you're like - until I say so."

She kept her eyes closed despite the gasping, awed crowd as a tall and bronzed man strutted across the stage and knelt on one knee. Sophie waited patiently until Steve said *now*.

She staggered, lightheaded, and Steve supported her. "Oh my god, I don't believe this."

He had been taking English lessons and the result was worth the effort, time and cost. "Sophie, please marry me? Please say yes."

Sophie buried her eyes, face, in her brother's shoulder, sobbing with relief that Juan had waited for her, grateful that someone so beautiful inside and out could love her so much. She took the ring she had rejected months before and placed it on her finger.

Clapping and cheering, whooping and whistling, tears and bursting, romance-starved hearts.

The lights dimmed and the song *Chasing Cars* echoed through the room, eerily enchanting and perfect for the moment. Hand in hand, they stepped from the stage and held each other tight, unaware of anybody but them, only hearing the haunting tune, only seeing each other's souls. Together at last, they danced.

Chapter 24
Darren Delaney

Darren couldn't understand why his head hurt so badly, it was unbearable, but he was unable to move his hands to the pressure points to relieve it. His eyes throbbed - darting stabs of pain, over, over - but he couldn't open them. And his abdomen and back felt like they had burst. Guessing it was the hangover from hell, he had never considered not drinking again before, but now... He wanted desperately to sleep, but the pain was too much.

He remembered the bar, the three girls... what were their names? And yes, he'd had sex, but couldn't recall which girl he had chosen. It hadn't been good sex; she had been too drunk for that.

Perhaps he should try hair-of-the-dog? He had stocked up for the week at the supermarket the day before - four bottles of brandy, two vodka, one single malt, and the fridge was filled with beer. Plus a few cartons of cheap wine. But he couldn't move a muscle. Maybe later, when the acuteness passed.

Did he hear voices? Had he broken his rule and brought a tart home? An odd sensation floated through him and he wandered if he was on a boat, on the sea, the gentle waves lulling the pain away. Sleep was beckoning and he gave no resistance, grateful for the blackness subduing his mind.

Close to the church hall, we came back to our place after the party, and Alan's sister assured Sophie over the telephone that she was coping fine with Jamie, that she had been fed and bathed and was sleeping peacefully. We shared a couple of toasts to the happy couple, to Sophie's birthday - and Alan's - and headed for bed at a reasonable hour, our sons on the sofas.

Harry got up at seven o'clock as usual, and chuckled to himself at the two sleeping bags with mops of hair popping from the top, surmising plenty of tea would be needed to ease the hangovers that would gradually drift to the table. He collected the paper from the doormat and dropped a couple of slices of bread into the toaster, filling the kettle.

A while later, he heard the postman and was about to collect the mail when, "I'll get them, Harry, you stay there and I'll bring them through."

I sifted through the letters for the one I had been anticipating and buried it at the back of the bureau, closing the lid silently. Breathing steadily to calm myself, I strolled to the kitchen.

Alan waited until he heard the door click shut and clambered from under his covers. Checking Steve was asleep, he nosily retrieved the letter and was surprised to see it was addressed to Sophie and bore a Spanish postmark. Curious, he debated whether to open it. No. His birth mother was up to something, but she was devious, so he needed to outwit her. He shoved it in the bureau.

Back in the sleeping bag, his mind went into overdrive, wondering what the letter was about. Thinking, thinking. Finally, Steve stirred, and Alan tapped his shoulder. "Steve," he whispered, "I need to talk to you."

Steve groaned, hand on head as he shifted onto his elbow. "What?"

"Shhh, we need to talk in private. I'll go to the bathroom, you come up in a minute or so and I'll let you in."

But as Alan trotted to the stairs, I popped my head through the kitchen door. "I thought I heard movement. I've just made a pot of tea; shall I pour you one? Do you want cereal? Toast?"

Alan forced a smile. "Sure, just the tea for now though. I'll be a few minutes, got to go to the loo." He patted his belly. "It's all that lager wanting out."

I smiled brightly. "Okay, see you in a minute."

Having heard the exchange, Steve crept silently up the stairs and tapped on the bathroom door, squeezing through when it opened, and Alan locked the door behind him. He explained, and Steve was also puzzled. "I thought all the business," he winked exaggeratedly, "in Spain had been done?"

"I know, so did I. We need to find out what the letter's about, because I could lose my job if anything gets out; I'm a copper after all."

"We could confront her, tell her we know she's up to something."

"Maybe." Alan scratched his head. "We can't be implicated, not in any way." The door handle turned and both men jumped, holding their breath. Alan pointed to the bath and Steve scrabbled in, pulling the shower curtain across. Alan flushed the chain and cracked the door. Sophie yawned. "Morning, Alan, I need to use the loo, I'm desperate. Do you mind?"

Alan's eyes darted to the bath, then he composed himself with a shrug, stepping onto the landing. "Sure. Don't be long though, I was about to take a shower."

Sophie chuckled, pushing the door to. "Go in my room for a minute, I don't want you listening."

Steve was horrified. He could tolerate a wee, but his sister emptying her bowel while he was in the room… He dragged the curtain aside and held his hands up. "Sorry, Sophie, I can't stay and listen to that."

Startled, hand on thudding heart. "What the hell is going on?"

"Let Alan back in, we've got something to tell you."

Sophie usually tried to avoid confrontation at any cost, but anger flared and she stomped down the stairs, followed by her timid brothers, lambs to the slaughter. In the kitchen, Harry and I stared at each other, disturbed from our breakfast by the noise.

Sophie retrieved the envelope from the bureau and ripped it open, examining the contents. Divorce papers. Rage bubbling, she stormed to the kitchen and waved the paper in the air. "What's going on Mary? Why did you hide my mail?"

Worried, I glanced at Harry, a frozen statue with a slice of half-eaten toast in his hand. "I, I, um…"

She marched around the table, snarling, arms flapping. "Stop babbling and tell me why you're intercepting my divorce papers. And I want the truth."

"Okay, here's the truth: I was dealing with your divorce for you because I thought it might be more stress for you, and you've been so distressed lately I thought…"

"Bollocks." Stunned silence.

"Calm down, please, there's no reason for shouting." Nervous, Harry turned to me. "Is this true?"

Ashamed, I had no choice but to come clean. "I did it to delay the divorce. If it goes through, you will lose everything you've worked so hard for, and it seems so unfair that the legal system won't recognise your input into that apartment. I did it for you, Sophie."

Awakened by the altercation, Juan entered and guided Sophie to a chair, sitting beside her. Debating, Harry understood my point, but was still confused. "I realise how much Sophie worked for that money, and it's a dreadful situation, but why would you invite Juan here to propose if she's not free to marry?"

I gaped at him, eyebrow raised. "Seriously, Harry, in this day and age?"

Flustered, he faced Sophie. "I know Darren is a nasty piece of work, a destructive alcoholic, but what is she supposed to do? Wait forty years for Darren Delaney to die before she marries again?"

Juan stared at Harry like a deer in headlights. "Did you say Darren Delaney?" Harry nodded and Juan's eyes boggled. "*Mierda, qué un lío*! I think I meet him before I fly to England." Steve, Alan and I shared worried glances. "He go to hospital, very bad, maybe *morir*, er, maybe die."

Harry and Sophie gasped in unison. "What?"

Juan shook his head, trying to find the right words. "No, no, he, er, how you say, beaten, and, er," he mimicked a knife stabbing his belly, "he cut, attack and steal from him, many men. He alive when I treat him, but not good. Lots of bad ill." He imitated a swollen head using hand gestures to his own. "Very big head, maybe he die now, I do not know."

Sophie sharply pushed her chair back and ran from the room and I followed, running up the stairs. Alan had mixed feelings. "So he was mugged, beaten badly and stabbed. Wow, I didn't like him, but that's pretty awful all the same. Do they know who did it?"

"No, thing like that, we see this all the time. Morocco men, not legal *residencia*, they steal for money, for identity. Is not good, but…" He shrugged, the sentence hanging in the air.

"So when are you going back to Spain? Will you be his doctor again? We need to know how he is." Harry was concerned.

Juan shook his head again. "No, I not go back now. Mary say I live here, with she and you, and I sell my house and buy one here. I marry Sophie and she and Jamie come live with me."

Sophie sat on her bed, stunned, and I held her hand. We didn't speak, each lost in our thoughts with the news Juan had delivered. Time ticked on, seconds to minutes.

Finally, Sophie stood, weak with shock. "I have to take Jamie to see him, that's if it's not too late."

"No." I grabbed her arm. "No. Why are you so forgiving to that man? He's a terrible person, and to be honest, not only could I see this coming, because he's vulgar when he's drunk and that's most of the time, but he treated you so badly he doesn't deserve your compassion."

Sophie tugged her arm back, resolute. "I need to do this for me, for my daughter. You don't get it, do you? If he dies and I haven't made peace, I will never be able to forgive myself, and Jamie deserves to see her father for a last time too."

In all honesty, I wanted to throttle her.

Alan and I insisted on accompanying Sophie, we didn't want her travelling alone, and Harry bought the tickets, despite having no wish to join us. Jamie behaved beautifully on the flight, gurgling and chewing her fingers to ease her teething gums, her angelic face drawing admiring smiles from the airline staff. We arrived at Palma just before midday.

We hired a car and Alan was soon accustomed to using the gearstick and handbrake with his right hand. Seeing Hospital General de Muro again brought unhappy memories back for Sophie and me and we were quiet, reserved. The receptionist directed us to the intensive care ward.

Sophie stood at the door and surveyed the man who had put her in the same position more than once and the sight of his battered body overwhelmed her, silent tears dripping from her chin. Collecting her emotions, she asked for five minutes alone with him and wheeled the buggy in, closing the door.

"Darren," unsure if he could hear, "it's Sophie." He raised a finger. She sat and took Jamie from the pushchair, holding her on her lap. "I brought Jamie to see you." The finger rose again.

His enlarged face was unrecognisable, with blackened puffy eyes deep set in a mound of swelling where his cheekbones should have shown. Scabs littered his skin and his ears were at right angles to his head. Three dressings covered the stab wounds on his torso and vast patches of purple-blue-black mottled where he had been kicked. Whoever had committed the horrendous attack clearly hadn't cared if he lived or died. Clinging to life, barely there.

I could see through the glass that Sophie was sobbing and after five minutes could stand it no more. Alan and I, turning my head to avoid seeing the injuries, joined her. "How is he?" I had asked Sophie, but Darren lifted the finger again. "So he can hear then?" The finger moved.

Alan saw countless battered people in his line of work and suspected he was unlikely to survive. He couldn't forgive Darren for mistreating his sister, and so badly, so the man's impending death was of no concern. Realistically, it would be beneficial to her and the child. "I think we should go."

A loud and monotonous tone, a red light flashing, frantic beeping. The room was suddenly heaving with medics and the three visitors were pushed aside as the crash team worked on the patient. Darren's body convulsed wildly, frighteningly, four nurses restraining him while a doctor injected him. And peace. The regular sound of his heartbeat on the monitor. The medics filtered away.

Sophie tapped a nurse's arm as she left. "Inglés?"

"*No, uno momento.*" She called to another nurse.

"Who are you?"

"I'm his wife. What just happened?"

"The swell on his head make the fit. He nearly have heart attack, yes? He sleep now, we make him sleep with medicine."

"Will he die?"

The nurse looked to the floor briefly and left without a reply.

Her tears spent, Sophie sat Jamie beside Darren, the father she would never know. "Say goodbye to Daddy." The finger was still.

She strapped Jamie into her buggy, and took Darren's hand, kissing it softly. "I'm sorry this happened to you. I know you can't hear me now, but I want you to know I forgive you. Goodbye Darren."

Chapter 25
Juan Murillo

Meanwhile, life at home hadn't been rosy either. The arrangement had been that Juan would have our spare bedroom until he and Sophie felt ready to progress with their relationship, but when Harry returned after dropping us off at the airport, he found Juan packing his suitcase. Perplexed by the constant drama and heightened emotions, he remained calm, suggesting they go for a drink and a meal to discuss whatever the problem was.

The pub was lovely, a couple of hundred years old with original features and a gentle ambience, a welcome to Britain's quaint history. Harry chose steak and kidney pie with a homemade crust topped with lashings of thick gravy, while Juan struggled to find something less bland. An impossible task, accustomed to abundant herbs and spices, he settled for beer-battered fish with chips and mushy peas. They tucked in hungrily, washing the food down with a pint of yeasty ale that made Juan squirm.

"She's still in love with her husband. I can't compete. She rush back to see him after all he has done to her. I not understand." Harry didn't either, but saying so wouldn't be conducive to solving the problem. "I leave good money job for her, leave my family, I take her back when she treat me mean. She give nothing back for me."

It was a reasonable argument, and Harry said as much, and without knowing Sophie's reasons for returning to Spain to see the man who had abused her so often, he had to assume. "Darren and Sophie's relationship was so intense and the aftermath has been a never-ending rollercoaster ride, I think Sophie needs closure to be able to move on and start anew."

But hot-headed Juan was adamant of his intention to return to Mallorca. "That's too easy, Juan, don't you see that you are also running away at the first hurdle. Stay another night at least, it would give us a chance to get to know each other better, and in all honesty I could do with the company." Despite his stubborn streak, Juan laughed; Harry was an excellent mediator.

They played Monopoly in the evening, Harry's favourite Mozart playing softly in the background, and smoked cigars over a balloon of cognac. It was a good evening.

And over tea and toast the next morning: "I like you, Harry, and I love Sophie, but I want, how you say, just me too?"

"Independence?"

"*Si*, my own room to live, not with you, not with Sophie."

Harry poured more tea from the pot. "I'm not picking the others up until two, so how about we go into town and visit some estate agents, see if there are any suitable flats available nearby?"

By the time Harry collected us, Juan had found a furnished two bed flat just a mile from our house. Generous as ever, Harry had signed as guarantor and Juan had paid the deposit, and he would be free to move in as soon as the background checks had been completed. Juan didn't want to be at our place when Sophie arrived back, so they collected his belongings and Harry dropped him off at a bed and breakfast on his way to the airport.

Sophie was astonished when she heard the news from her father. He explained how Juan had been feeling, but she wasn't interested, adamant that it wasn't unreasonable to see her dying husband - her child's father - for a final time, and she swiftly removed the ring for the second time, slamming it into Harry's hand to return to the deserter.

Exasperated by the ridiculous melodrama on both sides, Harry suggested she stay at ours for the night, but she flapped and sulked and demanded he take her home, rejecting my efforts to return with her. "I'm sorry, but I'm in a foul mood now, I'm better off left alone to calm down."

But after Harry dropped her off, his car rounding the corner, Sophie pushed the buggy to the shop and bought a bottle of brandy, intending to drink to oblivion after Jamie was safely in bed.

Despite concerns about living alone in a strange country, Juan settled in easily and his qualifications were in much demand in the failing NHS; he received a job offer and a work permit on the same day. Four weeks after his relocation, he began working at the Royal Derby in a similar capacity to his position in Mallorca. The money was reasonable, enough to pay the bills and have an enjoyable social life and savings too.

The nurses swooned over his boyish good looks and golden skin, especially his Mediterranean accent, and his genuine delight in life was a ray of sunshine on the wards. He welcomed the long hours as they kept his mind from wandering to Sophie.

He continued to meet with Harry over a few pints, gradually accepting Sophie's need for closure with Darren, but he remained distant from her while she worked through her emotions. Women and girls showed plenty of interest, but he politely declined every offer. He had emigrated for Sophie and was willing to wait.

Sophie, however, had found it harder to find a job than anticipated. The poor economic climate, dipping into a recession, made suitable secure positions in private business few and far between. Too proud to accept financial handouts, Harry and I ensured she didn't fall behind by buying a bag of nappies here, an outfit for Jamie there, and if she needed cash she would insist on paying us back once she found work. I suggested repeatedly that she claim income support, which fell on deaf ears, but after two months with no income except child benefit, and another rejection letter, Sophie sadly realised she would have to. Now her life was the antithesis of what she had expected it to be.

Sophie's long-time acquaintants, who had husbands and children, found it awkward now she was single, and their infrequent appearances gradually tailed off. She would take Jamie to the park during the day, or for long walks by the canal, playing peek-a-boo to make her chuckle. But once darkness fell, earlier each night as autumn drifted into winter, and Jamie was asleep, the brandy would ease the problems and help her to sleep.

Once immaculate, she had stopped bothering with her appearance; eyebrow-plucking, shaving, moisturising, nail polish - anything that made her feel beautiful - went by the wayside. What was the point? And inevitably, at a routine appointment with the doctor, she broke down, sobbing into Jamie's bodysuit as she clutched her tightly, spilling everything that had happened.

She had reached rock bottom.

A prescription for antidepressants, her name on the lengthy list to see a counsellor, and another appointment for two weeks ahead, the substantial weight on her shoulders had lessened that tiny bit by having spoken her story aloud.

Christmas Day was approaching fast and I was in my element arranging the festivities. Our three children and granddaughter, plus Steve's new girlfriend, Meena, were coming for the day and I couldn't wait. I hung metallic streamers across the ceiling and erected a tree, adorned with sparkling baubles and glittering tinsel, and filled the room with presents. The turkey was defrosting in a roasting tray and I had decorated a cake with fondant icing and pretty plastic robins. Treats, cakes, chocolates, biscuits, cheeses, and of course alcohol, everything to make the day special, memorable.

Harry and I had noticed Sophie's un-brushed and greasy hair, her prominent cheekbones and baggy clothes, but had put it down to new motherhood. It had never occurred to me she was depressed, taking Prozac; in my day we just got on with things no matter what. She had become a master at hiding the bottles of spirits she drank to excess, disposing of the evidence at the nearby recycling centre, so we knew nothing about her nightly binges and growing reliance. All we saw was what she wanted us to see: a doting mother and a happy child.

Harry's car pulled into the drive, so I put the bowl of pastry dough to one side and wiped the flour from my hands, greeting him at the door with a kiss. "How did it go?"

"Well, it was only a first consultation, so there's not much to tell, but he seemed like a good solicitor, knew what he was talking about. He said the first thing is to contact Darren's solicitor in Mallorca, but there's no point doing it over the Christmas period. Said he'd send a letter in the New Year. Cup of tea?"

I nodded, adding cold water to the pastry dough and pummelling with my hands. "Have you decided whether to tell Sophie or not?"

He poured hot water into mugs, milk from the fridge. "She won't talk about it, dismisses me every time I try. She's too polite to create a scene in front of Meena, so I'll tell her Christmas Day when the house is full."

"Sensible. I'm so pleased Steve's found someone at last. I can't wait to meet her, she sounds lovely. Good old Alan for introducing them. Did you ask him her position in the force when you spoke to him?"

He chuckled. "Firearms. I can't imagine a lady being a firearms expert, but that's what she is."

"Hey, sexist pig."

The doorbell sounded and Harry was pleasantly surprised to see Juan, inviting him in and offering tea and cake. "No thanks, I won't be here long, I just have a couple of questions to ask."

Wrapping the dough in a food bag, I said, "Your English has improved since I last saw you."

"Working in a hospital does that." He sat at the table with Harry. "I've been thinking. I understand now

276

why Sophie had to see Darren, and I think I've been too hard on her. I want to make amends; how do you think she'd take it if I apologised?"

"I think she would appreciate that. I know my daughter and you were special to her, there was a glint in her eye when she was with you that she never had with Darren."

Always plotting, I was miles ahead. "Are you thinking about having a relationship with her again."

Juan blushed. "I wanted to test the water first, but yes, I guess so. I really believe she could be The One."

"In that case, why don't you join us for Christmas?"

"No, Christmas is about family, I'm flying home tomorrow to spend it with *mamá* and *papá*."

There was no stopping me when I had an idea in my head. "But Sophie and Jamie could be your family soon, after the wedding."

He shifted uncomfortably and Harry gave me a look. "I don't know, she might hate me, tell me to get lost, then I'd have Christmas on my own."

"She won't, I promise."

Juan stood, eager to get away from my nagging. "I don't know. Thank you for offering, I'll speak to my parents and see what they think."

The front door closed and I punched the air with a triumphant 'yes'. Harry rolled his eyes. "You're incorrigible. That was not a yes."

"Yes it was. I have a feeling this is going to be the best Christmas ever."

Chapter 26
Christmas Day

Bright sun reflected from the glistening ground frost, but it was horribly cold outside, none of which mattered inside the cosily heated house that smelled delightfully of roasting turkey. I had spent the morning peeling, paring, preparing, humming happily to myself. There was nothing I had come to like better

now my circumstances had improved so dramatically than to mother and nurture my brood, and I was excited about seeing our children together again. Although Harry and I hadn't got around to arranging our wedding yet, I saw Steve as my own, especially as my three sons from my first marriage had ceased contact - with my blessing - years before.

Harry had braved the frosty and gritted streets to collect Sophie and Jamie, leaving me to lay the extended table with the finery that only came out once a year. I stood back to admire the scene that would have been a dream a year before.

Harry returned, shivering as he hung his coat up, and Sophie followed him in, carrying Jamie in her car seat. I hugged them tight, kissing Jamie's chubby cheek. "Happy Christmas, Mum. I'll just go and get the presents from the car."

Harry breathed in the tempting aroma. "Mmm, it smells gorgeous in here." He peered through the oven door at the steaming foil-wrapped turkey. "Are the boys here yet?"

"No, they'll be here soon. Can I get you a drink, something to warm you up?" Pretending to hide my glass with a cheeky grin. "Sherry, maybe?"

Leaving Harry to deal with the refreshments, I leant on the doorframe to watch Sophie emptying a bag of presents under the tree. "What?" she said, spotting me.

"You know, you're going to have the best Christmas ever, there's a special surprise for you today."

Sophie laughed as she sat on the sofa, taking a drink from her father. "Well, I'll look forward to that."

Steve and Alan had become inseparable since Sophie's birthday party, and Harry was overjoyed by their closeness, yet only I knew the real reason why. They arrived together and, clearly smitten, Steve proudly introduced Meena; we were stunned by her appearance. Given her job, we had expected a well-built and tall woman, but she was tiny, just over five-foot and delicate as a baby bird. She was beautiful, with flawless umber skin and shining raven hair that reached her waist, thick and healthy. It didn't seem possible that her dainty hands could fire guns and rifles with precision. Steve squeezed her close, worried she may be nervous, but she confidently stepped up to shake hands, hug.

And her strong grip said it all; I waved the pain from my hand behind my back as she said, "You must be Mary, Steve's told me what a wonderful cook you are, and by the delicious smell as I came in, I believe him." Then to Harry: "And you must be Dad. Thank you for inviting me today, it's really kind of you." Steve glowed, and Sophie's heart swelled, realising her brother had found the love he had wanted for so long. Meena hugged Sophie as if they were old friends. "I'm guessing you're Sophie. Steve adores you, says you're really close, so I'm really pleased to meet you at last. Where's little Jamie? I can't wait to meet your little bundle of fun."

Sophie laughed. "Cheeky bundle of mischief, more like. She's in the living room. Come on, I'll introduce you, but be careful though, she loves pulling hair."

Meena followed Sophie into the room, cooing affectionately at the baby, and Steve looked at Harry and me earnestly. "What do you think?"

"She's lovely, so polite and pretty."

Harry nodded vigorously. "Yes, a very pleasant young lady."

"Is it serious?" I was already planning a summer wedding in my head and was thrilled when Steve nodded, blushing.

Juan had driven himself crazy wondering whether to fly to Mallorca for Christmas with his family, or to try and make amends with Sophie again. He had eventually telephoned his mother and she said without hesitation that much as she would love to see him, she would love a daughter-in-law and babies more. He was to stop being an idiot and spend the day with the woman he loved.

Come Christmas morning he had a new dilemma: should he go for the meal, or wait until the afternoon? He had no appetite, but was fed up of pacing, wearing the carpet thin, and grabbed his keys and wallet, striding to the pub on the corner. He ordered a pint of bitter and sat in a quiet corner away from the revelling merrymakers at the bar. Lost in thought, Juan didn't notice the attractive blonde with chocolate eyes approach him, brandishing a piece of mistletoe. "Hey, handsome, how about a Christmas kiss?" Every part of him yearned for Sophie. *Her* blonde hair. *Her* chocolate eyes. But he was stubborn. He declined the kiss, but joined her at the bar for the rowdy celebrations.

The house was full of love, warm and close, which I had never experienced with my first husband and sons. That marriage had been all about the anger, the nastiness, the violence, my estranged sons probably in Her Majesty's custody for their criminal activities. I wondered if my heart would physically burst with contentment. But something was missing and it concerned me. I nodded for Harry to join me in the hallway, wiping my hands on my apron. "I'll be ready to serve up soon, maybe quarter of an hour or so."

"That's nice, I can't wait."

I whispered urgently, "No, you don't get it, Juan hasn't turned up yet, but if I hold the food back any longer the vegetables will spoil."

"I could phone him if you like?"

"Please, I need to know, I've set a place for him and everything. Let me know when you've spoken to him." I rushed back to the cooking, now reaching the manic phase, and was grateful when Sophie offered to help. Issuing breathless orders, I rushed from one place to another, lifting pan lids, stirring gravy, heating dishes. Harry waved from the doorway and I stopped briefly. "Well?"

"There was no answer." Sure he had gone to Mallorca after all, I felt like I had been kicked, but Harry gave me a quick hug, chuckling. "He's probably on his way, love, stop worrying."

"You think so?"

"Yes, now get on with my dinner, wench." He winked and I smacked him with the tea towel. "Do you want me to start carving the turkey?"

Never before had I experienced such a joyful relationship and the love I held for him was palpable. I thanked the god I didn't believe in for changing my life so remarkably, for giving me back the man I had always adored.

I called everyone to the table ten minutes later, while Sophie and I crammed steaming serving dishes along the centre, a platter of sliced turkey, gammon and pigs-in-blankets, two jugs of hot gravy. Steve strapped Jamie into her highchair, while Harry poured wine. When we sat at last, Sophie's brow furrowed. "Why's there an extra place setting?"

I glanced at Harry. "We were expecting another guest, but he's not here yet."

"Oh, who?"

I tapped my nose. "That's for me to know and you to find out. Now, help yourselves everybody, there's plenty here for us all to have seconds."

Harry laughed. "And thirds, I think, there's enough to feed an army."

The doorbell sounded and I smiled, relieved, while Harry went to let Juan in. We hungrily started to place meat, roast and mashed potatoes, vegetables, stuffing, bread sauce onto our plates, but stopped suddenly when Harry shouted.

Harry never shouted.

I dropped the spoon and rushed to the hall, and now I shouted.

Alan squeezed from his chair, worried, reached the doorway… the muzzle of a gun in his face. Hands in the air, he retraced his steps. Wide-eyed and terrified, Sophie stood and saw the gunman. Head spinning, everything went black and she collapsed.

Alan moved to help her, but Darren screamed, "Get away from her. All of you," aiming the gun at us all in turn, "hands up and walk slowly to the living room. Sit on the floor by the fire and don't move."

We obeyed and Darren followed us, sneering. Yellow eyes flashing, evil.

Woozy and disorientated, Sophie propped herself on her elbow, dragged herself up, glanced at the steaming dishes on the table, empty but for Jamie gurgling in her highchair. And then she remembered: Darren.

Darren Delaney was in her parents' house.

Darren Delaney had a gun.

Darren Delaney wasn't dead.

She fumbled with the harness on the highchair, grabbing her daughter, rushing to the hallway, the stairs. "Where do you think you're going?"

The gun was in her face, a vicious snarl showing how much he hated her. "I was just going to put Jamie…"

"Get in the living room."

We sat meekly on the floor, while Darren brandished the weapon, which Meena had already assessed to be a .357 Magnum. She surmised from two bulging pockets in a tool belt wrapped around his waist that he had plenty of ammunition, and a further pocket showed the handles of what she assumed to be knives or daggers.

Darren backed towards the open drinks cabinet and, keeping the gun pointed at us, poured a large brandy. "Courvoisier. You have good taste, Harold." He took a swig and sat on the sofa, amused by our faces as he waggled the gun back and forth. "You thought I was dead, didn't you?"

Sophie nodded lamely, clutching Jamie tightly to her chest. He had been so damaged when she had seen him at the hospital, and now his face was littered with scars that hadn't been there before, his left eye drooping, hooded. How could he survive such appalling injuries? But here he was, not only alive, but dangerous, insane.

Darren laughed wickedly. "You thought you'd killed me, didn't you? Did you all plan it, my so called mugging, or just you, Soph?"

The tremble in her voice matched her shaking body. "I don't know what you're talking about."

"Well, it doesn't matter anyway, because you're all going to pay for what you did to me."

Braver than I had ever considered he could be, Harry was intent on protecting his family. "I don't know what's brought you here, but surely we can sort things out without you waving that thing in our faces. Why don't we just sit down like adults and discuss why you feel disgruntled?"

Ochre eyes glistening, malevolent, he aimed at his father-in-law's head. "Disgruntled. Stupid cunt with your fancy fucking words. I'm not *disgruntled*, Harold, I'm here for revenge. You see, my memory came back, or most of it, and I clearly remember everything from the night you tried to kill me. I recognised your voices, I saw your faces when you were booting the crap out of

284

me." He aimed at me and I winced. "I saw you with the knife, bitch, I saw you stab me. You thought I was going to die, but I'm stronger than that. I held on because I was determined to make this Christmas the best ever. And I'm pleased to say," he laughed wildly, "that so far it is."

He pulled the trigger and the bullet burrowed instantly through my skull. I imagine my dying expression was one of stunned disbelief. I fluttered from my body - life to death - to the ceiling, saw my body topple to the floor, my family gasping, wailing.

Darren took another gulp of brandy, smirking, emotionless. "I always said she was a waste of space."

Jamie was screaming, frightened by the gunshot echoing deafeningly around the room, and shocked tears rolled down Sophie and Harry's cheeks.

Darren waved the gun from side to side. "Who's next?" He aimed at Steve. "You, dear brother-in-law. Poor little unlucky-in-love Steve. Have you worked out you're a gay boy yet? Hey? Have you come out yet?"

Meena was made of steel, eyes never wavering from the weapon, but her boyfriend shook his head, resigned to taking the next bullet; at least he would die in love, loved. "I saw you, Steve, I saw your pathetic anger as you booted my head, I smelt that revolting aftershave you insist on wearing; no wonder you can't get a girlfriend. Do you want to go next? Shall I pump a bullet into your brain?"

Steve swallowed, his mouth dry, facing his aggressor bravely, wondering how many seconds he had left.

But Alan was now the target. "And you, Mr Policeman, Mr Law-and-Order, protector of the citizens. Pig. You didn't protect me when you were kicking my head like a football, leaving me for dead. I guess right now you're trying to work out a way to stop me, aren't you? You'll be trained to fight, to self-defend, to disarm. What position should you get into? Where's best to tackle me so you can be the hero, save the day. You are, aren't you?"

Alan's teeth were gritted, fire raging from his eyes at the man who had coldly killed his birth mother. "And I will, too, you bastard."

Squeezing the trigger.

Alan's body slumped over mine, blood spurting from the hole in his neck, becoming a slow trickle as his heart stopped pumping.

Sophie couldn't breathe, couldn't understand, couldn't take any more. This was her battle, not her family's. Heart racing, tears flowing, choking. "Stop it, Darren, you don't know what you're doing. Stop it now."

He levelled the gun at her, stern, twisted with hatred. "Sit down, bitch, I know exactly what I'm doing. Months of rehab, learning to walk again, talk again, how to eat, dress; the whole caboodle. And with every new step I took, every new skill I relearned, I did it purely for this moment. And it's all your fault, you selfish bitch, because you chose to have a girl. You knew I wanted a boy, so you went and had a girl to hurt me. And then you planned to kill me. Were you there? Did you watch them doing it? Did it make you laugh?"

Her tears uncontrollable, Sophie's shoulders heaved, struggling for breath, deflated, confused, distraught. Meena, focused still on the weapon, grasped her hand, and suddenly she was the target. "Who's the Paki?"

A cold, hard glare. "A Paki is from Pakistan, I'm Indian. Get your terminology right, arsehole."

Darren chuckled. "Get you. I like feisty girls, fancy a quick shag after I've got rid of the shit?" Steve urged forward, but Meena held him back. "Don't tell me you finally have a girlfriend, gay boy? Makes a convenient front for your bum bashing, does it?"

"I'm not gay. Meena and I are getting married."

Darren swigged more brandy, chuckling. "Oh, really? Maybe, maybe not." A third deafening explosion. Steve slumped, lifeless, blood oozing from his pulped eye socket. "It won't be much of a wedding without a groom, will it?"

The doorbell sounded and Darren glanced at the survivors, nervous. "Who's that?"

Harry's life was worthless without me, his two sons, he was tired, his emotions dulled. "It'll be Juan, I expect. He was coming over for the day."

"Juan! Juan! Who the fuck is Juan?"

Hope filled Sophie, but dread too. She couldn't let him in, Darren would surely kill him. But he was their only chance of survival, wasn't he? What to do? "He's a doctor who treated me at the hospital," Mary was dead, she could take the blame, "Mary made friends with him."

A wicked, belittling snort. "So you replaced me then, found a blind and dumb idiot to shag you. Let's get him in here, shall we, see what he looks like." He edged to the hallway until he could see the front door and pulled another Magnum from his tool belt. Pointing one at the door and one at the group, he said, "Sophie, answer the door. Try anything funny, any of you, and the baby gets it."

Chapter 27
Help at Hand

The old couple next door had been enjoying a tame meal at the table, watching television as they ate, removing the need to converse with each other. At first they had thought the loud bangs were party poppers, knowing that Harold and Mary were hosting Christmas for the family, but the third explosion shook the picture on the party wall and Dora laid her cutlery on the table. "Daniel, I think something might be wrong next door."

"You and your imagination, woman." He shoved another forkful into his mouth.

"I think those could have been gunshots."

"Don't be daft," specks of food littered the table as he spoke, "we're in Derby, not Las Vegas." He swallowed the half-chewed food.

"I'm going to phone the police."

"You'll do no such thing, woman." Another mouthful.

Sedately, she wiped her lips on a napkin and strolled to the phone, found the number of the local station in the telephone directory, and dialled. "Hello."

Juan was shocked by Sophie's red and bloated face, tears glistening on her cheeks, and he instinctively reached out to hug her. "Get your bloody hands off my wife, arsehole."

Juan jumped, noticing Darren, a gun.

A gun aimed at Sophie's head.

"Get in the house and join the others on the floor." Juan followed Sophie, and Darren bolted the door. Seeing the bodies, the blood, he raced over; he was trained to save lives and maybe he could do something to help. "Leave them, they're dead."

Juan, the severity of the situation dawning on him, sat beside Sophie on the carpet. "What's going on?"

Darren hadn't expected Sophie's bloke to be such a catch and he had hated him on sight. He sneered, contemptuous. "We're having a little Christmas party, what does it look like."

Harry shifted, his aging joints seizing, mind racing. He still had a daughter, a grandchild. "Your glass is empty, Darren, why don't you pour yourself another drink?"

"Shut up, old man. Good idea, though, I think I will. Oh, by the way, I know you're thinking that if you get me drunk you'll be able to overpower me, but rest assured that won't happen. You'll all be pumped full of lead before I lose control." Tucking the second gun into the tool belt, Darren poured a fresh brandy and sat on the sofa. Jamie's incessant screaming was becoming intolerable. "For god's sake, will you shut that brat up. If it doesn't stop that fucking noise soon I'm going to pop it."

"No," Sophie shrieked, an overwhelming urge to protect her baby, "she needs feeding, she's hungry. And she's your child too. You wouldn't kill her, she's your flesh and blood."

"It's no child of mine. In fact, looking at fuckwit next to you, I reckon he's probably the father."

"How can you say that? I was always faithful to you. You know I was."

"So why is it, whore, that you've been shagging him when we're still married? Don't you consider that adultery?" The doorbell rang again and Darren rolled his eyes. "For fuck's sake, who is it this time?"

A ray of hope? Harry shook his head. "I've no idea, we're not expecting anyone else." The caller was hammering on the door now.

A movement through the patio doors turned Meena's head and she saw a colleague enter through the back gate. Darren followed her eyes and snarled. "Who the fuck called the police? Who's got a mobile phone?" The four prisoners shrugged, shaking their heads. "Get up. Go upstairs. Leave the brat here, I can't stand the fucking noise any more."

"No, she's terrified, I'm not leaving her." Sophie clutched her child tightly.

Guttural, furious, he shouted, "Drop the fucking brat or I pump it full of lead."

Fresh tears rolled down mottled cheeks to her chin. She strapped Jamie into her car seat, apologising softly, and followed the others to the stairs.

The officer could see the screaming child through the glass and radioed the find to his colleagues. Peering through, his stomach lurched; three bodies behind the armchair, blood spattering the walls and carpet.

The hostages reached the bedroom that had been Sophie's as a child, and Darren forced them into a corner, positioning himself away from the window. He listened keenly to the noises outside for a clue to what the police were doing. However, the two constables who had responded to the call reporting possible gunfire had been instructed to find a place of safety and await the armed response team, who were donning body armour as they travelled in the riot van towards the house, and Darren remained clueless.

Jamie wailed mournfully downstairs and Sophie was desperate to pacify her, cuddle her frightened tears away. But her own tears had dried up, skin tight from the salt, and she waited nervously for Darren's next move.

The silence seemed to go on forever, and Darren carefully edged to the window and peered through the net curtain, scanning the street, the paths, for any sign of activity. Nothing. No police, no squad cars. He sighed, relieved, but the horrified group in the corner were devastated, forgotten, left to die at the hands of a madman. Darren retreated to his place of safety away from the window and waved the gun. "You," to Meena, "what did you say your name was?"

"I didn't." The tiniest of the four adults, she was without doubt the strongest - professionally trained in martial arts, incredibly fit and agile, and an expert with guns - and her knowledge and ability was the best, if not the only, hope of survival for the hostages. But Darren was behaving erratically, could potentially take them all out on a whim, and she couldn't risk anybody's safety by making sudden moves. She stayed calm.

Darren chuckled to himself. "You're a cocky little bitch, aren't you? I think we should play a little game, me and you. Get up." Still. "Stand up, bitch."

"Why should I?" She hated cowards with guns. High school shootings, street shootings, they were weak; take the gun away and they were nothing.

"Because I told you to." Meena remained seated, confident, not allowing Steve, the man she had loved, to enter her mind. She had to stay in control, grieving

292

could come later. "Defiant bitch." He spun the barrel, yellow eyes glinting evil, and aimed at her head, cocking the hammer. Although terrified, she didn't allow it to show. "In that case, how do you fancy your chances today? This Magnum holds six bullets, I've shot three. So you now have a fifty percent chance if I pull this trigger."

"Wow, you can count as well, you are a clever boy." The others looked at her in disbelief and, angry, Darren fired. It was her lucky day, and she slowly, quietly, let her breath out.

The shot had scared Jamie and she was screaming again. Sophie couldn't stand it any longer. "Please let me get the baby, I'll make sure she doesn't cry, but she's too young to be left on her own. Please."

Darren briefly mulled the suggestion. "So you think I'm stupid enough to let you go downstairs on your own, try and get help, catch somebody's attention, whatever scheme you've got going on in your head."

"No, there's no scheme, I'm just worried for her, she's going to make herself sick if she keeps crying like that. Please."

His rage erupted, hatred spilling, bile. "You always thought you were smarter than me, made me out to be the dumb one. But you're not, who's the leader now, hey? Who's in control now? I wish I'd finished off the job earlier this year, got rid of you for once and all. I hate you so much. Taking away my right to have a son was a cruel thing to do, Sophie, cruel."

"It wasn't my choice, it was nature, I would have liked a boy first too."

"First!" Incredulous. "You mean you honestly thought I'd have another child with you after presenting me with that dumb thing down there."

He was losing control, emotions clouding his judgement, and Meena adjusted her position, prepared to pounce if the right opportunity arose. But he restrained himself, cackling venom. The moment was gone and Meena sighed, relaxing. "Oh, I see what you're doing. Trying to get me angry, are you? You were always good at that, you with your perfect vowels and your arrogant way. Fuck off am I falling for that one. The fucking baby stays down there. If it chokes on its spit, then who gives a shit."

Like Meena, Harry was waiting for the chance to do something - no idea what, he'd wing it - and he calmly motioned for Darren's attention. "Why don't you go with Sophie to get Jamie, then you'll be able to watch her."

"Oh, and leave you three up here to plan some kind of escape?"

"There's some…"

A voice on a megaphone; the room fell silent.

Keeping the weapon pointed at the captives, Darren began to pace, avoiding the area near the window.

The house was surrounded by the firearms unit, rifles aimed at every window and doorway, and the road filled with squad cars. Vultures, eager to see some bloody action on Christmas Day - far more fun than tedious television - tried to watch from the background, meaning valuable officers wasted time and attention ushering them to a place of safety from potential gunfire.

"We have you surrounded, come out with your hands in the air. I repeat, we have you surrounded, come out with your hands in the air."

Under cover of the tall hedges that lined the immaculate back garden, several armed officers quietly, swiftly, made their way towards the patio door. As expected, the door was locked. Speaking quietly into the radio: "No access at the back, do you want me to blow the lock?"

Team Commander Officer James Ellis crackled through. "Negative. Stay there."

The extensively trained negotiator had set up camp on the road and he waited for James to give him the go ahead. A nod. He spoke through the megaphone. "My name's Rob Barnes, I want to discuss what's going on. Can you open a window so we can talk?"

Darren sat on the carpet with no intention of opening a window; they would blow his head off. He had never considered the police would be involved when he had planned his revenge. Why had he not bought a silencer from the black-market too? How was he supposed to get out of this? It was all Sophie's fault, and she was going to pay. Dearly.

Negotiator: "How many people are with you?"

Damn the bastards, why did they have to turn up and ruin things? Every option he considered ended with his death. He had a good life, an apartment in the sun, sex with holidaymakers whenever he felt like it, a well-paid job, cheap booze.

Booze. He could really do with a drink right now. He thought of the Courvoisier on the drinks cabinet. Why hadn't he grabbed it before coming upstairs? If he went down, they would no doubt be at the back door - instant death.

Negotiator: "So how's it going up there? How about you tell me your name?"

The drink downstairs was all Darren could think of. He could send one of his captives down... they would let the police in. That amber liquid, warm, luscious. He needed it. It would help him think.

Dora had taken every side route possible while explaining what she knew of her neighbours and their situation, what could have led to the crisis now. Harold and Mary lived next door. They weren't married but were planning to be. They were hosting Christmas and their two sons, Alan and Steve, and daughter, Sophie, with her baby Jamie, were all coming. Sophie's ex-husband, Darren Delaney, had shown up, and another man whom she had seen a couple of times, possibly Sophie's new man. The gunfire had started after Darren's arrival.

PC Goldsmith radioed the commander. "I think it's a domestic, it's likely that the gunman is an ex-husband, Darren Delaney. Possibly eight hostages, one is a baby, six or seven months old."

The drink on the cabinet taunted Darren, he had to find a way of getting it. "Have you got any rope, Harold?"

"It's in the garage, do you want me to get it?"

"Don't try and be smart, it doesn't suit you." Drink. Brandy. All that alcohol down there and he was stuck in the bedroom, thirsty and craving a hit. He noticed his hands were shaking; he *needed* that drink.

Negotiator: "Darren Delaney?"

Drink. "I'm going to go out of the room and lock the door. Sophie, you're coming with me, you can get your stupid brat. But if it keeps screaming, I'm shooting it." Sophie followed him onto the landing and he took the key from inside the door, locking it and checking the handle. "If I hear a sound from in there, Sophie and the brat are dead." Down the stairs, tiptoeing, shifty.

Negotiator: "Darren, we know you're in there. What has happened to you to make you take such drastic action. You can tell me. I want to help you."

In the hallway, he instructed Sophie to go into the living room and get the whiskey and brandy, give them to him, and then return for the child. He figured that if anyone fired, she would take the bullet, not him.

"Movement by the door." The masked and helmeted officer held his Glock 45 GAP close to the glass, adrenaline flowing. The woman instantly raised her hands, her face a picture of terror, and he lowered his weapon slightly to reassure her. She walked to a cabinet and took two bottles. "Young woman in sight, hostage, I think. She's got some alcohol. She's gone out." He raised his weapon, relaxed it again. "She's back, taking the baby from its seat. She's gone again."

Darren unscrewed the brandy and took a long swig, grateful for the warmth, the comfort. He followed Sophie up the stairs, gun trained on her back, and they returned to the bedroom. The police could stay there as long as they liked now he had a drink in his hand, nothing else mattered.

Negotiator: "We can help you, Darren, but we need to communicate with you first."

Darren stirred, the voice hadn't sounded right, something was different. He moved the curtains aside and realised that his hostages had opened the small window in his absence. "You stupid fucking devious bastards, now they know what room we're in. We're going to have to move."

Darren was unaware of the microphone that had been placed under the windowsill outside; the police had heard every word. He trained the gun at each adult, then let it linger threateningly on Jamie. Back to Juan. "Juan! Juan! What stupid fuck type of name is Juan?" He slugged several gulps from the bottle, eyes not leaving the Spaniard, and aimed the gun at him again. A shot rang out and Juan slumped on the floor, clasping his belly with a weakening hand, moaning, growling. Sophie screamed.

The Team Commander: "That's gunfire. Blast the back door, storm the house."

Sophie applied pressure to Juan's abdomen to stem the blood flow. "Get your hands off him unless you want one too. Get up, all of you, we're going to the back bedroom, come on, move it, move it."

The muted sound of another gunshot.

Darren panicked and his mind whirred. The door. The back door. They must have shot the lock. "Get on your fucking feet, quick." Juan tried, on his hands and knees, trying to find strength. Agony. He collapsed into a ball on the reddening carpet. "Get on your fucking feet, I said." Juan was still, a foetus again. The other hostages were already on the landing and Darren waggled the gun at them. "Back bedroom, now. Keep away from the window." He turned back to the injured man and fired. Juan's body relaxed.

Now into the room, barricading the door with a chest of drawers, Darren heard people running softly up the stairs. Trying to count how many. It was impossible.

Outside the room, the officers trained their guns on the door, preparing to kick it down if necessary. "Darren, it's all over now, we have you surrounded. Come out of the room with your hands up."

"Go away." What was wrong with these idiots? He had the opportunity to blow the brains out of four hostages and they were nagging for him to come out. This wasn't how it happened in films. Darren slugged from the bottle as he decided what step to take next. "Give me the baby."

She clasped her daughter tight. "No."

He grabbed Sophie's arm and finally the opportunity Meena had been waiting for had arrived, he was off guard. Leg high, kicking the gun from his hand, and in a blink-of-the-eye movement grasped his wrist, twisted his arm behind his back, threw him on the floor, secured him in a stronghold. Darren struggled with his free left hand, feeling for the second Magnum. "Grab the other gun before he does."

Harry jumped on top, groping underneath Darren, grabbing in the tool belt and retrieving the weapon. He threw it across the room just as the door, splintered from a kick, flew open, tipping the heavy chest of drawers over. Six armoured officers stormed inside, weapons poised and ready to fire. A whirl of scuffling and Darren was handcuffed, led away, a life of alcohol free prison ahead of him. Safe now, Sophie raced to help Juan, desperately hoping he was still alive.

Everything was happening at once. Two officers leading the prisoner away, down the stairs, a car waiting outside to take him into custody. Meena excitedly speaking to another four, explaining her position on the police force, that she had been the one to disarm the gunman. More officers stomping up the stairs. Paramedics in the living room, assessing the bodies. Mayhem.

Sophie knelt over Juan's lifeless body, sobs wrenching, twisting her insides, regretfully wishing she had handled their relationship differently as her tears mixed with his spent blood.

A shot rang out.

Silence, but for the haunting echo that fired the gun again, and again, and again.

Chapter 28
Jamie's Future

Sophie sat on the comfortable armchair with her legs crossed and hands relaxed on her lap. She had finished relating the horrific Christmas Day, held at gunpoint by her ex-husband, who she had believed to be dead. The traumatic day that saw her lose a second mother, two brothers, her fiancé, and finally, her father.

"Dad was a gentle man, so placid, so calm, and when he lost my adoptive mother, Beryl, in suspicious circumstances - although it was formally recorded by the police as a mugging - it hurt him to the core. Mary, my birth mother, helped him a great deal, and as their relationship developed and we got to know my twin, Alan, who had also been adopted, we became a new family unit. Just as close, but with a couple of different members." She swallowed hard, keeping the tears at bay, hardening herself to the situation that never left her mind.

"He was sixty years old and had already lost one wife, then had to watch as his new love was killed, his two sons were killed. I think it took him over the edge. Once the police had left the room, he found the gun and shot himself through the temple. The post mortem said he died immediately and without pain. That was a blessing, if such a word exists any more.

"The only trouble is, he left me. I'd also lost everybody. My ex-husband was the lunatic who had committed these terrible murders, and my fiancé, the person I wanted to spend the rest of my life with, he was dead too. The only person I had left was my baby." She paused, composing herself and her mind.

"The funeral was dreadful. They were all cremated, well, my family, Juan's body was flown back to Mallorca for burial, and I never found the strength to visit his grave. I asked that they all be cremated together, but they couldn't do it as the furnace wasn't big enough, so I received four urns, and at home I mixed the ashes together to keep my family united in death as they had been in life.

"I tried, believe me, I tried. I moved into Dad's house, gave Jamie my old bedroom, although I sealed the door to the bedroom Dad killed himself in. But walking around the house brought flashbacks all the time, of the deaths, the violence that had occurred there. They increased the dose of my medication..."

"Which medication? And 'they' are?"

"Antidepressants. My doctor doubled the dose. But in the end I sold the house and moved to a remote village. Different area, different style of house, different furniture."

"Why was it important to make everything different?"

"I wanted to block away the images, the nightmares, the flashbacks, eradicate the memories that were consuming my life. It didn't work, though. They still haunted me. I began drinking heavily, which is ridiculous seeing as it was alcohol that caused so many problems with Darren, but it truly worked. I'd knock myself out with it, sleep, and when I woke up, I'd knock myself out again. It stopped me from being able to think."

He shifted his giant frame in the chair and rested his chin into his hands, leaning on the desk. "Which, of course, negates the effect of the antidepressants. You

302

had Post Traumatic Stress Syndrome, and realistically I think you'll agree that with alcohol being so involved, you weren't actually being effectively treated."

She debated for a moment and nodded. "Jamie had her first birthday, I did nothing for it, except bake her a cake. There was no party or anything. I didn't know anyone where we lived as I barely went out of the house, I was too scared. I even ordered my booze online and had it delivered. I wasn't looking after her properly and it broke my heart. I'd wanted to be such a good mum, I'd had plans and dreams when I was pregnant with her, but everything, my whole world, had imploded.

"When Social Services turned up at my door following an anonymous phone call - apparently I had been asleep in the garden and Jamie was left crawling around on the grass by herself - I was just too tired and too low to argue. They suggested they take her for a few days and, well, I've never seen her again."

"So in effect you've lost your entire family. Why didn't they bring her back, give you help to recover, I thought that was how they played it nowadays."

"I don't know, but I had no fight left in me. I felt so alone without my baby, she was the only thing I had to look forward to. The house was silent, no friends, no family, no career, no hope. I wanted out, so I took an overdose. I was sectioned and the rest you know." Sophie had said the words so many times she no longer felt embarrassed, just weary.

He glanced at the clock on the wall. "Well, the session's over for today I'm afraid, so I'll see you tomorrow, same time, okay?"

She nodded, resigned to what would happen next. On pressing a button, a nurse entered the room and helped Sophie into a wheelchair, steering her into the bright corridor, walking along to the end, where she keyed in an access code and they entered the secure unit. Moments later, they were back in her solitary room and Katherine helped Sophie onto the waiting bed, careful not to bruise the jutting bones of her skeletal, anorexic frame.

The nurse busied herself by the sink. "How did your session go today?"

"It was okay. We got to the end of my story at last. Now Doctor Carr knows all the reasons why I'm so fucked up."

"Now, now." Katherine injected olanzapine into Sophie's arm. "We're here to make things better but you have to be positive."

The psychiatric session over for another day - the only thing she had to look forward to any more - Sophie fell asleep within moments.

Harry and I, holding hands - always holding hands - with our sons, with Beryl, would watch her, moaning through the trees to try and get her attention. Every night was the same. She would wake from the drugs in the peaceful early hours of the morning and drag her pitiful body up the bed until she was seated. The task was clearly becoming harder, her refusal to eat making her weaker and weaker. They had tried feeding her through a tube into her stomach, but she ripped it out every time. They had tried rehydrating her through an intravenous drip, but she would pull the needle out. They had even restrained her at one stage. But, sitting

304

on the crisp white bed, in the crisp white room, restricting her dietary intake was the only part of her life that she had any control of.

She would silently climb from the bed, eager not to be disturbed by the night staff, and sit on the chair by the barred window, gazing out at the night sky, sometimes cloudy, sometimes oceanic and speckled with stars. An hour, maybe two, reflecting on her mistakes, listening to the soothing silence, her loved ones. We sailed free in the sky, our souls dancing eternally since she had scattered our ashes into the wind.

The serenity of the early hours.

For the guard who worked the gate at the high security psychiatric hospital, every night was the same too. The haunting, wasted lady at the window, ghostlike and pale, contemplating the heavens. He would often wonder why she did so, what she was seeing, so vulnerable and scared, yet also somehow at peace.

And the day her face didn't appear, he knew that if he were to gaze into the night as she had done, he would see her, flying through the sky as free as a bird, no longer restrained - imprisoned - by her mental condition.

Simply floating, tranquil and harmonious, and without pain.

With her family.

Biography

Author of Unlikely Killer, Deadly Angels, Black Park, Bonfire Night, Rings of Death and Hope's Vengeance, Ricki studies the mind, the psychology, of people with great interest, and writes to educate and involve.

www.ingramcontent.com/pod-product-compliance
Lightning Source LLC
Chambersburg PA
CBHW030936260626
47169CB00002B/499